I0643089

Harlriet Lewin Grote

Memoir of the Life of Ary Asheffer

Harlriet Lewin Grote

Memoir of the Life of Ary Asheffer

ISBN/EAN: 9783337332525

Printed in Europe, USA, Canada, Australia, Japan

Cover: Foto ©Andreas Hilbeck / pixelio.de

More available books at **www.hansebooks.com**

MEMOIR OF THE LIFE

OF

ARY SCHEFFER.

BY

MRS. GROTE.

LONDON:

JOHN MURRAY, ALBEMARLE STREET.

1860.

LONDON :
SAVILL AND EDWARDS, PRINTERS, CHANDOS-STREET,
COVENT GARDEN.

CONTENTS.

INTRODUCTION.

MANY notices—and some of them by confessedly accomplished pens—have been given to the world on the subject of the late Ary Scheffer's works. Some few particulars have likewise been published regarding the personal history of the painter; yet it has not seemed to me superfluous to add one more tribute to the memory of a man whose mind and character were as remarkable as his works are celebrated. Impelled by a tender and respectful regret for his loss, I propose to throw together, in a connected form, such incidents and particulars as I have been enabled to collect, relating to the life of Ary Scheffer, in the persuasion that they will offer to his friends and admirers a welcome addition to the " Sketches" which have already appeared: sketches which, taking them in a biographical point of view, certainly leave something to be desired.

It would be impossible, in retracing the career of this eminent man, to disconnect his personal life from his artistic progress. He had enough, it is true, of individual and even original character to compose, as it were, a separate and distinct current of existence.   But if the " Painter" be regarded as the exponent of the individual sentiments and inward feelings of the " Man," it may be said of Scheffer, with perhaps more propriety than of most other great artists, that his life was reflected in his works.

It will be my endeavour, in the following pages, to keep in view this double existence, whilst throwing into somewhat fuller light those qualities and those social and political relations which, in the case of Ary Scheffer, not unfrequently exalted the artist into the patriotic citizen.

H. G.

January, 1860.

MEMOIR

LIFE OF ARY SCHEFFER.

BORN 1795 — DIED 1858.

CHAPTER I.

1795—1818.

Family of Scheffer—His mother—Sacrifices made by her for her children—Early development of Ary's talent for painting—His mother's admonition—Her removal to Paris—Scheffer's earlier works—His brothers—Guerin—Sketch of the progress of art in France, from 1778 to 1828.

THE principal figure in the group composing the family of Scheffer is the mother, the object of the unbounded love and veneration of the three brothers, her sons. She may be said to have been, in truth, their sole parent, since she became a widow while the boys were yet of tender age.

The father of Madame Scheffer—M. Arie Lamme— was a Dutch gentleman, who took an active part in the resistance made in Holland to the Government of the Prince of Orange. That resistance having been put down by foreign intervention in the year 1787, M. Lamme found himself compelled to seek an asylum in Belgium: his house having been pillaged, and his life being considered in danger. His wife remained at

home, at Dordrecht, with their two children, a son and
a daughter.   After a while Madlle. Lamme, who was
tenderly attached to her father, obtained permission to
go and bear him company in his forced exile, which
she continued to do during two long years.   Madlle.
Lamme, being possessed of great personal advantages,
as well as of superior mental endowments, and being
altogether an extremely attractive young person,
naturally received more than one offer of marriage.
But, although she was far from indifferent to *one* of
her admirers—a distinguished officer in the French
army—she could not bring herself to quit her father's
side, and therefore resolved to reside with him until
he should be enabled to return to his native country.
After this return (I am ignorant of its date), she
accepted the hand of M. Scheffer, a German by birth,
pursuing the profession of a painter, though possessed
of a competent fortune.   Madlle. Lamme was mainly
induced to unite herself to this gentleman by the
circumstance of his residing in the same city with
her father (at Dordrecht), from whom she could
not bear to separate herself.   I believe that no less
than three children were born to M. and Madame
Scheffer prior to the birth of Ary, which occurred
in 1795.   Arnold and Henri were born successively
after Ary.   Ary manifested, at an early age, a
decided aptitude for drawing and painting: passing
hours in childish attempts at painting in his father's
atelier.   His general education, meanwhile, was
conducted by his mother, who devoted much of her
time to the instruction of her children; his father
affording him, at intervals, some assistance in handling the brush.   Towards the year 1804—that is to

say, when Ary was ten years of age, or thereabouts
—the extraordinary events flowing out of the French
Revolution changed the fortunes of Holland, which
became annexed to the French Republic. By a too
common exercise of arbitrary power on the part of
Buonaparte, then First Consul, the public Creditor
was subsequently partially despoiled: so that, on the
death of M. Scheffer, about the year 1809-10, his
widow found herself left with three children to support, and the remnant of a fortune once 300,000
francs in value, but now reduced to half that sum.

I must here pause a while to dwell upon the praise-
worthy conduct of Madame Scheffer, who for several
years prior to her husband's death underwent un-
ceasing fatigue in performing the office of nurse to
him; a duty which, it would seem, was not lightened
by the possession, on the part of the sufferer, of
qualities which sometimes constitute a just claim
upon one's sympathies.*   Not the less assiduously,
however, were the cares and sacrifices required
by the helpless man yielded by his high-minded
wife, who, it must be added, paid the cost of
her devotion by injuring her constitution. A long
illness ended in her contracting a heart affection, of
which her whole subsequent life bore the painful
effects. Her grief for the loss of a daughter, who
died at the age of five years, had also its share in
producing this change in her health.

---

* M. Scheffer was a man of honourable character, a respectable
artist, and an affectionate father—attached also to his wife, as he
might well be—yet his temper was sullen, reserved, and deficient in
sympathy towards those with whom he lived. Hence the domestic
circle was not a happy one.

The last offices rendered to M. Scheffer, the widow
next bethought her seriously how to provide for the
upbringing of her children.   The talent of her eldest
boy, Ary, was already so developed that he had actually
exhibited, in the " salon" at Amsterdam, a picture
which attracted much attention and approbation,
although painted before he was quite twelve years
old.   Henri, too, showed a promising disposition
towards the art, and Madame Scheffer thought that
the best course she could adopt was to foster and
encourage their talent, and to afford her sons suitable instruction in this line.   There could be no
doubt as to the place where such instruction could
best be obtained. That place was Paris.   She resolved to transport her family thither, but in the
interval, whilst she was collecting the remains of her
property together, and making her preparations for
this, to *her*, painful effort (for she was about to quit
the society of her own family, and her own native
land, to settle in a foreign capital, where she had not
a single friend), Madame Scheffer sent her eldest boy
to Lille, to pursue his professional studies under the
best teachers to be found there.   During the brief
residence of Ary *en pension* at Lille, his mother continually wrote to him letters, in which the combination of maternal affection and judicious counsels shines
out with touching effect.   I cannot refrain from introducing a quotation from one of these letters, as a
sample of this admirable woman's cast of sentiment.

" Si tu pouvais me voir embrassant ton portrait,
le quittant pour le réprendre encore, et les larmes
aux yeux t'appeler mon cher cœur ! mon fils chéri !
tu sentirais alors combien il m'en coute de prendre

quelquefois un ton de sévérité, et de te causer
quelques instants de chagrin. Je nourris toujours
l'espoir de te voir un jour un des prémiers peintres
de notre siècle, et même de tous les temps. Sois
assidu au travail, sois modeste surtout, et lorsque
tu pourras dire que tu surpasses les autres, compare
alors tes travaux à la nature, et à l'idéal que tu t'es
formé, et cette comparaison t'empêchera de te livrer
à l'orgueil et à la présomption."*

Those who knew Ary Scheffer will, I think,
join in admitting that his mother's admonition, to
avoid the effects of pride and presumption, was
respected to the letter.

Madame Scheffer would seem to have arrived in
Paris about the beginning of the year 1811, when she
lost no time in establishing her modest, frugal *ménage*.
The painter most in repute as a teacher at that time
was Guerin, and with him her son Ary was presently
placed as a pupil.

The young student acquired in this "atelier" a
certain amount of technical knowledge essential to
the practice of the art — such a knowledge as fits a
young man to go onward if the capacity reside

---

* "If you could but see me kissing your picture, then after a
while taking it up again, and, with a tear in my eye, calling you
my darling! my beloved son! you would then comprehend what it
costs me to use, sometimes, the stern language of authority, and to
occasion to you moments of pain. I cherish the fond hope of seeing
you, one day, take your place among the first painters of the age,
perhaps of any age! Work diligently, be above all modest and
humble, and when you find yourself excelling others, then compare
what you have done with Nature herself, or with the 'ideal' of your
own mind, and you will be secured, by the contrast which will be
apparent, against the effects of pride and presumption."

within him. His father had enjoined Madame Scheffer, when he was almost dying, to restrain Ary's propensity to compose pictures, at an age when the study of drawing, anatomy, and perspective was the more fitting occupation and preparation of an aspiring artist. Such studies, then, came to form the chief employment of Ary's life during the first years of his residence in Paris; but the exigencies of his mother's position impelled him to practise painting for profit before he was eighteen years of age. Madame Scheffer's means were so inadequate to the demands made upon them, and yet her desire to afford to her children all sorts of instruction was so dominant, that she became extremely pressed for money. Thus situated, it was natural that her sons should seek to supply the deficiency by working; and it was at this period that Ary began to produce those agreeable pictures, in which the expression of the gentler sympathies form the interest and the subject—a description of composition always certain to attract purchasers, and falling within the powers of execution at the command of a youthful hand. The number of these productions I take to have been prodigiously great. A few were placed among the exhibited works in 1859, but the bulk of them have doubtless been long absorbed into private collections, and are scarcely known out of them. I have had the advantage of obtaining a list of Ary Scheffer's works not exhibited in 1859,* and indeed little remembered by the public of this day. It is valuable as furnishing a kind of "chart" of the painter's progress—for pro-

---

* See Appendix F.

gress it was unquestionably.   It needs no remarkable
powers of observation or of critical skill to recognise the gradual enlargement of the scope of Ary
Scheffer's conceptions; the steps by which, as one
may say, his creative faculty ascended the slopes of
Parnassus; proceeding from tender yet familiar compositions such as " Le Baptême," " La Veuve du
Soldat," " La Mère Convalescente," " Les Enfans du
Marin," and the like, onward through the more exciting
subjects of national struggles, " La Défense de Missolonghi," " Les Femmes Souliotes," " La Bataille de
Morat," &c.; until, acquiring a more extensive range
of thought by reading and meditation, he arrived at
the point where grandeur of idea and poetical expression unite.   As, however, this view of Scheffer's
mental expansion will be farther amplified hereafter,
I resume my personal narrative.

The second and third brothers, Arnold and Henri,
were left at school in Holland, for the space of a year
or more, on Madame Scheffer's removal to Paris;
but in the year 1812 they also came and resided with
their mother in that capital.   Arnold showed a
general aptitude for learning, for languages especially, and he commenced the study of the Oriental
ones with zeal.   To aid him in this, Madame Scheffer
parted with the few jewels she possessed; she even
managed to dispense with the comfort of keeping a
regular servant: refusing herself, in fact, all indulgences in order to forward the instruction of her
sons.   Still attractive in person, she might easily
have married again, but this she steadily refused to
do, for their sakes.   Henri was undecided for some
time what profession to embrace.   He tried the study

of music at first, but finally decided on cultivating
his already pronounced talent for painting—with what
acknowledged success is well known to all who have
attended to the course of French art in the present
century. He, too, became a pupil, along with his
elder brother, of M. Pierre Guerin. Now this painter,
although not without merit, was far from capable of
directing the artistic education of such pupils. In
the first place, Guerin was a slavish disciple of the
school of Louis David, whose influence was sensibly on the decline already, not only among painters,
but with the public. The following passage, traced by
the pen of Ary Scheffer himself in 1828, and quoted by
M. Louis Viardot in his interesting notice on Scheffer
(in 1859), seems to me so instructive on this point
that I venture to reproduce it here.

" Cette période de cinquante ans (entre 1778 et
1828) embrasse la vie tout entière de l'école classique,
depuis sa naissance, au sein d'une réaction contre le
faux goût, la futilité, l'incorrection, et l'indécence,
jusqu'à sa décrépitude. Cette école, durant ses
années de virilité, ne l'a cédé à aucune autre ; elle a
marché avec une fermeté admirable vers le but ex-
clusif que sa tendance lui assignait; elle l'a at-
teint si parfaitement, qu'elle a fait un moment
illusion sur tout ce qu'elle laissait en arrière, et par la
puissance du talent, par l'attrait de la nouveauté, elle
a conduit toute une génération à n'aimer, en peinture,
que la correction des contours, à n'être sensible,
en fait de beauté, qu'au type des statues et des bas-
reliefs antiques. Après avoir contemplé, jusqu'à
satiété, des figures grecques et romaines, le public,
blasé sur ce plaisir, ne pouvait manquer d'en désirer

d'autres. . . . . l'art de peindre, loin d'avoir
pour bornes un certain type de dessin, ne se borne pas
au dessin lui-même; qu'il renferme encore le coloris,
l'effet, la reproduction fidèle des passions, des lieux,
des temps; que l'histoire toute entière, et non pas
seulement quelques siècles, entre dans son domaine.
. . . . . Dès qu'une école est tombée au dessous
d'elle-même, il n'est pas donné à celle qui la suit de
ramener les beaux jours de la première. C'est une
nouvelle ère qui commence, une nouvelle génération
qui s'élève, pour suivre le même chemin que celles qui
l'ont précédée, pour subir les mêmes vicissitudes de
faiblesse, de vigueur, et d'épuisement."*

---

* " This period of fifty years (from 1778 down to 1828) may be
said to comprehend the whole existence of the ' classic school,' from
its birth—engendered by the impatience of the public of the false
taste, imperfect science, insipidity, and coarseness which characterized the preceding condition of art—down to its final decay.
This school, in its best days, rose to a high level of merit. It
advanced with steady aim towards the particular object which it was
designed to further ; which, indeed, it attained so successfully, that
it threw a veil over its own shortcomings. By the captivations of
novelty, joined to great artistic capacity, it persuaded an entire
generation to concentrate its admiration upon the merits of correct
design in painting ; to admit of no other type, in respect of human
beauty, than that of the ' Antique,' as displayed in its Greek and
Roman sculptures. Having contemplated works partaking of this
character until the eye was downright weary of their correct unifor-
mity, the public began to hunger after some variety. . . . .
The art of painting, so far from being limited to the study of a
formal type or style of design and outline, is not bound to confine
itself within·this sphere of design itself. Its legitimate range com-
prises the employment of colour, of effect, the faithful representa-
tion of the passions of the soul, of local scenes of every time. It is
authorized to include all history, and not particular periods alone, in
its course. . . . . When a school has passed into a declining

But not only was the " atelier " of Guerin an imperfect medium of instruction, it was likewise wanting
in discipline; the pupils were not kept steadily to
their studies, and a general laxity prevailed both as
to the hours of attendance and to accuracy in work.
To use the expression of one of Scheffer's later friends
(M. Viardot), it was an " école qu'il traversa sans y
rien apprendre si ce n'est, comme nous l'avons tous
fait dans les colléges, l'art d'apprendre plus tard, et
par soi-même."*

stage of existence, it is beyond the power of the followers of that
school to recal the glories of its earlier days.   A new era must suc-
ceed it, a new generation must arise, though probably both will
pursue a corresponding circle; exhibiting the same feeble beginnings,
the same expansion and growth, and, finally, the same exhaustion."

* " A school, through which he passed, learning but little, beyond
the art of framing, in after time, a system of study for himself.   It
is in this way that most of us have gone through our college
period."

CHAPTER II.

1818—1826.

The Restoration—The brothers Scheffer become "Carbonari"—Lady Morgan's prediction concerning Ary—His introduction to the Orleans family—Anecdote of Ary as Instructor in Art to the Royal Children.

WE may perceive, from what has been said, that Ary Scheffer's professional education commenced amidst the ruins of an exhausted school.   The reign of the "Antique" was passing away, and as yet no teachers had arisen who could point the way to a fresh and untrodden path.   It was, however, a fortunate circumstance for Scheffer, that he was still young enough to be included in a movement which presently overtook him.   One which, for charm of novelty, for varied excellence, and for enthusiasm among its promoters, has had but few parallels.*

The first years of the Restoration, whilst they seemed to set loose the springs of talent and energy in every form of material progress, no less favoured a revolution in the arts.   The classic school everywhere gave way to the romantic; the conventional, again, to the sentimental and passionate.   Victor Hugo in dramatic literature, Rossini in lyric music, Géricault and Delacroix in painting—these led the van of the new

---

* Scheffer, at the moment when France was relieved from the dreadful compression of the first Buonaparte's reign, was only just "sprung to manhood."

movement. The young Ary also tried *his* hand, and in 1819 exhibited his picture of " Les Bourgeois de Calais," in which was discerned an evident intention to break through old traditions, and to aim rather at compositions clothed in expression and feeling. Occupied as he was on "easel pictures " calculated to attract purchasers, Scheffer, about this period, began also to cultivate portrait painting. We find him thus employed as early as 1818, at the Château de la Grange, the well known residence of General Lafayette.   In a letter of that date, written to Lady Morgan, the General tells her—" You will meet here a young painter of distinction, named Scheffer;" and afterwards, Lady Morgan herself, writing from La Grange, speaks of Scheffer as " a young but already celebrated artist, who is painting the General's picture." She adds, " Before breakfast I find all the young people at their easels, painting from models, in the ante-room;" these studies being presided over by Scheffer in person : for he united the pleasure of assisting the young people in their studies, with the steady pursuit of his own professional career.

Admitted, as it were, as a member of the family, to the society of distinguished visitors which gathered round his illustrious host, Scheffer naturally took a lively interest in their political discussions, and these happened to be, at that time, peculiarly exciting. The " élite" of the opposition which harassed the Government of the Restoration resorted much to La Grange, and it was no more than was to be expected, that Scheffer's ardent soul should be kindled by continual intercourse with these eloquent and high-minded conversers. The cast of Ary Scheffer's mind and sentiments was, undoubtedly, democratic—possibly repub-

lican.   At the period of which I am treating, however,
the aim and endeavour of the distinguished cluster of
men who were embarked in active hostility to the
Government of the day, was strictly " constitutional"
in character.

It was, in truth, as healthy and honourable a political agitation as perhaps ever occupied the national
mind.   The powers of Government were being un-
fairly strained, in the hope of restoring the ascendancy
of the priests and old " noblesse :" against this strove
a small but influential minority in the Chamber
—seconded, out of doors, by highly gifted writers,*
and secretly supported by most of the indepen-
dent thinkers in the kingdom.   The brothers
Scheffer became strongly influenced by political
sympathies.   They entered warmly into the general
confederacy, all becoming " Carbonari," and en-
gaging, even to a perilous extent, in the secret
organization then widely prevalent through France.†
Both Ary and his brothers, indeed, went so far in
these affairs, under the direction of General Lafayette
and other leaders, as to run the most imminent risks

---

* Paul Louis Courier, Benjamin Constant, Ch. Comte, Ch. Du-
noyer, General Foy, &c. &c.

† Les membres de la " haute vente" (a section of the Carbonari)
non deputés, que le général initiait habituellement à sa pensée per-
sonnelle, étaient MM. Joubert, Ary Scheffer, Laresche, Bazard,
et Trelat."—Vaulabelle, Hist. des deux Restaurations, tome vi. p. 9.

See also same vol. pp. 10, 11, 12, for some interesting particulars
respecting the projected rising in Alsace, in 1822, and the active
share which Ary Scheffer took therein, along with his brother Henri,
M. Armand Carrel, General Lafayette and his son, M. Joubert, and
others of their friends. After the failure of the plot at Béfort, Ary
actually affronted the danger of arrest, by re-entering the town to
ascertain what had become of Henri, who, luckily, had escaped in
safety.

in their own persons; Ary and Henri in the conspiracy
of Béfort (in 1822), whilst Arnold was actively con-
cerned, along with M. de Corcelles, in similar but
abortive efforts at Marseilles, from whence both of
them escaped only by extraordinary good fortune.
All these proceedings necessitated considerable expense, so that a " purse" had to be made up in order
to meet it.   Among those who were the most forward with their contributions, was the poor painter,
who worked incessantly to. acquire money for that
purpose, over and above the amount needed for the
maintenance of his family.*   Hear the words of the
friend already quoted :—" Scheffer n'était pas devenu
seulement le père de sa famille, il était, dès ce temps,
—il fut toute sa vie—une sorte de trésor commun, où
venaient puiser, dans leurs besoins, ses amis, ses con-
frères, où venaient puiser toutes les infortunes.
Jamais il ne sut refuser un secours ou un service."†
   At La Grange there commenced an intimate
friendship, which lasted through long years, between

* On a pu voir, par les faits que nous avons cités, que les dépenses
de la société étaient le résultat de sacrifices que s'imposaient ses
membres : les plus riches comme les moins heureux.   C'est M. de
la Fayette qui fit les sacrifices les plus considérables."—Vaulabelle,
tome vi., p. 126.
   The same author also tells us that the members of the "Haute
vente" practised military exercises, and that M. Thierry, along
with others, was "drilled" by M. de Corcelles, the unsuccessful
envoy of the Republic to the Pope in 1849.
   † " Scheffer had become, not only the father of his own family,
but from this period—as, in fact, during the whole of life—he was
regarded as the holder of a ' stock purse,' into which all might dip
their hands when money was wanted.   Friends, brother-artists, all
who were in need, had recourse to Scheffer's kind aid, for to no application could he turn a deaf ear."

Scheffer and Augustin Thierry, the celebrated histo-
rian.   Lady Morgan, then sitting for her portrait
in Paris, to Berthon, one of the eminent "face
painters" of that period (1818), mentions them in
her diary :—" To-day Aug. Thierry and Ary Scheffer
sent up their cards, and were, of course, admitted
with acclamation. I met with these two gifted young
men at La Grange, since when, we have opened a
mutual account of goodwill and intimacy.   They
have both started fair for posterity, and I am quite
sure will reach their goal . . . . . When the two
artists had discussed the merits of the portrait, which
Scheffer observed was 'better than his own' (which
Berthon begged permission to see), the conversation
turned entirely on politics—both, Liberals in the
extreme, and Thierry, by his great historical acquirements, well suited to the task which I see he has
begun.   I had difficulty, from the freedom with
which they spoke, in believing we were not living
under the protection of a constitutional government."
—*Diary*, pp. 222-3.

The excellent mother of these ardent youths had
to undergo much anxiety, not to say apprehension,
on their account, at the period of which I am now
speaking, viz., between the years 1818 and 1823.
One of the brothers thus states the circumstances in
which she and her sons then stood.

" Nous étions de jeunes hommes, et nous étions
dévenus Français de cœur et de passion; et comme
tels, nous étions entrés dans le mouvement politique
de notre époque. La jeunesse en 1819 nourrissait contre la dynastie des Bourbons cette défiance et cette
haine qui fit explosion générale en 1830. Elle vou-

lait, dans son impatiente ardeur, dévancer le sentiment
général, ou le faire éclater dès les prémières années
de la Restauration; et dans cet espoir, des conspira-
tions, des sociétés secrètes, s'étaient formées, dont nous
faisions parties, dans lesquelles même nous avons
figuré au premier rang.   Notre liberté, notre vie
même, couraient des périls dans ces tentatives. Notre
mère ne l'ignorait pas, mais elle respectait nos convictions, et ce que nous regardions comme des devoirs.
Elle, qui n'auroit pas survécu à un de nous, ne nous
empêcha pas de risquer notre vie; et il y eut un moment où elle nous permit, à tous trois, d'aller courir
des dangers auxquels nous n'échappâmes que par
miracle.   C'était de la tendresse maternelle poussée
au plus haut degré, car je le repète, la mort d'un de
nous eut été la sienne."*

---

* "We were all young men, and were become Frenchmen with our
whole heart and soul: as such, we entered into the political agitation
of our times. The youth of France entertained towards the
Bourbon dynasty, that general mistrust and dislike, which came to
a regular outburst in the year 1830. With the impatient ardour of
early manhood, they would have brought about a much earlier
'cataclysme,' had they found means to inflame the public feeling sufficiently. With this view, conspiracies, secret societies and schemes,
were set agoing, in which we all bore our share ; I may even say
that we played a leading part in them. Our personal liberty, our
life indeed, was imperilled by these proceedings. Our mother was
not uninformed of them, but she respected our convictions, and
what we looked upon as our duty. She would hardly have survived
the loss of any one of her three sons; notwithstanding this, she
never forbade us to risk our heads: in fact, there was a moment
when she permitted us, all, to plunge into dangers, out of which
we escaped, as it were, through a miracle of good fortune. This
was pushing maternal tenderness to its extremest verge, for, I
repeat it again, the death of any one of us would have brought *her*
to her end."

But, after the untoward result of the well-known conspiracy of Béfort, in 1822, as well as of some others, less important, the excitements of political feeling began to give place to habits of assiduous labour on the part of the Scheffers. Ary's pencil was taking a higher range; his reputation was augmenting, and his works found a ready sale at good prices. If ever this interesting being had an interval of exemption from care or from suffering, perhaps it was at this period. Yet even now it was clouded by anxiety, on the score of his beloved mother's health. She endured repeated attacks of the disease of which mention has already been made, the result of her former fatiguing exertions; violent palpitations of the heart threatening, in the years 1825–26–27, to deprive her sons of their admirable parent. In the intervals of her complaint, however, Madame Scheffer occupied herself in copying the best of the pictures painted by her own sons (for she had a respectable talent for the art), and in reading the works of the most esteemed authors of the day, on political, literary, and even philosophic subjects: her conversation was, in fact, so enriched thereby, that her society had a great attraction for all who were permitted to enjoy it.

Ary would seem to have cultivated portrait painting a good deal at this stage of his career, although never from preference. (See p. 97.)

Among the most carefully executed of the portraits, about this date, was that of Madame la Duchesse de Broglie, which I am inclined to rate as one of Scheffer's best. It was a fine subject that he had to deal with, and the result was most happy. It is to be regretted that this portrait did not appear among the exhibited works in 1859, as it would doubtless have added new lustre to the fame of the painter.

It would be doing injustice, perhaps, to the proficiency acquired by Scheffer at this stage of his career, if I did not also bestow the passing tribute of praise fairly due to his picture of "Le Baptême" (of 1823). For unaffected sentiment, happy arrangement of the figures, and, I will add, agreeable colouring, it reminds us of Greuze; a painter who greatly influenced the artistic taste of his countrymen, and doubtless that of Scheffer among the rest.

Between the years 1825 and 1830 was the period, during which a different class of compositions, wherein strong action and sentiment prevail, were executed: such as "Les Femmes Souliotes," "La Défense de Missolonghi," "La Rétraite d'Alsace," "La Bataille de Morat," &c. I will only observe, in reference to them, that although a certain measure of ability and progress appears therein, yet there is unquestionably a want of clear and harmonious colouring, as well as of concentrated effect. Since he so far surpassed these productions later in his career, I prefer to take small account of this phase of it, unless perhaps to note the portrait of M. Destutt de Tracy, which is at once impressive and pleasing.

In the year 1826 Ary Scheffer was introduced into the family of the Duke and Duchess of Orleans, by the Baron Gérard. This event was destined to exercise a sensible influence over his whole life, the closing days of which were, as will be seen hereafter, consecrated to the fulfilment of duties whose original source is traceable to his first entrance into the domestic circle of Neuilly. Within this circle were contracted relations of the purest and most delightful character. The poetic and sentimental side of Scheffer's mind found nurture and encouragement, whilst his love of political progress derived support from the pronounced disposition of the head of the house towards liberal ideas.

The special functions which were assigned to Scheffer in this family, were those of instructor of the children in drawing and painting; but the professional talent being combined with rare mental capacity and much intellectual culture, the Duke and Duchess of Orleans, both fully capable of appreciating such a companion, grew fond of having Scheffer about them. Thus, from the "instructor in art," he gradually passed into the familiar and attached friend; not—as a recent French writer has thought fit to term it—" Le complaisant serviteur d'une famille royale bourgeoise:" a relation in which it was morally impossible that Ary Scheffer *could* stand towards any family, "royale" or "roturière."*

---

* As illustrative of the self-respect and independence of the young painter, I will here mention an anecdote, which may be relied upon as authentic. During one of the lessons which, at a later stage, Scheffer was giving to the children of the Royal family, one of the brothers forgot the respect due to the master, and used some unbecoming expressions towards him. Scheffer banished the offending Prince from the lesson. The Queen interposing to obtain a remission of this penalty, Scheffer resigned his appointment. The brothers and sisters were so grieved and discomposed at the loss of their master, that they begged and entreated him to resume his position; yet he was inexorable, until the King, adding his own earnest endeavours, Scheffer was induced to give way, and he presided anew over their artistic studies. But he made it a condition that the mutinous pupil should never more join in the lesson, and he was, accordingly, excluded. I am afraid it must be added that this incident was long remembered by both parties.

On the return from Italy of M. Ingres, the sight of his pictures would seem to have awakened Scheffer's emulous admiration of that painter, whose distinguishing qualities happened to lie in the very direction in which Scheffer was, then, least proficient. M. Ingres' style possessed the elevation, the noble forms, of the ancient school, whilst the mastery he showed over the mechanical portion of the art commanded the homage of connoisseurs, no less than that of the general public.

It is obvious that Scheffer's taste received a strong bias from the contemplation of the works of Ingres, for whom, thenceforward, and indeed to his latest hour, he professed a deep admiration and respect.

One of the first examples of Scheffer's altered mode of composition was a picture from the *Faust* of Goethe—"Faust in his Study."* After this, appeared

---

* Goethe's wonderful poem of "Faust" furnished to Scheffer a subject of which his imagination seems never to have tired. Itself, perhaps, the most remarkable creation of the eighteenth century, "Faust" opened up to his view the vast field of metaphysical speculation. Profoundly as it explores the mysterious relations between the sensual and the intellectual natures of man, whilst exhibiting the varied workings of human passions and weaknesses, "Faust" deals likewise with the tragic element, in a way to touch the deepest chords of sympathy. This combination of the powerful and the mystic, with the tender vein of poetic fiction, awakened in Scheffer's soul, images, which would appear to have floated around his fancy to his latest moment.

Even after he had addressed himself to the illustration of biblical subjects, see how his pencil fondly returns to his Faust!—to the great vivifier of his meridian hour. But to whom, I ask, does *not* this immortal poem recur, at intervals, who has once been lifted, by its wondrous charm, out of the real world in which we live and move, into the boundless realms of imagination ?

the " Margaret at the Spinning Wheel," in which the
abject depression of the young maiden is depicted
with tenderness and pathetic truth.   It has been
cited as one among Scheffer's best productions; yet
I am forced to confess that the colouring strikes
me as monotonous, sickly, and faded, and the attitude of Margaret as unimpressive.*   Far higher in
merit may be ranked his " Margaret at Church,"
where the faculty of " expression," in which Scheffer
now confessedly rose to distinction, is employed in a
striking manner.   The whole composition attests the
care and meditation of a superior mind; the ingenious
apposition of common, indifferent figures, intent upon
ordinary, familiar duties, as against the conscience-
stricken, heart-broken Margaret—her attitude, her
sombre dress, the concentrated feeling indicated by
her countenance, the meaning implied in the position
of the hands,—all combine to rivet the spectator's
attention upon this painfully interesting work.

Inspired at this period by the powerful poem of
Lord Byron, Scheffer painted " The Giaour," a work
which may fairly claim to be placed high in the series
of Scheffer's single figures, as well for vigour of handling as for the exhibition of vehement mental emotion.   The absence of colour here rather adds to than
weakens the effect of the picture, by which the
amateur will naturally be reminded of certain works
of Murillo, Alonzo Cano, Juanes, Morales, and other
Spanish masters—often executed with as little aid
from colour, yet producing a grave, solemn impression.

---

* I have reason to believe that a much finer picture of this same subject exists in Holland, in the collection of M. Nottebohn. (See p. 54.)

CHAPTER III.

1827—1830.

Charles X.—Grand Review of the National Guard—Arbitrary proceedings of M. de Villèle—Indisposition of Madame Scheffer.

HAVING reached the point at which I conceive the
talent of Ary Scheffer to have received a new, lofty,
and poetical impulse, I will suspend the thread of his
artistic progress for a moment, in order to return to
that of his "civilian" duties and personal history.
It is in conformity with the design indicated in the
first page of this humble memoir, that I endeavour to
keep both of these two currents in view: so far, at
least, as it is permitted to me to delineate the personal
course. But it is necessary to preface what I shall
have to relate, by a review of the state of public
feeling, and the aspect of political affairs, in 1826 and
following years.

The first acts of Charles the Tenth's reign (beginning
with 1825) were marked by a disposition so unmis-
takeable towards absolute rule, that all liberal Frenchmen were kept, as it were, on the alert: expecting
that measures might very likely be resorted to, on
the part of the executive government, deeply affecting the permanent interests of the nation. The
minister at the head of affairs in 1826 was M. de
Villèle, himself by no means so thoroughgoing a
partisan of absolutism as many others of his class,

yet too fondly attached to the exercise of power not
to endeavour to preserve it by trimming between
the commands of his master and the risks of opposition. Defeated, by the strenuous efforts of the
Liberals in and out of the Chamber, in a *projet de loi*
bearing upon the procedure of the courts of justice,
upon the liberty of the press, upon individual secu-
rity—said *projet* being, in fact, an attack upon public
liberty in all its aspects—M. de Villèle's government
became sensibly discredited, and lost much of its
power. Nevertheless, "Il persista," says M. Villemain, "dans d'autres rigueurs; ménaça, destitua,
et crut pouvoir se faire craindre par des brutalités de
police."

Not long after experiencing this check, the King
thought fit to order a grand review (at the end of
the month of April, 1827) of the National Guard. M.
de Villèle demurred, urging the danger of the step;
M. de Chateaubriand, even, deprecated it, going the
length of addressing to Charles X. himself a respectful letter, in which, along with other contingencies,
he hinted at the possibility of a popular demonstra-
tion in Paris: ending with a recommendation to the
King to dismiss the actual ministry, and to construct
in its place, one which should be presided over by
M. le Duc de Doudeauville and M. le Comte de
Chabrol. No notice was, however, taken of this re-
monstrance. The review was held, giving occasion
to various uncomfortable manifestations of public
feeling; among the rest, some of the companies of
the National Guard cried " à bas Villèle," in passing
before the windows of the " Ministère des Finances,"
in the Rue de Rivoli. This insult was too much for

the minister's stomach, and he consequently pressed upon the King the necessity of dismissing the National Guard altogether.*   Backed by M. le Baron de Damas, M. de Clermont Tonnerre, M. de Peyronnet, and M. de Corbière, the incensed minister carried his point, and not only got rid of the National Guard, but re-established the censure of the Press; persuaded as he was (like another French minister, of our time) that, so long as he could depend on the support of a majority in the Chamber, all was safe. Much dissatisfaction being shown, however, out of doors, M. de Villèle, farther irritated by the able attacks directed against him in print, took the bold measure of dissolving the Chamber.   The electoral colleges signified, by their choice in the new elections, their disapprobation of the course pursued; and it may be worthy of record that M. Royer Collard was now elected for no less than seven places.

Thus the "lull" which had succeeded to the discouraging incidents I have mentioned as occurring towards the close of Louis the Eighteenth's reign, was, in 1827, quickly exchanged for fresh activity in the ranks of the malcontents.   The public were aroused to displeasure by the arbitrary proceedings of M. de Villèle, and the veteran "Carbonari" once more buckled on their armour for resistance. La Grange was still, as ever, the stronghold of Liberalism.   One of its cherished "habitués," Charles Comte, had been exiled and persecuted for his writings; but now, recently returned to France, he lent his able assistance in "the good cause."   Scheffer

---

* See Villemain's "Chateaubriand," Paris, 1858.

resorted, as heretofore, to General Lafayette's
"château," as well as to his hôtel in Paris: and
being personally connected besides with the advanced
members of the party, he was thoroughly cognizant
of all that went on in the way of political agitation.
With the ardent temperament which characterized
him, nurtured from his cradle in the love of freedom
and of the public good, and sharing the councils of
the most distinguished leaders of the Opposition—no
wonder that Ary Scheffer's life was now one of
fatiguing excitement. To quote an expression of a
contemporary writer (in speaking of General Foy's
death):—"La vie politique use les hommes de cœur
aussi rapidement que la vie du champ de bataille; ses
luttes, ses émotions, les veilles, le travail, brisent
surtout très vite les nobles organisations."

Madame Scheffer's chronic complaint again, in
1827–28, caused to Ary, as well as to her other
sons, cruel apprehension; so that, between the political ferment around him, his pressing need to labour
at his profession, and his anxiety for the prolongation
of his beloved mother's life, the strain upon Scheffer's
mind and nervous energy was at this time considerable.

CHAPTER IV.

1830.

Political discontents—Elections of 1830—La Grange—Revolution
of July—Ary's mission to Neuilly—M. Thiers—Lafayette—
Offers made to the Duke of Orleans.

TOWARDS the spring of 1830, the principles between
which the destinies of France appeared to oscillate,
i.e., that of an undisguised despotism, or of a constitutional *régime*, were obviously about to receive a
solution in one or another shape.   The audacious
step taken by Charles of dissolving the Chamber, set
all the Liberals in motion.   Each man flew to his
post, and the " exaltation" became as lively as it was
far-spreading.

   I may here take leave to mention, perhaps, that
at this precise juncture, Mr. G. and myself happened
to be on a visit at La Grange itself, where a scene
was passing calculated to make, and to leave, ineffaceable impressions.   It was in the month of May,
1830, that, on one of the mornings of our stay, there
came to La Grange a numerous body of electors
of the " arrondissement," for which M. Geo. Lafayette was a candidate for re-election.   The general
elections being close at hand, it was desirable that
the electors favourable to him should communicate

personally with him and the General.   I think that
about forty of them sate down to breakfast along with
the family, in the great hall of the château, and a
striking sight it was to us, as I well remember.   The
General sate in the centre; I was placed by his side,
and the numerous branches of the family dispersed
themselves among the company at different parts of
the table.   The cordiality, courtesy, and good feeling
which reigned amongst this large assemblage, it was
most pleasing to witness.   The repast was plain and
abundant; but little " talk" prevailed, and no healths
were drunk, although wine formed, as usual, the
common beverage.

After the "dejeuner," the house guests withdrew,
and the electors held a long consultation on the business
which had brought them thither, with their hosts.
The spacious courtyard of the château, into which we
strolled the while, was crowded with the vehicles in
which these good people had travelled (many from a
long distance) to La Grange. Every sort of "patâche,"
cabriolet, char-à-banc, and " cariole," was there: all,
of course, covered with dust and dirt, the harness
equally begrimed: cleaning of wheels and harness
being a practice nearly unknown (at least at the
period of which I write) among the rural inhabitants
of the provinces.   The horses found ample stable
room and provender on the premises.

In Paris, and at other places on our homeward
route, the animation which we found everywhere prevailing on the subject of the elections, attested the
importance of the crisis.   Wherever we stopped to
change horses, the villagers—women as well as men—
came flocking out to interrogate the postilion about

the elections. " Est-il nommé, M. Harlay?* dites
donc!" *A postmaster* — " Le Roi veut donc une
nouvelle chambre!   Eh bien! nous allons lui en
envoyer une," &c. &c.

We had quitted the shores of France shortly prior
to the grand, the almost sublime, uprising of July,
which " settled the business," for that time at least;
but I have a peculiar inducement to enlarge upon this
preliminary matter, because the political events of
1830 happen to bring Scheffer before us, not as a
painter, but as an actor on the stage, in the part of
an active and influential " citizen."

The ferment into which Paris was thrown by the
news of the famous " Ordonnances" gave occasion to
the surmise that matters were likely to come to some
forcible collision.   On the morning of the 28th July,
Scheffer, being abroad early in the streets, met a political friend going towards the " barrière." " Ho!" quoth
Scheffer, " why, your steps are turned in the wrong
direction; you ought to stay in Paris, and stand by
your friends at this critical juncture." " Ah! my
dear fellow, you must know that *I* am not a fighting
man, and I foresee that there will be a hard struggle
between the soldiers and the people."   " I expect no
less," rejoined Ary; " mais la partie est engagée, et il
faut la jouer."†   The friend, nevertheless, went his
way, and, sure enough, the conflict quickly commenced—with what ardour and what unflinching
bravery we all of us well recollect.   Scheffer was

* M. Harlay was the Liberal candidate for the " Pas de Calais,"
in 1830.
† " But the game is begun, and we must play it out!"

among those who fought unceasingly through two of the "glorious days" which crowned the resistance with victory.

On the morrow of the third and decisive day of July, that is to say, on the 30th, Scheffer, fairly tired out with the efforts of the three previous days, was in his own house in the Rue Chaptal (the same in which he continued to reside until his death), when he was surprised by the entrance of Monsieur Thiers.* " Eh bien! Scheffer, me voici! j'ai besoin de vous : j'ai tout fait."† " Comment, '*tout fait?*' "‡ calmly inquired Scheffer. " Well, I mean that I have been to the Hôtel de Ville, seen the members of the Municipal Committee, seen the 'Chefs de partis' at Lafitte's, and, in short, I am the bearer of a communication to the Duke of Orleans, which you must assist me in conveying to Neuilly." " Tiens!"§ replied Scheffer; "so, you mean that I am to go with you as a kind of commissioner from the leaders of the party?" " I do," rejoined M. Thiers, 'and for this reason, among others, that you are known to keep good horses in your stable; for, look you, we can go in no other way

---

* It may be well to remind those of my readers in whose recollection such facts have ceased to dwell, that MM. Thiers, Carrel, and Mignet were perhaps the earliest as well as the most courageous initiators of the resistance to " Les Ordonnances." M. Thiers especially, then " rédacteur en chef" of the journal, *Le National*, exercised the ascendancy which his rare talents and activity of mind justly claimed over his fellow-citizens, turning it to good account at this momentous epoch.

† " Well, Scheffer, here I am! I want you : I have done everything that was necessary."

‡ " How! done everything?"

§ " Hey-day!"

than by riding on horseback." "That is certain," quoth Scheffer; "the barricades would render the passage of a carriage impossible." "But stay," said Thiers; "how shall I manage about my *montûre?* I shall never be able to sit one of *your* great beasts." Thereupon Scheffer hastened to the stables of young Ney (son of the Marshal), with whom he was on intimate terms, and, borrowing a small, nimble nag for his friend, they started on their important errand.

The barricades presented, in truth, some obstacles to their progress, but Scheffer being a practised horseman, leaped his horse over them. M. Thiers could not manage matters quite so actively. The mob, however, good-naturedly aided him to scramble through, lifting him, almost bodily, over the piles of stones, &c., horse and all, laughing heartily at " le petit commis" for his bad horsemanship. As M. Thiers rode in white stockings and shoes, and wore spectacles, I suspect that his personal appearance did afford some scope for the light-hearted jokes of " le peuple" on that morning.

When, at length, the two gentlemen found themselves fairly outside of the walls of Paris, a number of men of the lower class crowded about them—" Où allez-vous donc, Messieurs?"* " Cela ne vous régarde pas."† " Eh bien! then we shall send some of our fellows with you, to *see* where you go to." A couple of " blouses" accordingly accompanied them, each mounted on horseback, and armed. The party had not trotted far on their road before Thiers said, in a

---

* " Whither are you bound, gentlemen ?"
† " That is no concern of yours."

quiet tone of voice, to his companion, " Ecoutez, mon
cher! you are a good rider, whilst *I* may very
easily get a tumble before I reach Neuilly; and if
this should happen, my hat will inevitably roll off,
and the *mandât* which, before we set off, I put therein
for safety, may be discovered, and then I shall get into
trouble: I beg you will take charge of it."   Scheffer
took the paper, and placed it in his breast pocket.   It
was a sort of *blanc seing*, to which the names of Lafayette, Lafitte, Marshals Lobau and Gérard, and
one or two other leading men, were appended.
The Duke, it was expected, would, on looking at the
paper, frame some sort of "declaration" in reply to
the missive.

At the Bridge of Neuilly, Scheffer wanted sadly to
get rid of his neighbours in the "blouses."   Pretend-
ing to descry some of the King's troops at a distance,
he cried out, " Ah! here come our friends, I see; it
is the royal guard!"   Whereupon the two attendants
judged it prudent to wish them "good morning," and
to turn their horses' heads the other way.   The two
envoys quickly arrived at the Château de Neuilly.
M. Scheffer (from whose lips I learned what has been
related above) gave me no details of what passed
within its walls, except to mention one circumstance,
viz., that Madame Adelaide, addressing her brother,
had said, "Sire! conduisez-vous en Roi."*

Let me halt a space here to invite attention to the
singular fate of Scheffer, in reference to his connexion with the family of Orleans.   We have seen
that he was the first to open up a prospect of the

---

* "Sire! pray behave as becomes a king!"

crown of France to his royal patron, in 1830—
eighteen years later, it is again Scheffer, as we
shall find, who, by pure accident, hands the King
into the "rémise" which bears him away from his
capital—never more to return—a dethroned monarch
and a fugitive!

The Duchess of Orleans (so says at least Vaulabelle) reproved Scheffer for venturing to suppose that such a proposal as that of which M.
Thiers and he were the bearers, could be acceptable
to her husband. "That M. Thiers should have done
this," said her Royal Highness, "does not surprise
me. *He* knows but little about us; but you, Sir,—
you who have been admitted to so close an intimacy
with this circle, *you* might have appreciated our
sentiments more correctly."

But I must not permit myself to linger too long
over the details of the negotiation, as between the
leading members of the Liberal party and deputies on
the one side, and the family of Orleans on the other.
They are to be found abundantly distributed through
the various memoirs which have been published,
relating to this singularly interesting and—I may
add—creditable passage of French history. One
feature of the transaction, however, I must call
attention to—I mean the pertinacious endeavour
of General Lafayette to turn to account this rare
opportunity, by obtaining some sort of pledges,
or guarantees, for the future better administration of the Government. He would, I really believe, have insisted on obtaining better terms for
the popular party—even whilst accepting the Duke

of Orleans as King* — but for the uncertainty
felt by a considerable number of persons, as. to
the relative force of the Royalist troops and the
people. The situation was, undeniably, critical:
and it is nowise surprising that, since the scales
hung vibrating between the courses open, the emphatic counsel of General Sebastiani, to make sure of
at least the advantage of ridding the nation of
Charles X., should be effectual; nor, that the Assembly
should, on the proposition of M. Lafitte, declare, "à
l'unanimité" (minus three voices), for appointing M.
the Duc d'Orleans Lieutenant-General of the kingdom. MM. Labbey de Pompierès and Corcelles,
it must be added, loudly insisting on coupling
the invitation to that Prince with stipulations and
conditions; M. Villemain, on the other hand, crying
out, "that they could not pretend to have any right
to change the dynasty."

This latter protest falling utterly flat upon the
Assembly, twelve names were drawn out by lot
to form a commission, which was ordered to wait,
forthwith, upon the Duke of Orleans. [This was a few
hours after Scheffer had returned from Neuilly.] The
commissioners found him not at his residence in the
Palais Royal. Neuilly was too near St. Cloud to be

---

* See the letter which he addressed to the Chamber, then
actually deliberating ˙on this point, on the 30th July, by the
hands of M. Odillon Barrot (secretary of the municipal commission), who, clothed in the uniform of an officer of the National
Guard, carried it in person to the Palais Bourbon. (Vaulabelle,
vol. viii. p. 347.)

safe for them, so a messenger was dispatched, bearing
a letter signed by the commissioners, and he, having
managed to get upon the trace of the missing Duke
(whom he discovered alone in a secluded summer-
house in the park of Neuilly), brought back an answer
that his Royal Highness " would come to Paris on the
following day." " To-morrow !" cried M. Lafitte (who
was the very soul of the party in whose name the offer
was tendered), " let him come this instant, if he
values his chance;" and the messenger started afresh
for Neuilly.*

One single individual remained closeted with M.
Lafitte, at midnight, in his own hôtel (July 30) : it was
M. Benjamin Constant.   The slackness of the Duke
occasioned to M. Lafitte some misgivings as to the
result of the serious measure which had been taken.
He said to his companion, " I wonder what will come
of it all, to-morrow?"   " To-morrow," replied with
his habitual *légèreté*, Benjamin Constant, " why, very
likely to-morrow *we* shall all be hanged !"   The ur-
gent summons of M. Lafitte, however, determined the
hesitating Prince to repair to Paris.   He came on
foot, attended by two military friends, towards midnight : and slipping through the crowd, unrecognised,
entered silently the gates of the Palais Royal, " le
Roi du lendemain."

---

* Souvenirs de Bérard.

CHAPTER V.

(REIGN OF KING LOUIS PHILIPPE.)

1830—1835.

Government of Louis Philippe—The Princess Marie of Orleans—
The King orders pictures for Versailles—Scheffer accompanies
the King's eldest son to Antwerp—Appearance of the " Francesca di Rimini"—Birth of his daughter—Generous conduct of
Ary's mother—Correspondence relative to new government.

THE new order of things encouraged, in most of
the Liberal party, hopes of a more approvable system
of government.   M. Odillon Barrot was named Pre-
fect of the Seine, M. Charles Comte, his friend, Pro-
cureur du Roi, and others, of declared popular
opinions, received appointments.   Scheffer's adhesion
to the Orleans ascendancy was of course quickened
by feelings of personal attachment to that family, and
he continued to be their frequent visitor, as formerly.
The King gave him orders for pictures suitable to the
galleries of Versailles, whilst the heir apparent (now
become Duke of Orleans) bespoke and purchased
others, of a stamp more congenial with the painter's
own choice and impulses.   The young Princess Marie,
lately sprung to womanhood, studied and worked as a
pupil with Scheffer, and in the master presently found
a devoted friend.   Their characters, as well as their
tastes, happened to fall in with each other, and there
is little doubt but that the liberal and patriotic ten-
dencies which existed in that charming young per-

son's mind, derived strength and confirmation through
her conversations with her master.   I have heard
this alluded to in a tone somewhat akin to censure,
but feel persuaded that Scheffer would never have
sought to *engraft* his own opinions upon the daughter
of his sovereign.   Finding the spontaneous dispositions of the Princess accord with them, however, he
could hardly do otherwise than allow her to perceive
the coincidence.

By all good Frenchmen, the memory of this interesting young Princess is. regarded with affection
and reverence.   Cut off in the morning of life, endowed (as she was) with gifts of every kind, and a
heart which throbbed with the truest love of her
country—she left a sort of saint-like, luminous track
behind her, at her too early departure.   Ary Scheffer
was grieved to the soul for her loss, for few persons
knew and valued the Princess better than himself.
I am, fortunately, able to present my readers with
a sketch of her character, as well as of his relations
with her as "professor," which cannot fail to be acceptable.   The sketch is precious, as coming from
Scheffer's own pen, but it is, moreover, traced with
judgment and a finely discriminating hand.

Arnold Scheffer had once the intention (though it
remained unfulfilled) to compose a biographical
sketch of the Princess Marie of Wirtemburgh.   He requested his brother to aid him, by furnishing some
"notes" respecting her early years; and Ary wrote
down what follows,* in the year 1839.

"Les 'notes' que tu me demandes, mon chèr

---

* "To furnish you, my dear Arnold, with what you require of

Arnold, sur les travaux et sur les idées de la Princesse
Marie, sont très difficiles à faire.

" Elevée à la façon de toute princesse, par Madame
de Malet, personne fort instruite, fort pieuse, mais aux
idées les plus bornées possibles, elle était, *Enfant,* la
petite princesse la plus impertinente, la plus étourdie
qu'on puisse imaginer. Mais tout en se moquant de
ses maîtres, elle apprenait ce qu'il fallait apprendre—
langues vivantes, histoire, etc. etc. Un seul maître,
(M. Pradher) eut le mérite—par une severité non in-
terrompue, mais sans un mouvement de colère—de
lui inspirer du respect—elle lui devait en outre, un
talent de musicienne assez distingué.

" Les leçons de dessin que je lui donnai depuis l'âge
de douze ans, n'avaient jamais été qu'un passe temps
pour elle et pour moi.—Elle faisait peu de progrès,
et n'a jamais su dessiner une tête même d'après la
bosse. Quand sa sœur ainée s'est mariée, cette jeune

---

me, viz., some particulars respecting the Princess Marie of Orleans,
is no easy task for me to attempt.

"She was brought up after the manner of all princesses, by
Madame de Malet, a person of education, and religiously disposed,
but having exceedingly narrow and restricted ideas of things. The
Princess was, as a child, impertinent, heedless, and wild to a degree ;
yet she learned what she was taught—languages, history, and so
forth—though habitually indulging in saucy sallies at the expense of
her instructors. One of these alone (Mr. Pradher), managed to control the Princess, and, by an inflexible sternness, untinged with angry
temper, to inspire his pupil with respect. He also directed (and with
ability) her musical talent, which, in itself, was above the ordinary level.

"Such lessons as, from the age of twelve years and onwards, I
had been in the habit of giving her, were never much else than an
amusing pastime, either for master or pupil. The Princess made
but slight progress, and could at no time draw a head correctly,
from the plaster model. Upon the marriage of her elder sister, this

fille, jusque là si étourdie, etait devenue tout d'un
coup triste et reflective.   Elle me demanda sérieuse-
ment de lui donner des leçons capables de la distraire
et de l'occuper, tout en me disant que de copier l'en-
nuyait à mourir.

"Elle essaya de faire des compositions de sujets
historiques et de les colorer au lavis.   Dès le prémier
essai, tout son talent, tout son imagination me furent
révélés.   Dans l'éspace de deux ans elle fit plus de
cinquante dessins, tout composés, tout trouvés d'expression, avec une originalité et un bonheur très
remarquables; mais tous très incorrects de dessin, et
bien médiocrement colorés.   Les idées etroites de
Madame de Malet, les craintes de la Reine, et mon
respect, à moi, pour la pudeur de jeune fille, empê-
cherent les progrés de dessin et d'execution.—Ne
pouvant copier que des figures drapées, (et très drapées) elle a toujours ignoré la structure du corps hu-

---

young girl, till now careless and unreflecting, became all at once
serious and pensive.   She entreated me earnestly to afford her
instruction of a nature to occupy and interest her mind, and to
distract her attention from the loss she had sustained; but she
added that, 'as to setting about to *copy*, it was too tiresome an
affair by half for her to attempt it.'

"So she took to composing historical subjects, washing them in
with water colour.   The very first trials which she made, revealed
to me the existence of undoubted talent, and of her imaginative
faculty.   Within the space of two years, she executed more than
fifty drawings; all of them showing a certain power of design,
carried out with originality and good general effect, though faulty
in drawing, and but indifferently coloured.   The contracted notions
of Madame de Malet, the scruples of the Queen, and the reverential
feeling in my own breast, as towards maidenly purity and reserve—
all these offered serious impediments to regular artistic instruction;
so that, being restricted to the copying of draped figures, (and

main. Ennuyée de toujours bien composer, et de
toujours mal dessiner, elle prit le dessin en dégout, et
me demanda un jour si je ne pourrais pas lui donner
quelquechose à faire de moins monotone, et que tout
le monde ne ferait pas comme elle? Ennuyé moi-
même, de corriger tous les jours des bras cassées et
des jambes tordues, je l'engageai à essayer de la
sculpture, que je n'avais jamais faite, et dont la nouveauté était aussi attrayante pour moi que pour elle.

"Le premier essai fut le petit bas-relief de *Goetz
et Martin*, composé simplement, l'execution étant tout
à fait l'enfance de l'art.

"Ce premier essai n'était pas encourageant, mais le
jour même où cet essai révenait du mouleur, le livre
de Quinet, 'Ashéverus' se trouvait sur la table : elle
venait de le lire, composa et ébacha sur le champ,
Ashéverus, à qui l'ange Gabriel défend l'entrée de sa

---

those *abundantly* draped,) the Princess remained, of necessity, wholly
unacquainted with the structure of the human body.

"At length, weary of composing cleverly, and executing unskil-
fully, she became out of humour with her drawing ; and one day she
inquired of me, 'whether I could not find something for her to do,
less dull and monotonous, and less like what other people did?'
To say the truth, I was myself somewhat tired of having continually
to correct her bad drawing of legs and arms, often distorted and out
of all shape. I suggested, then, to the Princess the idea of trying
her hand at modelling and sculpture : a walk of art wherein I was
equally unpractised with herself, and which therefore offered to both
of us the attraction of novelty.

"Our first essay was the small bas-relief of 'Göetz and Martin ;'
very simply designed, and executed with the imperfect skill of mere
novices. This was not a very encouraging beginning, certainly ; but
it happened that on the day when the plaster cast of the clay model
was sent home, M. Quinet's book, 'Ahasuerus,' fell into the hands of
the Princess. She began a group forthwith, of 'Ahasuerus refused
admittance within the abode of the Angel Gabriel.' In this 'bas-relief.'

maison.   Dans ce bas-relief, l'instinct de sculpture se
révèle : la connaissance des plans, une forme particu-
lière et originale, une expression frappante, denotant
une vraie vocation d'artiste.   Dès ce moment elle
prit la passion de la sculpture, et moi, pour dire vrai,
la passion de lui donner des leçons.   Pendant qu'elle
travaillait, je lui cherchais des sujets à exécuter ; dans
Quinet, puis dans Schiller, qu'elle ne connaissait pas ;
puis dans Goethe.—Le premier sujet qu'elle prit fut
' le Reveil du Poëte,' qu'elle composa entièrement, dont
je lui dessinai seulement quelques têtes sur papier.—
Ce bas-relief est, pour quiconque a le gout de l'art,
une chose admirable de conception, et pour tout
homme qui peut juger de la difficulté vraie, une chose
hors ligne.   La manière dont instinctivement elle a
deviné les plans multipliés de ce bas-relief, et dont les
caractères divers des personnages sont indiqués, ne
peuvent vraiment se comprendre dans une jeune fille
qui, en sculpture en était à son troisième essai, et qui
n'avait lu les poëtes et romanciers que sous la direc-

---

was now disclosed the indubitable instinct of a sculptor. Along with
a perception of distances (by diversity of surface), and quite an original style of arranging the figures, there was joined so much of expression, that the whole thing bore evidence of a true vocation for the art.

"From this moment, a passion for sculpture took deep hold of the
Princess, and I must own that I felt scarcely less pleasure in giving
her lessons in it.   Whilst *she* was at work, *I* sought out suitable
subjects for her to execute ; in the works of Quinet, then in those
of Schiller (which were new to her): and later, from those of
Goethe.   Her first choice fell upon ' le Reveil du Pöete,' from which
she ' composed' the whole of a bas-relief: my aid being rendered by
drawing heads for her on paper.   Viewed as an ideal piece of
sculpture, and furthermore, as a triumph over recognised difficulties,
this performance must be regarded as something extraordinary in
itself; but, as the production of a young girl, who was actually only

tion d'une gouvernante devôte.   Après ce bas-relief,
elle fit le modèle de bronze de 'Jeanne à cheval;' la
conception est entièrement d'elle, la figure de Jeanne
est bien trouvée, mais dans l'exécution matérielle je
l'aidai beaucoup.   A cette époque le Roi avait com-
mandé à Pradier, notre premier statuaire, une statue
de Jeanne d'Arc, pour Versailles.   Mal inspiré, Pradier fit un modèle qui ne rendait nullement cette
noble figure; alors le Roi commanda un autre projet
de statue à sa fille; la Princesse accepta, apres m'avoir
consulté, mais à condition de faire *aussi* la grande
statue, si le modèle réussissait.

"Ce fut au moment de commencer ce travail qu'elle
perdit Madame de Malet.   Cette pauvre femme, qui,
tout en idolatrant son élève, la querellait du matin au

---

at her third attempt in modelling, and who had read works of poetry
and fiction under the sober influence of a gouvernante of strict
piety, this work is truly surprising; the gradations of the ground
plan, and the characteristic indications of the various personages
introduced, being managed with singular and happy ingenuity.

"After completing this 'bas-relief,' she modelled the 'Joan of Arc
on horseback,' of which the conception is entirely due to herself.   The
figure of 'Joan' has much merit, but in the manipulation of this
model I gave the Princess a good deal of help.

"About this period, the King had bespoken of Pradier—our most
approved artist in statuary—a monumental figure of Joan of Arc,
for the museum of Versailles.   Pradier chanced to be in no happy
vein at the moment, and so produced a design, which fell far short
of the mark.   The King, not feeling satisfied with it, asked his
daughter to try and invent another; she accepted the commission,
after consulting with myself, but coupled her acceptance with this
stipulation—that should her design be successful, she should be
entrusted with the execution of it in the marble.

"Just as the Princess had begun upon this task, she lost Madame
de Malet.   To this poor woman,—who, whilst she idolized her
young charge, nevertheless tormented her from morning to night,—

soir, mais dont la bonté et le dévouement désinte-
ressées rachetait tout l'ennui, reçut de la Princesse
Marie durant sa maladie, des soins de fille. Elle ne
quitta pas sa vieille gouvernante pendant plusieurs
jours et plusieurs nuits, et reçut son dernier soupir.
La séparation avec sa sœur avait operé un premier
changement dans son esprit; la perte de sa gouvernante changea complètement son cœur; ses regrets
pour cette pauvre femme ont duré tout sa vie, et à
chaque instant elle invoquait son souvenir. Madame
de Malet m'avait beaucoup aimé; à cause de cela
surtout, la confiance de la princesse pour moi redoubla.
Elle me fit chercher au moment ou sa gouvernante
venait d'expirer, et je puis dire que jamais je n'ai vu
douleur plus vraie, ni plus touchante.

"Au bout de peu de temps je la forçai de ré-
commencer à travailler. Une grande composition

---

the Princess rendered the tender offices of a daughter; attending
upon her as such, assiduously, all through her illness. She would
not quit her sick chamber during several days and nights, until she
at length received Madame de Malet's last breath. The devoted
affection and disinterested character of Madame de Malet, had
caused her tiresome, querulous ways to be forgiven by those about
her, insomuch that the Princess mourned over her loss with genuine
regret. The parting from her own sister had brought about the first
change in her character; the separation which now took place by the
death of her 'gouvernante,' affected her feelings profoundly, and indeed shed a painful reminiscence over her whole after life.

"Madame de Malet had always shown partiality towards myself,
which encouraged the Princess to repose confidence in me. When her
'gouvernante' died, she sent for me to come to her, and I may say
that never was grief more sincere or more affecting to witness.

"In the course of a little time I persuaded her to resume work
again. Her attention first fixed itself upon a grand composition,*

---

* "Ahasuerus" is the title of a French tale, or sort of "biblical
novel," *I believe;* but I have never seen the book.

'd'Ashéverus' l'occupa d'abord—En haut, Dieu : dans
le milieu le Christ portant sa croix, et le Juif qui lui
refuse de se reposer à sa porte—a droite les tribus
primitives descendant l'Himalaya — à gauche, les
monuments de la civilisation Egyptienne, Grécque et
Romaine; en bas l'enfer, recevant dans ses bras les tro-
phées des batailles qui ont terminé les grandes epoques
historiques.   Tout cela, merveilleusement arrangé et
bien dessiné, aurait fait honneur à tout artiste distingué.

Elle commença la grande figure de Jeanne d'Arc.
L'experience materielle lui manquait ainsi qu'à
moi.   Au lieu d'exécuter cette figure en terre,
qui est facile à manier, nous imaginâmes de la
faire en cire.   Elle tomba deux fois, s'affaissa une
troisième; puis toujours impossibilité d'avoir des
modèles.   Malgré toutes ces difficultés, cette statue
est la meilleure statue moderne de Versailles.   La

'Ahasuerus.'   Above she placed the figure of the Deity ; in the
centre Jesus Christ, bearing the cross, and the Jew who refuses
him permission to rest beneath his porch.   On the right, native
tribes descending from the Himalaya mountains : on the left,
monuments indicative of Egyptian, Greek, and Roman civilization.
In the lower part of the design are represented infernal personages
receiving the trophies of battles which had closed one or other of
certain great historic periods.   All this, wonderfully well handled,
and skilfully composed, might have done credit to no matter what
artist, however distinguished.

"She then set to work upon the modelling of her celebrated
figure, 'Joan of Arc watching by her Armour,' in attempting
which, both the fair sculptor and myself found ourselves very deficient in the mechanical experience required.   Instead of moulding
the form in clay, we took it into our heads to model it in wax.   It
fell to pieces more than once, then it bent down at a third attempt ;
furthermore, living models were unattainable.   For all this, the
statue finally came out the finest *modern* figure to be found at
Versailles ! Not alone does its impressive attitude, its simplicity,

noblesse, la simplicité, et un admirable caractère
feminin la distinguent des vulgaires productions qui
l'entourent, parce qu'elle porte non seulement l'em-
preinte du talent, mais surtout l'expression de l'âme
élevée de son auteur! Le succès de cette statue fût
immense; les adulations ne manquèrent pas, mais
jamais je n'ai vu un mépris plus grand pour les
flatteries, que celui qu'elle éxprima; quoique bien
méprisante dans cette occasion, comme, du reste,
toujours pour l'entourage officiel, elle était ravie
comme un enfant, du succès de son œuvre parmi le
peuple, et surtout parmi les soldats.

"Depuis .elle fit 'la Pérîe' portant aux pieds de
l'eternel les larmes du pêcheur repentant—l'ange à la
porte du ciel—le groupe d'Ashéverus et Rachel—le
buste de sa sœur et de son fils—deux petits groupes
équestres, et 'le Pelerin' de Schiller. Dans chaque
œuvre subséquente, il y avait progrès. Le travail

---

and its distinctive feminine character contrast favourably with certain vulgar productions among which it stands, but it carries upon
itself the stamp both of the genius and the elevation of soul possessed by its author.

"The success which attended the appearance of this statue was
prodigious. The most flattering applause was lavished upon it, yet
I never saw flattery received with greater indifference than by this
Princess. Though always manifesting, more or less plainly, her
contempt for the 'official tribe' around her, she was as delighted
as would have been any child, at the success of her work among *the
people;* and, more than all, with the admiration bestowed on it by
the soldiers. •

"Succeeding to the above came—I. 'The Peri' bearing the tears
of the repentant sinner to the foot of the throne of grace. II.
Angel at the gates of Heaven. III. Ahasuerus and Rachel. IV.
Bust of her sister, with her son. V. Two small equestrian
groups; and VI. the 'Pilgrim,' from Schiller. In each of these

était dévenu une telle passion pour elle, qu'à l'insu de sa famille elle y donnait une partie de ses nuits. Elle rêvait une vie élevée d'artiste, et d'éxercer une grande influence sur les arts en France. Elle lisait tout ce qui pouvait développer son intelligence; œuvres de science, comme œuvres d'imagination; tout était lu, et bien compris par elle. Elle admirait tout ce qui était, ou paraissait, grand et beau. Les larmes lui sont venues dans les yeux quand elle apprit la mort de Carrel, qu'elle jugeait, pourtant, très bien, être l'ennemi le plus dangereux de sa famille. Son cœur avait toute la foi religieuse qu'un noble cœur de femme peut contenir, mais son esprit osait aborder toutes les questions, et ne réculait, en discutant, devant aucune de leurs conséquences. Avec ses gouts d'artiste, avec l'élèvation de son esprit, avec sa bonté de cœur (qui était toute autre chose que la bonté

---

performances, and in some which followed, decided and progressive improvement was discernible. The occupation had, indeed, taken such hold upon her that, unknown to her parents, she would actually sit up at night to pursue it. Her settled dream was, to lead the life of an elevated, conscientious artist, and thus to exercise a beneficial influence over high art in France. She chose for her studies books calculated to ripen and develope her intellectual faculties. Scientific treatises, imaginative works, everything was read, and read with profit, by her. All that seemed great and worthy of admiration she prized at its full value. Thus, on learning the sad end of Armand Carrel, the tears rose to her eyes, notwithstanding that he was, and that she knew him to be, perhaps the most formidable among the enemies of her house.

"In the heart of this Princess dwelt a religious faith, such as became a noble, womanly heart. Nevertheless, her ardent mind sought to penetrate into subjects offering certain difficulties, without fear of being led into danger by the inquiry.

"The artistic tastes of the Princess, the lofty range of her under-

banale des grands) elle devait se trouver en désaccord continuel avec l'entourage royal. Elle avait le senti-ment aristocratique, mais n'était nullement *Princesse*. Toutes ses amitiés d'enfance, elle les avait réligieuse-ment conservées jusqu'à sa mort. Avec un senti-ment de patriotisme français très exalté, elle avait pris une haine profonde pour ce qui se passait en France. Sa maladie et les derniers mois de sa vie, mois de souffrance, dont elle savait la fin avant de quitter la France, sont un exemple de grandeur et de resignation."

In 1832 the King requested Scheffer to accompany his eldest son to Antwerp, where the siege operations were being actively carried on: General Baudrand, the military governor, as it were, of the young Duke of Orleans, having the responsible charge of him on

---

standing, and the sterling benevolence of her heart (which was quite a different thing from the 'kindness' often present in the royal character), all combined to engender a coldness and contra-riety of views between herself and the persons composing the Court of her royal father. Her sentiments were of the kind termed aris-tocratic; still she was, properly speaking, in nowise the 'Princess.' Such early friendships as she had contracted in her childhood were religiously cherished and cultivated up to her dying day. Ani-mated as the Princess was by patriotic ardour in desiring the wel-fare of her country, it was to be expected that what was passing before her eyes in France should inspire her, as it did, with pro-found disapprobation and disgust.

"Her pulmonary disease, which lasted several months—months of physical suffering—was borne by the Princess with a resignation and courageous self-command worthy of herself. She was aware, indeed, of the inevitable fate which hung over her, even before she took leave of her family to go to her new home in Wirtemburg.

"A. S., 1839."

this expedition. Scheffer had enjoyed, from the first, the confidence and respect of the young Prince, and he contributed in no small degree to influence his character and form his opinions, in such manner as to prepare him one day to fulfil "the hopes of France."

As a circumstance closely connected with my subject nearly coincides in order of time with this period, I will here mention that, in the summer of 1830 Scheffer became the father of a female infant. It is less common in Paris than in England, for young men to contract improvident marriages, and to imperil their whole future prospects from inability to exercise the virtue of self-control. But in place of the casual indulgences of the passions — ever fraught with injury to a man's humane and generous feelings—Scheffer had formed a more exclusive and satisfying connexion. The name and quality of the person to whom he had attached himself, remained untold, down to Scheffer's closing hour. All that is known, even to his intimate friends, is, that she died, not long subsequent to the birth of her child.

After watching over the infant with paternal care (it was nursed in the country) during seven years, its existence came to Madame Scheffer's knowledge, when she, without hesitation, proposed to her son to acknowledge his daughter, and allow it to be carefully educated under her eye, at their own home. Madame Scheffer acted in this affair like a generous and high-souled woman; I may add, like a far-sighted mother. Still, she could not have divined the extent of the benefit which she thus prepared for the future of her beloved son. It will hereafter be seen that, from the filial attachment and the noble qualities of "Cornélie" (so the young girl was called), Scheffer, in his latter years, derived some of the brightest of the few cheering rays of happiness which illumined his otherwise clouded existence.   But to resume the artistic thread.

We will take this up at the point of time when the greatest of the products of Scheffer's poetic pencil burst upon the world of art—the "Francesca di Rimini," as it is called, though " Paolo" is almost as important a figure in the group as herself.   When first exhibited in 1835, in the Salon du Louvre, it excited universal curiosity and attention.   I scarcely know how to speak without presumption of this most impressive work, at the present day, seeing that its commanding merits have assigned it a place among the *chefs d'œuvres* of our century. Nevertheless, my cordial appreciation of all the beauty and romance which breathes forth in this composition—of the felicitous grouping of the two figures—the fine treatment of the flesh, the grace and tenderness present in the Francesca, together with a certain " halo " of spiritual existence diffused over the scene—my profound appreciation of all this, I repeat, would, if yielded to, easily tempt me into enthusiasm.   The picture was immediately bought by the Duke of Orleans, and, at the sale which took place of the property of his family, after the Revolution of February, 1848, it passed into the possession of the Prince Anatole Demidoff, who placed it in his gallery at Florence.*

The year 1835 was indeed a marked epoch in

---

* See, for some particulars of this picture and its "repetitions," Appendix (D), especially of the " Replica" which figured in the Scheffer Exhibition of 1859.

Scheffer's artist career.   He had illustrated the conceptions of three true poets—Goethe, Byron, and
Dante: rising in power at each successive stage, and
by the last composition taking rank, confessedly,
among the most distinguished painters of France.

The amount of labour, thought, and attention
which Scheffer brought to the production of the picture in question, must have been enormous.   In
truth, his technical education having been so imperfect, he was forced to climb the steep of art by drawing upon his own resources, and thus, whilst his hand
was at work, his mind was engaged in meditation.
He had to try various processes of handling—experiments in colouring—to paint and repaint, with tedious
and unremitting assiduity.   We shall see indeed, in
the progress of this memoir, how lasting was Scheffer's
consciousness of the incompleteness of his early training in what related to the craft, and to the precious
secrets of the " palette."

But Nature had endowed him with that which
proved in some sort an equivalent for shortcomings
of a professional kind.   His own elevation of character, and his profound sensibility, aided him in acting upon the feelings of others through the medium
of the pencil.   To use his own words:—

" Pour être artiste, il faut avoir en soi un sentiment
élevé, ou une conviction puissante, dignes d'être exprimé
par une langue qui peut être, indifféremment, la prose,
la poesie, la musique, la sculpture, ou la peinture."*

---

* " To be a true artist, one must possess, within oneself, a certain
elevation of sentiment, with deep and powerful convictions, worthy
of being expressed by one or other of the arts—by prose composition, poetry, music, sculpture, or painting."

And again, " C'est que réellement, l'artiste le plus eminent n'a rien créé ni rien inventé; il a seulement rendu fidèlement les impressions du beau, du sublime, et du bon, qu'il a reçues de la nature entière. Je dis *expressément* la nature entière, parceque à coté des parties palpables qui s'adressent à nos yeux et à nos sens, il y a cette partie qui parle diréctement à notre âme, sans interprète matériel visible," &c. &c.*

The passage here quoted forms part of an "address to his pupils," in whose progress and welfare Scheffer always took a paternal interest. He was accustomed to supply them with funds to enable them to make the journey to Rome and other cities, in the pursuit of their professional studies; and many of the copies of old masters' works, brought back by the young *élèves*, were purchased by Scheffer by way of encouragement to them to persevere.

We will again suspend here the course of the " painter," to retrace the political current of existence, which ever ran side by side with the other. We have seen the doleful issue of the efforts made by the Liberals of France during the last "decade" of the Restoration, down to 1830. Those which they made, in harmony with the public sentiment of the nation,

---

* " To speak strictly, the most accomplished artist has neither invented, nor created anything: he has, simply, striven to reproduce, faithfully, those impressions of the beautiful, the sublime, and the pure, which he has derived from all nature. I say, advisedly, *all nature*, because, over and above those obvious qualities which address themselves to our eyes, and to our senses, there exist in nature unseen influences, which affect our mind and feelings, without passing through any material medium."

in that memorable year, having been crowned with unexpected success, it was a season of hope, almost of exultation, which followed upon the accession of Louis Philippe of Orleans.

But the spirits of the Liberals were not long in becoming affected by sinister apprehensions. One after another (M. Odillon Barrot among the earliest) of the Liberal party were dismissed, and the march of political affairs grew less and less conformable to the expectations of the "Gauche." Perhaps I may be forgiven for introducing in this place, an extract from a letter addressed to myself by a member of the French Chamber, himself of no mean personal distinction. It will serve to enlighten the reader upon the opinion entertained of the "government of July" at this early stage.

"Paris, Avril 3, 1832.

"Que dites vous de la marche déplorable que suit notre gouvernement depuis qu'il a été créé et mis au monde? Je m'imagine que nous vous faisons pitié, si même nous ne vous inspirons pas un sentiment encore moins flatteur. Nous avons pris un peu de tous les régimes qui nous ont précédés; la corruption du Directoire, les fanfaronades et les brutalités de l'Empire, l'hypocrisie et la lacheté de la Réstoration. Tout cela, mis ensemble, ėt bien mélangé, forme un composé qui s'est appelé "le Juste-milieu." Je me hâte de dire, pour l'honneur de la France, que c'est le gouvernement le plus impopulaire que nous ayons vu depuis un demi siècle. . . . .
Le Juste-milieu a trouvé le moyen de grossir tous

les partis; il multiplie tous les jours le nombre des
Républicains, des Légitimistes, des Napoléonistes;
mais tous paraissent également à craindre.   C'est, au
reste, ce qui fait la principale force du ministère et de
la dynastie de Louis Philippe.   Notre révolution a
été faite trop vite et trop facilement: le pouvoir était
sorti des mains des patriotes presqu'avant qu'ils se
fussent apperçus qu'il y etait tombé.   Ils ont manqué
une belle occasion de donner à la France une organi-
sation complete; ils ne la retrouveront plus. . . .
    . . . Nos amis, et particulièrement le Général
Lafayette, sont un peu découragés: ils ont presque
perdu l'ésperance de voir rentrer le gouvernement
qu'ils ont contribué à fonder, dans des voies nationales.
Ils se réprochent probablement, d'avoir été trop con-
fians, et cela ne peut qu'augmenter leur tristesse.   Il
faut dire aussi qu'on les a cruellement trompé, et
qu'il ne leur etait pas permis de supposer que la
fausseté serait poussée si loin."*   .   .   .   .   .   .

---

* "What say you to the deplorable march of affairs here ?   Me-
thinks it is enough to inspire you with a sentiment of pity, perhaps
with a sentiment still less flattering to us.   We seem to have united,
in our present Government, the various defects exhibited under
former 'régimes'—the corruption of the Directory, the boastings
and brutality of the Empire, the hypocrisy and meanness of the
' Restoration.'   All these, well mixed and stirred together, compose
what is termed our ' Juste milieu.'   To be just, I ought to add that
this is the most unpopular Government which has existed in France
for half a century. . . . .   This 'Juste milieu' has contrived
to swell the numbers of every section of politicians.   Each day adds
fresh strength to the Republican, to the Legitimist, to the Bona-
partist parties; but they seem, all, to inspire fear and dislike.   In
fact, it is this which constitutes the principal force of both the
ministry and the dynasty of Louis Philippe.   Our revolution has
been made too rapidly, and too easily.   The directing power passed

(*From another Correspondent*).*

" Paris, 1832.

" Je ne sais aucune nouvelle interessante à vous mander en politique; nous vivons dans un état de malaise et de découragement bien pénible; les mêmes ' mangeurs de budjets' que nous avons eu sous tous les régimes, ont pris pour eux tous les avantages de notre révolution.   Ils se sont emparés de l'esprit du roi, et lui ont persuadé que ceux qui l'avaient placés sur le trône voulaient le renverser; et enfin ils ont si bien fait, que nous sommes absolûment, à present, comme nous étions sous la restoration."†

---

out of the hands of the patriots, almost before they were conscious of its having fallen into their possession.   They have missed an excellent opportunity of bestowing upon France a complete organization : one which they never will overtake. . . . . Our friends, especially General Lafayette, are somewhat disheartened ; they have nearly relinquished all hope of seeing the Government, which owes its existence to them, pursue a course beneficial to the nation.   They probably feel that they have been much too confiding, but this only serves to depress their spirits further.   One cannot but allow, however, that they were cruelly ' *taken in*,' and that they could hardly have been prepared for so large an employment of the art of dissembling." . . . .

* M. Jean Baptiste Say.

† " I have no news of any interest, as regards politics, to send you ; we live in a condition of uneasy discouragement which it is hard to endure.   The same ' budget devourers' whom we have had under every successive ' régime,' have secured for themselves all the advantage of our revolution ; and these people have got round the King, and have made him believe that the party to whom he owes his throne are bent upon dispossessing him of it.   In short, they have managed matters so completely their own way, that we are, literally, at this present time, precisely where we were under the Restoration."

The above extracts will serve to furnish a notion of the extent to which political disappointment prevailed among the advanced liberal party in France. They must for the present close the subject of public affairs, whilst we return to that of Scheffer's personal life and occupations.

CHAPTER VI.

1835—1847.

Death of the Princess Marie—Scheffer's close attention to his profession—His great love for his mother—Remarks on some of
Scheffer's works—His advance towards excellence—Causes of
this—Spirited colloquy with the King—Advice to his daughter
—Her marriage.

THE loss of the Princess Marie about this period,
together with the visible decline of Madame Scheffer's
vital powers, served to throw around the path of her
sons, depressing influences ; so that although, as an
artist, Ary Scheffer was now followed, flattered, and
admired, his inward life bore the impress of discouragement.

The necessity under which he lay, of working incessantly, in order to furnish the means of fitly educating
" Cornélie," [in addition to his usual current expenditure,] had doubtless its use in forcing his mind to fix
itself on subjects apart from the distasteful realities
of the day.   Arrived, after years of toil, at a somewhat more complete mastery over mechanical difficulties, Scheffer produced, with more or less rapidity,
a number of pictures of importance between 1832 and
1838.   Portraits of the King (on horseback), of the
Duc d'Orleans, of the Queen of the Belgians (full

length), of Marshal Lobau, the Prince de Joinville, of General Ney, Professor Marjolin, and others, fall into this category; yet, during this same period, Scheffer's ideal pencil was scarcely less active than his imitative one.   Not to mention the splendid performances discussed in the preceding chapter, we are likewise indebted to it for the two " Mignons,"* for the " Margaret coming out of Church," the " Roi de Thulé," and the grand composition of " Le Christ Consolateur."   The " Mignons" became the property of the Duke of Orleans, and were bequeathed by him to Count Molé, with whose descendants they have remained.

As embodying this romantic creation of Goethe's fancy, the two figures in question have always possessed peculiar interest, not only for the connoisseur, but for all educated beholders.   Few have ever, I believe, gazed upon the sad, forlorn aspect of the friendless maiden without feeling profoundly touched. And why?   A single figure in complete repose,—poor, wan, half-clothed, half-grown,—how does she manage to move you?   How?   The girl has a soul: full of deep, refined sentiment; it is a real and genuine melancholy, and both the expression of the face, and the attitude, tranquil and passive though this be, forcibly unlocks your sympathy, and draws you with emotion and tender pity towards the poetical being before you. Such an effect is precisely that which so many painters strain after, and which it was Scheffer's especial gift to attain.   Exceptions have been taken to the treat-

---

* A third, " Mignon and the Harper," was painted some years later.

ment of these figures; *ex. gr.*, their hardness of outline, their heaviness of colour, some imperfect drawing
in the feet and ankles, and the like. To such criticism
one can only oppose the wide--spread attraction which
the " Mignons" possess: recollecting that Rubini
moved us even to tears, when almost without a
voice; that Thomas Moore captivated all listeners
with scarcely a *musical* tone in his; and that Pasta
reigned supreme with but slender advantages of
person, and limited vocal power—all of these effects
being produced by the magic touch of sympathetic
genius.*   The vast field of art offers, in truth, so
many varieties of excellence, that the best critic is
he who keeps his mind open to the merits of every
style.   I fear, however, that we shall ever continue,
in a certain sense, sectarians in art: special idolatry
being a more animating and agreeable state of mind
than that to which a catholic and equitable judgment
would conduct us.

In the year 1839 Scheffer completed two pictures,
the painting of which he had evidently felt to be a
" labour of love :" both of them representing the likeness of his incomparable mother. For truth, dignity of character, moral beauty, and the serenity
of declining age, the single figure portrait must be
ranked very high.   Colour there is little or none, but
here, this circumstance, as in some other examples of

---

* In our own day, in the height of English enthusiasm for Jenny
Lind's lyric talent, critics were not wanting, who hammered away
weekly at proving that the " Swedish Nightingale" could not sing
Italian music. But learning is not always a match for sensibility,
especially when multitudes concur in a common sentiment of admiration.

the master, rather tends to heighten than diminish
the effect.   However much I admire this portrait, I
still venture to question the propriety of laying out
the hands and arms on two parallel lines?   It somewhat formalizes the "pose," detracting from its feminine grace.   Yet the painter must have had his
reasons for this arrangement, if one could but have
learned them! The second work pourtrays the beloved
and venerable woman in her final moments, giving
her blessing to the daughters of her two sons.   It
tells of pious resignation, and the tender feelings
which filled her whole being when her sons or their
children were present.

The grateful love and devotion borne by Scheffer
towards his mother formed, through her life, the
moving, the dominant spring of his actions.*   No
wonder, then, that the grief which Ary (and it must
be added, her other sons) felt at the loss of this sole
parent† was poignant in the extreme, and suggestive
of what our own Thomas Gray, the poet, wrote to a
friend when suffering under a like bereavement:—
" I felt, then, with all my full heart, that one *can*
have but *one* mother!"

It strikes me that some of the productions of
Scheffer's hand, during the period immediately succeeding to 1839, are chargeable with a certain languor

---

* Where a son and mother have been united by similar strong
bonds of love and mutual confidence, it may generally be presumed that both individuals possessed moral qualities of a high
order.

† This event took place in the summer of 1839, after repeated
attacks of illness, both of the old complaint and of fever : the three
brothers receiving the last sigh of their expiring mother.

and tameness. The portrait of Madame de Fitz-
James, for instance, with her three children, executed
in 1842—a work which would have been more suit-
ably deposited elsewhere, than in a collection intended
to do honour to the painter. Neither will the " Christ "
of this period bear comparison with others of a later
date ; the " Laissez venir à moi les petits enfants,"*
being, in my view at least, quite unworthy of Scheffer's
reputation. We are in some sort justified in sup-
posing this languor to have been the consequence of
his mental sorrow, because shortly afterwards his
better vein of composition returned, with more than
its former *élan* and vigour.† In 1844 appeared " Les
Rois Mages," a work which evinces progress in his
method of colouring, as well as a greater boldness of
style. The heads of the " Magi " are powerfully
painted, with a cast of the oriental in character. We
are, it is true, still among *facts* here ; not much of
" ideality " looks out in " The Three Kings." But we
have not long to wait, before another and a loftier
composition salutes our eager eyes, in " Les Saintes
Femmes :" not in the " Salon," however, this time,
whither Scheffer sent no more pictures after the year
1846. He is known to have felt a kind of impatience
of the judgment of " the crowd," and therefore pre-
ferred exhibiting his pictures in the " studio," to the
discriminating few, rather than to the general gaze.
As the " Saintes Femmes " (finished in 1847) may be

---

* No. 51 in Catalogue, 1859.

† I must not, however, omit to mention one picture of the date
of 1841, " The Annunciation to the Shepherds," in which may be
found examples of human beauty and expression, of great merit.

regarded as properly opening that phase of Scheffer's artistic course in which his later triumphs were achieved, I take leave to offer some few remarks upon the unquestionable advance made by him, about this time, in his treatment of biblical subjects.

Scheffer was at this period entering upon his fifty-second year, an age when a full experience of men and things usually brings its fruit, in the form of what the French term *désillusionnement.* His enthusiasm for the public weal, which had animated him to both active and passive sacrifices during the plenitude of his powers, was effectually damped by the mortifications which he, along with other high-minded Frenchmen, was forced to submit to under the new dynasty. Disgusted by the vulgar politics " buzzing" around him—farther depressed in spirits by the disastrous death (in 1842) of the heir to the throne, on whom he had placed his last fond hope of future better days for France—Scheffer drew closer and closer to his art: ceasing to connect himself with public affairs, otherwise than as a member of the National Guard (in which he held the rank of Captain), performing its duties and obligations like other men.

In the comparative seclusion of the Rue Chaptal, and with a taste and judgment ripened by long practice and thoughtful meditation—seeing little company beyond a few privileged friends and amateurs of art—Scheffer's imagination had more ample leisure than heretofore for attentive and sustained concentration on lofty and sacred subjects. I believe (in spite of what Diderot says) that in order to excite profound emotion

in others, in any walk of art—painting, acting, or sing-
ing—you must either experience such in your own
person, or arrive at a strong belief of its presence by
a previous effort of fancy.   Such effort is, however,
only fruitful when pursued in solitude, and under
perfect abstraction from disturbing forces.   The secret
of Scheffer's advance in the power of investing his
compositions with a deeply sentimental charm, lay, as
I conceive, partly in his strict devotion to his art,
partly in a greater abstinence from the external com-
merce of society.*

"Les Saintes Femmes" (which by some is looked
upon as Scheffer's masterpiece) became the property
of the Duchess of Orleans, a lady well qualified to
judge and appreciate its merits.   Few of the author's
works on scriptural subjects have met with more
extensive admiration than this picture, which may
be said to approximate to the highest type of pictorial art; whether we contemplate its purity of
design, the harmony of the sober colouring, or the
almost celestial expression of the two rapt female
heads.

Shortly after this grand effort (as though his mind

---

* Although he kept up his connexion with the Tuileries, it was
the widowed Duchess of Orleans, and the young Count de Paris,
whom he saw most of; the last-mentioned taking drawing lessons
of him at intervals.   With this section of the Royal family, indeed,
his interest was peculiarly lively.   Nevertheless, I may venture to
affirm that the attachment he felt for the whole family ranked
among the foremost of his friendly and grateful affections.   Towards
Louis Philippe himself, Scheffer's earlier sentiments became, latterly, unavoidably tinctured with displeasure, and he saw the King
but seldom after the year 1840.

sought change and relief in treating purely human concerns) Scheffer painted his " Four Ages."*

A lady (a countrywoman of ours) distinguished for her knowledge and cultivation of art, speaks of this picture with warm eulogy, thus,—

" The ' Four Ages' is a gem! a small, long picture.

I. Two children—boy and girl—playing together.

II. An older girl and a youth, (the maiden seated, with her back to him) half shy, half sulky, who have just discovered that their hearts are beating.

III. A middle-aged couple, staidly loving; and lastly,

IV. A feeble old pair, each tender of the other's infirmity.

" This is an exquisite picture—a sweet lesson of life—a type for each age."

The same pen makes mention of the " Margaret at her Spinning-wheel," also in the collection of M. Nottebohn (not the one which was exhibited), as follows :—

" The Margaret—life-size—is a picture of more than common excellence, adding to all his pathos the most gorgeous colouring. The flesh is warm and transparent, and her high-backed chair and yellow curtain behind, are quite Venetian. It is the finest *art*, in technical matters, I have yet seen by Scheffer."

Of " The Annunciation to the Shepherds"—also in M. Nottebohn's possession—the correspondent, quoted above, has the same high opinion as myself. See p. 61, note (†).

---

* It belongs to M. Nottebohn, of Rotterdam, but was not among the works lent by that gentleman to the Exhibition of 1859.

Under the date of 1846 we find some compositions of first-rate interest and merit. Among the foremost may be cited the "Faust and Marguerite in the Garden," "Dante and Beatrice," and the "St. Monica with St. Augustin;" each of these embodying a different form of sentiment, yet each, one of an absorbing kind. The first of these—widely known through the engraving—whilst indicative of tender, amorous feelings, nowise trenches upon the "modesty of nature." A young and handsome couple, finely drawn, standing in a natural attitude (an attitude, by the way, in some sort original in itself), expressive of newly awakened love, must ever be a subject possessing universal interest and attraction, independently of its connexion with Goethe's great poem.*

The "Beatrice and Dante" is intended to imply another phase of the passion. The poet, represented in a rapt, admiring, confiding state of mind, is gazing up at Beatrice, whom he regards as his quasi-celestial guide to the empyrean regions of bliss. These two impressive figures, however, can hardly suggest any other than spiritual or mystic relations, and fall, properly speaking, under the head of "poetical creations."†

---

* Of late years a print has been seen in every print-shop of London, calling itself "The First Kiss," which affords an example of the absence of the very quality which one admires in Scheffer's composition: it is, in fact, but a vulgar production, designed for "the million," to their misfortune !

† The discovery at Florence of an original portrait of Dante, by Giotto, of the date of 1300, coinciding with the commencement of this picture, Scheffer employed a young painter to go and make a copy of this head for him, in order that he might reproduce, on his own canvas, the best attested likeness of the great poet.

F

The St. Monica, again, combines the historical
with the religious element.   In the fulness of faith
is discerned the rapidly departing spirit, clinging to
mortality only through the ties of maternal affection;
whilst St. Augustin, her son, is agitated by the conflict between his reason and a filial sympathy with
his mother's convictions.   All this is wonderfully
well expressed by the painter.   I may here quote the
words of a friend (an " habitué" of Scheffer's "atelier") in reference to this solemn subject:—

"Je n'oublierai jamais l'émotion que cette composition me fit éprouver quand je la vis, esquissée légère-
ment à la craie sur la toile; il n'y avait pas à se
méprendre sur le sens et l'attribution de chacune de
ces deux figures; mais Scheffer *seul*, peut-être, était
capable de les rendre ainsi reconnaissables sans un
détail de costume, sans un accessoire indicateur."*

Scheffer was now acknowledged as the most effective living painter in the walk of religious Art.   The
St. Monica, indeed, produced so permanent an impression that several copies of the picture have since
been made; all of them in the artist's own " atelier."
The original remains, I believe, to this day in the
possession of the Queen Marie Amélie.   The *best*
" Replica," perhaps, is that which Scheffer bequeathed
to his daughter; another copy, I have been informed,

---

* "I shall never forget the emotion with which I first caught
sight of this composition, although merely sketched on the canvas
in white chalk.   There was no mistaking the purport and the intention apparent in each of these two figures.   But Scheffer alone,
perhaps, was capable of stamping them with a character so fraught
with individual meaning as to be recognisable, in spite of the absence of costume, and of all accessories of detail."

is in Poland; a third graces the " salon" of an accomplished English lady in London, for whom it was expressly painted; and I am not sure whether these three are all that exist.

I have spoken of the friendly intercourse which Scheffer maintained with the Royal family; the Comte de Paris became, in his turn, a pupil, thus furnishing a new link in this long-standing connexion. An anecdote which I once heard, from undoubted authority, will serve to show how undeviating was Scheffer's self-assertion in his relations with the Tuileries. The King had entreated him to compose a design for a monument, wherewith to adorn the little edifice erected on the spot where his lamented son, the late Duke of Orleans, met his death. Scheffer willingly set to work, and after a time brought his drawing to show to his Majesty. Having attentively studied it, the King said, "It is just the thing, and quite meets my wishes: Pradier shall execute this." " Pardon, Sire," replied Scheffer, " mais Pradier n'en est pas capable." " Et pourquoi non?" inquired the King. " Parceque, votre Majesté, Pradier a fait, ces dernières années, trop d'objets de métier pour vendre." " Eh bien, n'importe! c'est toujours Pradier qui le fera." " Pardon, Sire," said Scheffer (deliberately), " mais Pradier-ne-le-fera-pas." " Comment, *ne le fera pas?* Eh! si je l'ordonne?" " Ce sera encore la même chose; la volonté de l'artiste aura plus d'autorité sur lui que les commandes du monarque même."* The

---

* " Pardon, Sire, but Pradier is not equal to the task." " And pray why not?" " Because, your Majesty, Pradier has made too many things to sell, of late years, or ' shop' articles." " Ah, well,

King now became irritated at this quiet, yet firm resistance to his will, and, losing his temper, he began
to use somewhat strong language, so Scheffer quitted
his presence.

On the next morning, while at work at his easel, he
was informed that an " officier d'ordonnance du Roi"
wished to see him. " Oh, ho!" said Scheffer to himself, " I think I know what *this* means." And the
officer proved to be, as Scheffer supposed he was, the
bearer of most apologetic messages, on behalf of his
Majesty, for his vehement behaviour on the previous
evening. Other interviews ensued between the King
and his artist friend, wherein the former strove to
bring Scheffer over to his own wishes, and to prevail
on him to accord his sanction to the plan of employing
M. Pradier. But nothing would avail. Scheffer in-
flexibly withheld it.*

His beloved " Cornélie" was married to M. Marjolin, a physician of repute, about the year 1845. She
had no children, and the doctor being much absent
from home, on professional duties, his young wife,
naturally, came often to her father's house, affording
him the sweetest comfort which such relationship has
to bestow. Madame Marjolin could handle the brush

---

that is no matter; Pradier shall do it, all the same." " Pardon,
Sire, but I say Pradier will *not* do it." " How, *not do it!* And
what if I order him ?" " That will make no difference. The
wishes of the artist will carry more weight with *him* than any command, even that of a monarch."

* The memorial chapel (at Sablonville) of the heir to the throne
was, ultimately, ennobled by a truly admirable work, from the hand
of a genuine artist and sculptor, M. le Baron H. de Triqueti: after
his own beautiful design.

too, and occasionally worked at the easel in company with her father.*

It was for Scheffer an effort of no small amount, to separate himself from his child; especially at an age when her character was forming itself in a manner corresponding to his hopes, and when she herself was gradually becoming the friend in the daughter. But no selfish considerations ever found entrance into Ary's mind. His conduct was invariably regulated by his ethical doctrines, in great as in small affairs. The following extract from one of his letters of this date will afford confirmation of what is here stated:—

" En t'unissant à un homme que j'aime comme un fils depuis longtems—en assurant ainsi ton bonheur, autant qu'il est permis aux hommes de compter sur l'avenir—je n'ai eu en vue que toi. La meilleur preuve de mon amour est dans le sacrifice énorme que je viens de faire, en me séparant de toi au moment où tu devenais pour moi une amie. . . . ."†

But however pleasing it be to recal passages tending to elucidate the character of Ary Scheffer, I must not detain the reader too long on secondary topics, and will therefore proceed with the main stream of events connected with this period.

---

* The father of M. René Marjolin, the husband of Cornélie, had been the attached friend of Scheffer and his mother for years, and had alleviated the sufferings of the latter by his care and his superior skill in medicine.

† " In consenting to your union with a man whom I have long loved as my own son, and thus providing for your happiness—in so far as it is permitted to us to count upon its attainment—I have thought only of yourself. The best proof I could give of my affection is, that I sacrifice so much in parting with you, and *that* at a time when you were growing capable of being my friend."

CHAPTER VII.

1848—1849.

Ominous state of political affairs—Interview with the Duchess of
Orleans—Flight of the King and Queen—Scheffer conducts
the Duchess of Orleans and the Comte de Paris to the Chamber
of Deputies—Proclamation of the Republic—Scene on the Place
de la Concorde described.

THE grave and ominous signs of danger to the monarchy which manifested themselves—particularly in
1847—to all far-sighted politicians, and which were
emphatically interpreted from the " tribune" of the
Chamber, in January, 1848, by the late M. Alexis
de Tocqueville, filled Scheffer with uneasiness. He
had taken no share in politics, personally, for a
long time: feeling little sympathy in the sterile con-
flicts of party, and discouraged by the apparently
hopeless degradation of mind and opinion which then
prevailed in France among the electoral body.

The expected hurricane arrived, and swept away
the Orleans dynasty, as we all remember. Indeed, the
curious history of that startling change cannot fail to
be read and re-read by our children's children, with
undying interest and emotion.

I had the good fortune to receive from Scheffer's
own lips various intimate details relating to these
eventful times. His manner of recounting occur-

rences wherein he had taken part, was both captivating and impressive, and always conveyed the
idea of absolute exactness.   It was my habit to make
memoranda of incidents communicated by eye-wit-
nesses, relating to public affairs, with a view to assist
my own recollection.   I here reproduce some passages,
which can hardly fail to interest the reader.

I have already alluded to the fact that Scheffer was
in the habit of giving lessons, in general art, to the
youthful Comte de Paris.   On the Sunday which preceded the Revolution of February, he repaired to the
Tuileries for that purpose.   It was two days prior to
the day on which it had been announced that *the*
" Banquet" would be held.   Whilst he was engaged
with the Comte de Paris, the Duchess of Orleans
looked in at the door: " Scheffer," said she, " when
you have done with Paris, come to my private room;
I want to speak to you."   Accordingly, the lesson
being ended, Scheffer went to the Duchess.   " What
do you think," said she, " about this banquet affair?
Do you entertain any apprehensions as to the consequences which may ensue from its being held?"
Scheffer replied, " Madame, I think that the precau-
tions which have been taken are sufficient to warrant
the belief that no danger is to be anticipated, and
that the affair will pass off without any serious results,
for this time.   But your Royal Highness must allow
me to add that, unless some concessions are made to
the reasonable demands of the nation, some fresh
manifestation will not fail to arise, which may not
perhaps be quite so effectually resisted."

The Duchess coloured.   " Scheffer!" exclaimed her
Royal Highness, " it is a highly improper proceeding

on your part, to glance even at the possibility of any danger to the monarchy."

Scheffer bowed respectfully—was silent—and withdrew.

On the very next day (Monday) a friend of Scheffer's (a gentleman holding a high position) brought him a letter to read, which he had just received from M. Odillon Barrot. It informed him of the decision taken by M. Barrot and his friends, to renounce their design of holding the "Banquet" on the Tuesday; assigning as the reason, their disinclination to provoke a conflict with the authorities, in the then excited state of the public feeling. "Give me the letter," said Scheffer; "I will carry it to the Duchess of Orleans, who will thank me, I am sure, for bringing her this good news some hours earlier than she would naturally learn it." Scheffer hastened to the Tuileries, found the Duchess, and showed her the letter. Her eyes filled with tears as she perused it. "How good of you, to bring me this welcome news, Scheffer! but I must have you come with me into the King's cabinet, to communicate it to His Majesty." "Your Royal Highness must excuse me," replied Scheffer; "le Roi et moi nous ne nous sommes jamais aimés; I would rather that your Royal Highness carried in the news alone."* She did so. After the lapse of a few minutes, she returned. "The King is delighted," said the Duchess; "but do you know that he could not help observing, in his jocular way, 'Voyez, donc, quels drôles de gens que

---

* "The King and I were never very partial to each other."

ces Messieurs là! dès qu'on leur montre le *bout du corne*, ils vous tournent le dos!'"*

Scheffer went his way, reflecting upon the incurable presumption which characterized the King. "He gave himself credit (said Scheffer) for having, by a clever display of resistance, frightened off the assailants of his power, yet he entirely neglected to ascertain what means were really at his disposal for its defence." (See Marshal Bugeaud's published letter, now known to have been addressed to M. de Lavergne.)

It was towards noon on the morning of the 24th February, 1848, that M. Scheffer, having been on duty (as Captain of the National Guard) ever since daylight, met M. Oscar de Lafayette, who was in search of him. "Scheffer," said Oscar, "it is mighty disagreeable to be obliged to expose one's life for a monarchy which one does not esteem; but nevertheless it is our duty, and we must go and defend it at all price." Scheffer assented. They repaired to the garden of the Tuileries, and posted themselves on the terrace under the windows of the King's apartments. There was a great quantity of straw strewn upon the steps, which had been placed there to enable the Dragoons to ride down the steps into the garden, from the other side of the château. They sat down on the straw, and after some time a voice was heard, calling upon Scheffer by name. Scheffer heard it, "but," said he, "I was too much absorbed with the thoughts which the grave events passing before me engendered, to pay any attention to the call."—

---

* "Only look at these people! No sooner do they catch sight of even the 'tip of the horn,' but they take to their heels."

"Scheffer!" again cried the same voice, only this time still louder. "Who calls?" cried Scheffer. "It is I, the Queen." Scheffer sprang up, approached the château, and perceived the Queen at the "croisée." He said, "What does your Majesty want with me?" "I want you," said she, "to assist in conducting us out of the château. The King has abdicated, and we are going to depart." Scheffer and Oscar Lafayette immediately entered the château, in the intention to ascend to the King's apartments; but they had not got half way up when they met the King and Queen, their sons, and sons' children, together with the Duchess of Orleans, and *her* two sons, all coming hurriedly down the stairs. The Queen said, "Scheffer, keep close to the King, your uniform will inspire respect." The King gave his right arm to the Queen, and they set out, proceeding through the gardens by the "grande Allée," and not "by a secret passage," as has been foolishly asserted. Scheffer walked close to the King, on his left side: the rest of the party following in their train; these consisting of perhaps ten or a dozen persons. Among the group was Scheffer's own brother, Arnold, who had joined them on the way through the gardens.* A small escort of cuirassiers accompanied the party, to protect them on each side. Nobody spoke a word, except on one occasion, when an officer, unmindful of a bough of a tree, which hung low, was swept off his horse by it. The King suddenly stopped and said, "Pray, somebody go and assist that officer."

---

* He had been thrown into prison some years previously by Louis Philippe for writing against his government.

When they reached the " Grille," which opens on the
" Place de la Concorde," there was found a considerable mass of people, and Scheffer had some uneasy
misgivings as to what might happen.   There were no
carriages provided, as has been stated by M. Thiers
and others.   But two public carriages—not " Fiacres,"
but what are called " Remises"—chanced to be within
hail, and were accordingly brought by one of the
attendants to the spot at which the royal party had
arrived.   Scheffer, knowing the impossibility of getting them away unrecognised, took off his " Schako,"
and waving it in the air, called out to the people—
" Le Roi part, vive le Roi!"   The people offered no
opposition, but very few voices responded to his
cheer.   Scheffer then assisted the Queen into one of
the " Rémises," the King after her; then one child
after another was taken on to their laps, until five souls
were in the carriage, and it could hold no more.   The
King kept calling out, "Où est donc mon portefeuille?
Sauvez mon portefeuille, pour l'amour de Dieu!"*
Scheffer caught the portfolio from the hands of one
of the attendants, and threw it up to M. Dumas, who
had mounted beside the coachman.   The second
carriage having been filled in like manner with the
first, the Royal party drove off at a rapid pace (still
escorted by the Dragoons), and took the road to
Passy, along the " Quais."

There remained now standing on the Place de la
Concorde, the Duchess of Orleans, with her two sons,
M. Jules de Lasteyrie, M. Scheffer, and (I think) two

---

* " Where is my portfolio?   Pray, for Heaven's sake, do not
lose sight of my portfolio!"

or three more Royal personages; perhaps the Duchess of Montpensier, but whom they were I really cannot specify. Just then M. —— joined the party, and offered his arm to the Duchess of Orleans, and thus all re-entered the garden of the Tuileries. The noise of the insurgents pouring in numbers down the Rue de Rivoli sounded alarmingly upon their ears. " M. —— !" exclaimed Scheffer, " you must allow me to say that your name is not held in sufficient respect for you to be of any use to the Duchess of Orleans; you had better leave us; I will take care of her Royal Highness to the best of my ability." ——, without making any answer, at once quitted them. The Duchess now took Scheffer's left arm, and he held the young Comte de Paris with his right hand, followed by M. Jules de Lasteyrie with the Duc de Chartres. They retraced their steps towards the château. When they reached the centre of the gardens, Scheffer heard a loud crash in the direction of the Rue de Rivoli. The mob had forced the iron gates, and were thronging into the gardens. Scheffer called out, " Vive la Duchesse d'Orléans !"—" Vive le Comte de Paris !" The mob, although offering them no molestation, seemed uncertain whether to respond or not. The young Comte de Paris took off his cap, and bowed repeatedly to the populace. The boy manifested no symptom of fear, preserving entire self-possession. One of the mob cried out, " Un roi ne se découvre pas !"

They passed out of the Grille on to the " Quai," and walked along by the river side to the Chamber of Deputies. Scheffer stood near them during that terrible, stormy scene, which ultimately resulted in

the proclamation of the Republic. M. Jules Lasteyrie, after this was over, managed to get the
Duchess out, through the President's garden, and
conducted her (as is well known) to the "Invalides."
The Duc de Chartres was placed, during the tumult,
in some part of the building. Scheffer told the
Duc de Nemours that the young boy was in a place
of safety, and that the Duc himself had better
"get out of the way," his person being well known.
The Duke asked one of the National Guard to lend
him his uniform. The man did so, putting on the
Prince's clothes in exchange; and so the Duke made
his way out. "I could not have quitted this place,"
said he, "until I knew that Chartres was safe."*

---

* At the moment when the Royal family reached the "Pont
Tournant," as I have related above, and were taking leave of one
another, a member of the Chamber (M. Léonce de Lavergne) was
proceeding across the Place de la Concorde, arm in arm with another
'Député," to the Salle Législative. He saw a group of persons at
the spot where the leavetaking was going on, with white pocket-
handkerchiefs raised to their eyes, among whom some little agitation was perceptible. The carriages were driving off, when General
———— walked across to M. de Lavergne, and said (without a
previous "bonjour!" even), "Voila le Roi qui part!" "Ah!"
replied M. de Lavergne, "où va-t-il?" "Peutêtre à St. Cloud, peut-
être à Rambouillet, ou à Dreux; que sais-je?" "Comment? vous
ne savez pas où?" "Mais—c'est que le Roi a abdiqué!" M. Lavergne, in relating this incident, added, "La coupole du Panthéon
m'auroit croulé sur la tête; que je n'eusse pas été plus atterré—je
demeurai stupéfait!"—(*Translation.*) "There goes the King!"
"Ah! and *whither* is he going?" "Perhaps to St. Cloud—perhaps
to Rambouillet, or Dreux; how can I tell where he is going to?"
"But what! you do not *know* where?" "Well, but you see—the
King has abdicated!"—"Had the dome of the Pantheon come down
about my ears, I could not have been more astounded. I stood
motionless and speechless!"

CHAPTER VIII.

1849.

Election of Louis Napoleon to the Presidency—Intervention in
Roman affairs—Scheffer's dissatisfaction—His visit to Holland
and Eisenach—Letters from Scheffer to his daughter—Return
to Paris—His house described.

1849.—At the date which this narrative has now
reached, we close the chapter of the " Monarchy of
July," so far forth as its substantive attribute—political power—is in question.   The events which succeeded to its expulsion were highly exciting.   In the
memorable struggle of June, 1848, Scheffer fought at
the head of his company during all three of those terrible days; and I have heard it stated that he showed
ability as a leader, no less than cool, undaunted
bravery.*   After the election of Louis Napoleon
Buonaparte to the Presidency, Scheffer became somewhat hopeful of the march of public affairs; all the
more, since he saw, in the chief members of the President's first Ministry, men of whose public conduct
he had approved, and with one or two of whom he had
even entertained friendly relations.   M. Léon Faucher,
for instance—a man who joined to a character of spot-
less integrity very extensive knowledge, and an accu-
rate acquaintance both with the internal economy
and with the requirements of his country.

---

* See Appendix (G).

But the interest with which all well-wishers to the prosperity of the Republic watched the course of this Government received a check of the most disheartening kind, when the fatal decision was taken (in May, 1849), to send an army, under the command of General Oudinot, to stifle the efforts of the Roman people to fling off their oppressors. It was not difficult to discern, in the strenuous advocacy of this fratricidal policy by M. de Falloux, the deeply-seated source of the opposition to Roman independence. The clergy of France had too much at stake to suffer the Papal throne to be imperilled, and accordingly made its preservation by French arms a condition of their upholding the Government of the President.

I cannot afford to bestow more than a passing notice on this deplorable mistake, the retributive consequences of which not only overtook, rapidly, its authors, but the embarrassments arising out of which still continue to perplex the ruler of France. I will restrict myself to the assertion that Ary Scheffer, along with all true-hearted patriots (and especially with his brother Arnold), felt profoundly displeased at the use made of their power by the party calling themselves "le parti de l'ordre." He, in common with other good Republicans, foresaw that the angry, I may say the insulted feelings of the popular minority in the Chamber would thenceforward impel this minority to hamper and obstruct the President's Government, and, by inducing a discordant and unmanageable temper in the whole assembly, infallibly bring about, sooner or later, the ruin of the Republic.

Impatient and dissatisfied, Scheffer resolved to absent himself for a space, and to make a visit to his

native country, Holland; but in his way thither he
halts at Brussels.   Here is an extract from a letter
written thence, under date October, 1849, in which
he speaks of the Queen of the Belgians as follows:—

"J'écris encore de Bruxelles, chère fille, étant resté
chez la Reine Louise jusqu'au 6ᵐᵉ Octobre.   Elle a
été comme toujours, parfaite. Tant de choses s'étaient
passées depuis la dernière fois que je lui avois parlé,
que nous avions long à dire.   Il est impossible de
réunir plus d'élévation, plus de bon sens, et plus de
grace féminine, qu'elle ne possède.   Je suis très fier de
m'être trouvé d'accord avec son opinion sur bien des
choses graves, étant en dissidence avec l'opinion
générale, &c. &c.*

On another day he says, writing from Amsterdam
(October still):—"Ce matin j'irai admirer le beau
portrait de Rembrandt que nous avons vus ensemble,
au musée, il y a cinq ans. J'ai déjà une envie terrible de travailler, et d'être de retour dans mon
atelier.   .   .   ."†

Again : "Je suis déjà extenué de fatigue, et je brûle
de me retrouver au milieu de mon atelier.   .   .   .   .

---

* "I write again from Brussels, my dear daughter, having stayed
with the Queen Louise up to the 6th October.   She was, as ever,
delightful.   So much had happened since I last conversed with her,
that we had a vast deal to talk over.   It is impossible for any one
to unite, with true feminine grace, more elevation of mind, and more
good sense, than the Queen possesses.   I feel proud of the coincidence which exists between us on many important points, respecting which I differ from the received opinions."

† "To-day I am going to see that fine Rembrandt portrait which
you and I saw, five years ago, at the Museum.   I feel a strong in-
clination to be at work again, and to get back to my 'atelier.'. . ."

J'ai un desir démesuré d'être de retour chez-moi, et n'était la crainte de passer pour un fou, ou un 'original'—ce qui est équivalent ici—je me sauverais à toute vitesse. . . ."*

The extract which follows affords us an insight into Scheffer's opinion of his own capacity and his deficiencies. A more interesting disclosure of a great artist's candid estimate of his own powers, it would be difficult to find in the history of the class.

Oct. 1849.—"Voilà huit jours que j'ai quitté le travail! je croyais que cela me réposerait la tête, et le contraire me parait arriver. Il est vrai que j'ai vu une quantité de belles choses qui redoublent mon désir de me remettre à peindre. Je sens si bien tout ce qui me manque—non pour compléter mon talent, ce serait folie d'y songer—mais pour rendre suffisamment ce que je désire exprimer, et pour avoir un côté toute à fait saillant. Quand on voit cette vérité si frappante d'expression, chez les anciens peintres Allemands, cette perfection de forme et de beauté chez les Italiens—puis, l'exécution forte et saississante des peintres Hollandais—je sens que je suis un 'Mittelding,' et cela je n'aurais pas dû l'être; et je tacherai au moins de ne pas le rester dans le peu que je pourrai produire encore. . . ."†

From Rotterdam, Oct. 1849.—"Aujourd'hui j'ai

---

* "I am tired beyond endurance, and feel a craving to be again in the 'atelier.' The desire to be once more in my own house is indeed so strong, that, but for the fear of being thought a lunatic, or—what comes to pretty much the same thing here—an eccentric character, I should certainly make short work of my return journey. . . ."

† "Here have I been eight days without working! I fancied that I should feel refreshed by rest, but the very opposite effect

beaucoup et très bien peint; cela me fait grand plaisir, d'être de nouveau au travail. Je me porte bien, mais je m'ennuie beaucoup d'être séparé de toi et de mes frères. Dis à Henry que son tableau de Prêche Protestante est admirable, que son petit tableau chez Jacobson est charmant. . . . . . Je travaille beaucoup, mais malgré toute la diligence que je pourrai y mettre, cela me prendra plus de temps que je ne croyais. Tout le monde est parfait pour moi ici, et me trouver, ainsi, hors du monde turbulent, aurait un bien grand charme pour moi si je t'avais avec moi."*

It is to be presumed that Scheffer was occupied,

---

seems to have ensued. It is true, I have seen a quantity of fine things, which redouble the desire within me to get back again to my painting. I am well aware of my own weak points—(to think of ever becoming a complete painter would be idle)—and of what is wanting on my part to render, in an effective shape, all that I wish to express, as well as to claim for my works something like a distinctive stamp. When one beholds the truth and force of expression displayed in the works of our old German masters, the perfection of figure-drawing and of beauty in the Italian painters—and again, the dexterous and commanding power of hand possessed by the Dutch —I seem to feel myself but half a painter—and *this* I certainly ought not to have been; nor will I continue such, if I can help it, during the time which is still allotted to me to produce in. . ."

* " I have painted a good deal to-day, and painted well; it gives me much pleasure to be once more busy. I am quite well, but I miss the society of yourself and my brothers. Pray tell Henry that his picture of the ' Protestant Preaching ' is an admirable performance, and his little picture at M. Jacobson's is also a charming thing. . . . I am very closely at work, but notwithstanding all my diligence, it will take me a longer time to complete what I am about than I calculated it would do. Every one here is full of attentions towards me, and indeed, to find myself so far removed from the noisy world would cause me genuine satisfaction, if you were but at my side. . . . . ."

during his stay in Holland, in painting for Dutch commissions; otherwise it is difficult to account for so
many of his works being distributed among the collections, public and private, of that country.   The
early associations he had contracted with his native
land were with Scheffer always pleasant to recur to,
whilst the ties of kindred still existing there, helped
to maintain the connexion unbroken.   M. Lamme,
his cousin, pursued the same profession as himself,
and indeed holds at this day the honourable post of
keeper of the museum at Rotterdam.

From the Hague, whither he had proceeded
in order to pay his respects to the Queen of the
Netherlands, he writes of her Majesty in high terms,
thus :—

"J'ai trouvé en elle, comme on m'avait prévenue,
une femme de la plus haute distinction.   .   .   .   .
Elle m'a paru d'une grande beauté, me rappelant les
portraits de ma mère quand elle était jeune.   Je
travaille beaucoup, mais, comme toujours, peu satis-
fait de ce que je fais.   On est charmant et parfait
pour moi, mais je m'ennuye à mourir, d'être loin de toi
et de mes frères.   .   .   .   ."*

A little farther on we find that, notwithstanding the
inflexible modesty which guards him from self-delu-
sion, Scheffer has arrived at a consciousness of possessing a "something," which is not present even in

---

* "I found in her, as indeed I had been led to expect, a woman
of real distinction.   She appeared to me exceedingly handsome,
and reminded me of the portraits taken of my own mother, when
she was young.   .   .   .   I work steadily, but, as is usual with me,
am not over-pleased with the result of my labours.   I am treated
most kindly by all here, but am weary with longing for my brothers
and yourself.   .   .   .   ."

the great works of the Dutch and Flemish masters.
One can enter into the complacent feeling under
which he avows it :—

"J'ai vu ici de merveilleux tableaux de la vieille
école hollandaise.   Je commence pourtant à éstimer
un peu plus mon propre talent.   .   .   .   .   Je
crois que j'ai touché une corde dont les autres n'ont
pas essayés.   Quand je reviendrai chez-moi, je crois
que j'aurai fait des progrés."*

There it is—*the* secret, which enables Scheffer to
arrest and enchain the attention of the beholder who
stands before his compositions.   *The* secret, I repeat
—which cannot be imparted to another—of kindling
the intelligent sympathies, through the medium of
art.   Even while gazing upon the masterpieces before his eyes, he recognises the absence of that peculiar, subtle charm, for which his own best works are
prized; namely, the true " outlook" (as the Germans
have it) of the emotions—be they what they may—
by which the persons portrayed are supposed to be
animated.

A little later he writes :—

"J'ai revu aujourd'hui mon tableau de la Madeleine au pied de la Croix,† qui est vraiment beau. . ."‡

From the Hague again :—

---

* " I have seen here some marvellously fine pictures of the ancient
Dutch school.   Nevertheless, I begin to think somewhat more
highly of my own talent.   .   .   .   It seems to me that I have
managed to touch a chord not hitherto attempted by others.   When
I return home, I fancy that there will be found indications of my
having made progress."

† Painted 1845.

‡ " I saw again this morning my picture of the Magdalen at
the foot of the Cross, which, positively, is a fine thing."

" J'ai diné chez le Roi, qui m'a parfaitement ac-
cueilli. Il parait que ma vieille méthode, de dire simplement la vérité aux princes, m'a encore fort bien
réussie ici."*

Here is a trait of honest paternal pride. Writing
to his daughter he says:—" La Reine m'a beaucoup
demandé si la petite Mignon ressemblait à quelqu'un
qui me fut cher? Je lui ai dit que c'était ton portrait.
Elle m'a fait compliment, ce cas étant, de ma fille."†

Once " set agoing," we find Scheffer extending his
travels as far as Eisenach, in order to pay a visit to
the Duchess of Orleans—

" J'ai trouvé la Duchesse d'Orleans très bien; ses
enfants fort grandis—l'ainé ayant fait, en tout, des
progrès étonnants . . . J'ai été reçu comme je m'y
attendais—parfaitement?"‡

" La Reine (Marie Amélie), qui a toujours été si
excellente pour moi, me fait demander de tous côtés
d'aller la voir. . . . Mais aller en Angleterre me
répugne—je ne sais pourquoi."§

---

* " I dined with the King, and was most agreeably welcomed. I
suspect that my old habit of simply speaking frankly to princes,
has served me usefully in this city."

† " The Queen wanted very much to know if the little Mignon
had any resemblance to some one who was near and dear to me?
I informed her that it was your portrait: whereupon she complimented me upon having such a daughter."

‡ " I found the Duchess of Orleans in good health. Her children
much grown — the eldest, especially, has sensibly improved in
every respect. I met with a most cordial reception, as indeed I
anticipated."

§ " The Queen (Marie Amélie), who has always been so kind a
friend to me, manifests an earnest desire that I should go and see
her. . . . but the idea of going to England is repugnant to me
—I hardly know why."

At Rotterdam, whither he returned on his way home, in order to finish some pictures which he had begun there, (possibly those now in the possession of M. Nottebohn?) Scheffer was complimented by the Society of Arts and Sciences of that city, at a numerous "réunion" of the members. Being obliged to acknowledge the honour done him, he made a "speech" in the Dutch language, which was much applauded; I doubt not deservedly. He talked so well in social converse, that he could hardly do otherwise than speak eloquently in public.

It is agreeable to find him admitting, after some two months' absence from Paris, that

" Cette absence de tourments a été d'un grand bien pour moi, sous tous les rapports. J'ai retrouvé du calme et de la résolution; depuis longtemps j'avais perdu l'un et l'autre."*

It was about Christmas, 1849, it would seem, when Scheffer regained his own residence; that secluded "rus in urbe," in the Rue Chaptal, wherein the elements of a genuine "home" were present. Two spacious "ateliers," two plots of flower-garden, together with good stabling and "Rémises;" a large, branching cedar tree shaded the "cour," the approach to which was closed by gates. The house (which he occupied entirely) was of moderate size (though quite as large as his modest ménage needed), and its interior presented an aspect of elegant comfort. Some of Schef-

---

* " This exemption from all worry has been of great service to me, in more ways than one. I have recovered my tranquillity and my firmness of purpose; both of which had well nigh deserted me for some time past."

fer's most valued pictures—that of his mother among the number—adorned the "salon."

I think that he must have painted the "Amour Divin et l'Amour Terrestre" during the winter which succeeded to his journey in Holland and Germany: a work wherein unveiled beauty of form, and unusual fulness of colour, evince a resolution on the part of the painter to try his hand, for once, in a style more exclusively "realistic" than was his wont. There is present in this picture more artistic skill in delineating what may be termed voluptuous nature, than Scheffer usually displays. The remark which suggests itself to the spectator is, perhaps, that the "terrestrial" candidate unquestionably bears the palm from the "celestial" one.

CHAPTER IX.

1850—1856.

Fidelity of Scheffer's attachment to the Orleans family—Death of
Louis Philippe—Journey to England—His enthusiasm on be-
holding the Elgin marbles—His marriage—Madame Scheffer—
Ary's interior life—His recreations—Madame Hollond.

THE attachment felt during so many years by
Scheffer towards the Orleans family was nowise
damped by the change in its fortunes.* Towards the
dethroned Queen, indeed, he seemed to become even
more attentive and tenderly respectful, than before
the storm of February, 1848. A friend, writing
about Scheffer, expresses himself on this subject as
follows:—

"Il se sentait plus à l'aise, disait-il, depuis les mal-

---

* The decree compelling the Orleans family to sell the property
they possessed in France, caused the chief portion of the pictures
painted for that family by Scheffer to be thrown into public
competition. He wrote a letter to his esteemed friend, Mr. Salis
Schwabe, of Manchester, proposing to that gentleman to become the
purchaser of one or two of them—particularly of his "Christ Consolateur." Mr. Schwabe responded to this desire by authorizing an
agent to bid for this work, as far as the sum of 50,000 francs.
But the picture was bought by a gentleman of Amsterdam named
Fodor, for a sum exceeding that price. The ex-Queen of the
French retained her "St. Monique;" the Duchess of Orleans her
"Saintes Femmes," (now the property of the Count de Paris). The
'Francesca" passed into the hands of Prince Demidoff.

heurs de la famille royale, pour lui témoigner une
fidèle amitié. Il éprouvait, en peignant pour la Reine,
une émotion profonde et vraiment réligieuse, qui
donne un caractère de beauté sombre et superieur
à celles de ses compositions dont la destination fut
telle."*

The repugnance entertained by Scheffer to the idea
of visiting England was therefore overborne, when,
in 1850, the ex-King of the French succumbed to the
common fate.   On learning the news of his ancient
sovereign's decease, Scheffer put aside all other feelings in presence of the duty which he owed to the
royal family at Claremont, and he repaired thither,
arriving in time to pay the last homage to the mortal
remains of "Louis Philippe of Orleans."   He wrote
to his daughter on reaching Claremont a hurried
note:—

"Août, 1850.

" Je n'ai qu'un moment pour t'écrire : je suis à Claremont.   J'ai trouvé toute la famille, comme je m'y attendais, admirable.   La Reine, qui n'a voulu recevoir
personne d'autre, a voulu me voir.   La Duchesse
d'Orleans m'a beaucoup parlé de toi," &c.†   After

---

* " He felt himself more at liberty, he said, after the misfor-
tunes of the Royal Family, to testify his sincere friendship towards
them.   In painting for the Queen, his feelings were tinged with a
character of religious earnestness, which imparts a certain sombre
charm to those compositions which were destined for her."

† "1 have but a minute to write to you. I am at Claremont.
I found all the family, as indeed I expected to do, in the best dispositions towards me. The Queen, who has seen nobody else, was
good enough to admit me to her presence. The Duchess of Orleans
talked to me much of you," &c. &c.

taking his leave of the illustrious mourners, he made
a brief stay in London, where he went to view the
antiquities in the British Museum.   He writes of
them in the following strain of enthusiasm:—" J'ai
mis le temps à profit en visitant le musée des marbres du Parthénon à Londres. (Tu sais le fameux vol
de Lord Elgin.)   Rien dans l'art, chère enfant, n'ap-
proche de cette beauté, de cette noblesse, et *de cette
verité.*   Ces êtres surnaturels ont dû exister; ils vivent
encore dans ces débris!.   Tant qu'on n'a vu les
marbres, rien n'en donne l'idée; les plâtres à peine.
Je veux absolument revoir cela avec toi .   .   .   ."*

It was during the spring of this same year (1850)
that Scheffer first entered the conjugal state; uniting
himself with the widow of his friend General Baudrand, a lady of English descent.   She possessed a
superior mind, a winning deportment, and an amount
of personal beauty still considerable, though it *had*
been greater.

Madame Scheffer exercised great influence over
her husband, who, on his side, regarded her with
tender consideration and sincere affection.   But

---

* " I profited by my short stay to visit the British Museum, where
the marbles from the Parthenon are deposited.   (You know all
about the famous *theft* committed by Lord Elgin ?)   Well, my dear
child, nothing, in the whole range of art, can come up to them, for
beauty, for grandeur of conception, and *for truth.*   Those immortal
beings must positively have existed: nay, they live even now, in these
very fragments !   So long as one has not beheld the marbles themselves, no copies can convey a just idea of what they are, not even
the casts in plaster.   We must absolutely see these, together, one
of these days."

Madame Scheffer was of a very delicate, fragile constitution, to which was, unfortunately, joined a disposition impatient of rivalry in every form, whether
of man or woman, friend or relative—nay, even of
Scheffer's passionate pursuit of his own art.   These
circumstances, I regret to say, led to somewhat painful results.*   Poor Madame Scheffer fell into the
deplorable error, of which many, otherwise estimable,
women have been the victims; viz., of requiring that
her husband should not only love *her* above all other
things, but should love nothing beside.   Scheffer's
widely diffused sympathies and absorbing occupations
forbade such exclusive feelings.   He loved his brothers—some few intimate friends, and, more than
all perhaps, his daughter.   He was fond of children,
as well as of the company of eminent men of letters
and artists, who, when permitted, eagerly sought
his.   During the day time, he applied his whole
mind and faculties to his art, with unfading devotion.
Pleasure he rarely sought abroad — in fact, he
seemed to care little for any amusements, commonly
so called, after 1850.†   But Ary Scheffer was

---

* " Madame Sophie Scheffer had, as her friends all recognised, a
thousand fine qualities.   She only needed a better regulated understanding, to have rendered her lot, and her home, each, a happy one.
For want of self-discipline, and the discernment to estimate, justly,
the amount of attention which she might expect from a man so rich
in friends, admirers, and disciples—for want of this, I regret to say,
Madame Scheffer sometimes embittered their common existence, by
her exigence, and by her too exalted craving for the monopoly of
her distinguished husband's time and thoughts.

† Scheffer took some interest, however, in devising, from time to
time, fanciful and historical " costumes," for eminent actors and
actresses : rejecting the traditions of the " Théâtre Francais," as

keenly sensible to the charm of good instrumental music, especially when given in the " atelier," as it was by some of the best musicians in Paris—MM. Maurin, Sabbatier, and others, frequently playing there, *en amateurs*, at his wife's invitation. The delicious harmonies, and even the mysterious and learned " rêveries" of Beethoven, seemed to kindle and stimulate his fancy : and I have seen Scheffer yield himself up to the fascinations of sound with a sort of dreamy enjoyment, such as is rarely attained by persons who have not cultivated musical knowledge.

The highly gifted Madame Viardot, as also her husband—himself a studious votary of art in its noblest forms—were among the most welcome and familiar of Scheffer's "habitués:" and since, along with Madame Viardot's vocal power was united a talent for pianoforte playing of a superior kind, Scheffer had often the pleasure of listening to her tasteful execution of the best compositions for that instrument.

Two works fall, in order of time, under the date of 1851, the year succeeding to Scheffer's marriage. I allude, 1, to the portrait of General Cavaignac, and, 2, to the " St. John writing the Apocalypse." The former is undoubtedly among his best efforts in this

----

obsolete. In later days he invented stage garments for Madame Ristori, of whose brilliant talents Scheffer was a sincere admirer, and of whose striking lineaments a record remains, painted by his hand.

line, whilst the head of the Apostle has been justly
regarded as one of Scheffer's most decided "successes"
when attempting the grand Ideal.   It is indeed a
striking and impressive picture, reminding us of the
older masters of Italy, such as Fra Bartolomeo, or
perhaps Ludovico Carracci.*

The two Eberhards (" Le Coupeur de Nappe," and
" Le Larmoyeur") were likewise the product of 1851.
Pictures each highly extolled by critics of ability, but
which, I am free to confess, never captivated my
fancy. Their composition may display merit, but
the colour of the " Larmoyeur" is so opaque, heavy,
and pasty, that I never could look on it with any
satisfaction.†

A work, ascribed by the catalogue to this date,
was, I feel persuaded, rather the fruit of 1852.   I
allude to his charming likeness of Madame Hollond.
Admirable as a portrait, Scheffer has rarely painted
one more interesting to amateurs.   Since my reasons
for changing the date of this performance are inter-
woven with circumstances too notable to be lightly
passed over, I must be permitted to dwell, for a space,
upon the grave events of December, 1851.

---

* It formed part of the choice collection of the late Mr. Salis
Schwabe, and was lent for the Exhibition of 1859 by the widow of
that lamented gentleman.

† I have, since seeing it last, found reason to believe that the
" medium," and pigments, employed in painting this picture have
become blackened and injured, which partly accounts for its (in my
view) want of attractiveness.

CHAPTER X.

1851.

Violent end of the Republic—Scheffer's profound disappointment—
His incapacity for work—This surmounted by appeal made to
his pledged word—Paints portrait of Madame Hollond.

ALTHOUGH the state of public affairs, in the autumn
of 1851, seemed to forbid any sanguine hopes of the
" Republic" prospering, as such, still the friends of
liberal government clung to the chances of a solution
of the actual difficulty, as between the President and
the Assembly, in some form which might at least
avert the horrors of fresh civil war. Scheffer certainly
had no expectation that the knot would be cut in the
violent mode which *was* employed by the President.
The effect which the astounding incidents of the 2nd,
3rd, and 4th December produced upon him, was therefore bitterly painful—I may say, overpowering.

I called at his residence within a day or two of the
terrible slaughter of the Parisians in their houses
and in their streets—that is to say, as soon as it was
prudent to venture forth. I found Scheffer at home,
and alone with his wife. The interview was, in a
measure, at once solemn and sad. The collective
ruins of thirty years' illusory hopes and struggles
stood before me, as it were; * whilst in the few

---

* Whilst this visit lasted, neither of us sate down.

broken phrases which Scheffer's emotion permitted of his uttering, was revealed the anguish of final despair.

It would have argued a want of reverence and sympathy towards this noble but aching heart, to seek to maintain the conversation beyond a few minutes, and I accordingly withdrew. Madame Sophie Scheffer followed me into the court—" You see how he suffers!" whispered she :—I pressed her hand, but said nothing—what was there to *be said?*

Shortly after this visit I repaired again to the Rue Chaptal. In the atelier into which Scheffer's morning visitors, when admitted, were usually introduced, (he painted in another), I found M. le Comte Adolphe de Circourt waiting. Scheffer was not long in joining us. At first he seemed so full of mortifying thoughts as to be incapable of talking; looked haggard and dejected; whilst his voice, when he did let fall a few sentences, was veiled by grief-stricken, subdued tones. After a little time, he related how that he had, on learning the arrest of the Generals (early in the morning of the 2nd December), put on his uniform, summoned his " Tambour," and gone forth to try to collect together the members of his "Company," with the view to rally round the legal government of the nation. " But," he added, " the indifference, not to say the reluctance to ' turn out,' with which my appeals were met, so discouraged me, that I gave up the effort, and returned home. The Chamber," continued Scheffer, " has lost its hold upon the country : nobody will stir a finger for it. All is up with the *Republic*."

M. de Circourt now drew from his pocket a paper—I think it was a newspaper—wherein was given a long list of persons newly arrested, of whose probable destination nothing could be learned.   The reading of this document aroused Scheffer's ire beyond control: his eyes seemed to flash fire; he paced the atelier with wavering steps, giving vent at intervals to his feelings by emphatic exclamations inspired by his honest, just wrath.   The scene was one not to be forgotten.*

The memorable event, which is commonly known as "the coup-d'état," has been the theme of such endless volumes of controversy, and is even now viewed in such different lights, according to the cast of sentiment of the individual who judges of its complexion, that it would be quite out of place were I here to expatiate anew upon its character.   I conceive that it will continue, as hitherto, to divide the opinions of those two great sections of society—the upholders of moral obligation on the one side, the partisans of triumphant violence on the other—which are likely to compose the human family throughout all time.   I only wish that it were permitted to me to hope that the former section would, one day, outnumber the latter!   But to resume—

---

* If there be a spectacle touching on the morally sublime, it is that of a high-souled man, conscious of having strenuously laboured for his country's weal, in every way open to him, during his whole life, who beholds that country's laws and liberties abrogated by the audacious employment of military force.   This was not, however, the only occasion on which I had the pain of beholding such a sight.   Among the noble, patriotic, and pure-minded Frenchmen, with whom it has been my good fortune to be acquainted, three of the most distinguished may be said—figuratively speaking—to have "died of their wounds;" namely, Léon Faucher, Ary Scheffer, and lastly, Alexis de Tocqueville, of whose mental anguish I have been, in each case, a sympathizing witness.

It happened that, very shortly prior to the catas-
trophe which, as I have observed, put the finishing
stroke to the many political disappointments which
Scheffer had already endured, Madame Hollond had
arranged to sit to him, for a portrait of herself. I
must here note in passing, that, at no period was
Scheffer partial to this employment of his talents; so
far from it, that he sought to evade commissions for
portraits; putting so large a price upon them as
would, he flattered himself, deter people from giving
him orders. For Madame Hollond, however, he was
less unwilling to undertake the task, since that lady
and her husband were included in the circle of his
friendly acquaintance, and, moreover, her face and
head offered an interesting subject to paint from.

Accordingly, Mr. and Madame Hollond went about
the 6th or 7th of December to Scheffer's house (by
appointment, made some time in November) to commence the sittings. They found him in so perturbed
a frame of mind, that there was no possibility of
getting him to begin work. He walked about the
" atelier" like a restless spirit, saying " he would *try*
and arrange about the attitude, dress, &c., in a day
or two." Eventually, they quitted the house, engag-
ing to return within that space. Again the same
incapacity—the same vain result. As Madame Hollond sincerely sympathized with Scheffer's feelings,
she entertained some scruples about importuning him
on the subject; when one day, after a renewed attempt, equally infructuous with former ones, Madame
Scheffer spoke to her friend thus, in private—" Dear
Madame Hollond, you have but one chance of prevailing with Ary to set to work, and that is to remind

him of his *promise* to paint your picture. So long as he can put you off, and escape the effort needed to vanquish his depression and fix his attention, he will do so. You must observe how wretched he is; he can neither eat, nor sleep, nor paint; nothing can distract his mind from the deplorable spectacle now passing before his eyes, and I really grow seriously uneasy about him. By touching his *sense of duty*, you employ the only means of arousing Scheffer, and I beg of you to try it; indeed, to see him once more at his ' chevalet' would be a welcome relief to myself."

The appeal was kindly and discreetly made, and, after a resolute struggle with himself, Scheffer commenced the portrait; but it must have taken some weeks to complete, and thus, I have ventured to place this interesting work among the products of 1852.

CHAPTER XI.

1852—1853.

Ary's close devotion to his professional occupation—His aversion to general society increases—Occasionally receives guests at home —Charm of his society for them—Illness and death of Arnold Scheffer—Commencement of deranged action in Ary's heart— Its origin—He adopts his little nephew, Ariel.

In the spring of 1852, I took a country house in the environs of Paris, and, during several months, had the pleasure of seeing Scheffer frequently at his own house: sometimes also, his anxious wife would persuade him to drive out and dine with us, at our "villa" at Ville d'Avray. Madame Scheffer, being a devotedly attached wife, used every effort in her power to divert his thoughts, and to furnish him with some recreation which might prevent his confining himself so incessantly within the four walls of his atelier. He would pass whole days therein, painting till the light failed him, without even taking a walk: in hot, summer weather, too.* Riding on horseback was for many years a favourite exercise of Scheffer's; but, though he still kept saddle horses, Madame Scheffer now observed with regret, that he no longer cared to mount them. After the coup

---

* His mind dwelling painfully upon the humiliation of his countrymen under the new government, he disliked the sight of the swarms of military whom he met if he walked about the streets of Paris.

d'état, he secluded himself more and more from the
Paris world; would hear nothing, ask nothing, about
political affairs, and went but rarely abroad.

Although, as I have said, Scheffer clung unremit-
tingly to his art, as the solace—as the *medicine*, I
may call it,—to his wounded soul, he would occasionally indulge in the enjoyment of society; entertaining
his guests handsomely at his board, and delighting
those around him by the clear sense, the varied knowledge, and, I may add, by the malicious pleasantry
with which he would occasionally animate the repast.
As for telling a story, few could equal him, in my
judgment: whilst no man ever had a keener appreciation of wit and intellectual gifts in others than
Scheffer manifested, when these were present.

He had found time, during long years—especially
in winter, when want of daylight abridged his painting hours—to read most of the standard works in the
literature of France, England, Germany, and Italy:
each in the original tongue. I have heard him say
that, having made acquaintance with most of the best
writers, he took little or no pleasure in reading books
of a secondary order, even though they might possess
great merit in their way. But the books of the Old
Testament were perhaps those most frequently seen
in his hand, during the last eight years of his life.
The study of pastoral, primitive, rude forms of
society,—with the touching episodes here and there
occurring in the history of those early peoples—had
an unfading attraction for Scheffer; whilst it served
to prevent his mind and thoughts from brooding
over the actual state of things in France. Still, it
was from the New Testament that the larger number

of his sacred compositions were taken; for he loved to dwell upon the humanizing influences, and devotional feelings, connected with the mission of Jesus Christ, whose ideal lineaments it was ever his loftiest ambition to pourtray.

If the cup of *political* bitterness seemed now drained, by the complete extinction of all Scheffer's hopes of political progress, there remained abundance of sorrow in store for him of a personal kind.

His brother, Arnold Scheffer, fell ill about the beginning of the year 1853, and whereas he had no relative to attend upon him at his own residence (being a widower), Ary offered to receive him in the Rue Chaptal, whither he accordingly removed in the month of April.

Not only was Arnold housed, and attended, and cared for, ministered to by Madame Scheffer and by Madame Marjolin, (aided by the kind household servants,) but Ary himself habitually passed the *night* near the sick man's bed. Month after month was this pious duty discharged by the devoted, compassionate brother, to the evident detriment of his own constitutional powers.

All persons acquainted with even the elements of physiology recognise the influence of mental states over the functions of the heart. That susceptible and vital organ was, in Scheffer's case, about to experience the ill effects of prolonged anxiety, further augmented by unwholesome habits. His bodily frame and organization was by nature one of manly vigour, and of equally distributed forces. But what human machinery could have resisted the unfair burthen laid by Scheffer upon his ? To say nothing of the traces left by the mortifications he had gone through, (in reference to public affairs), Scheffer imprudently neglected the commonest precepts of a sound " hygiéne"—sitting perched on his " échelle," stooping over his canvas, the livelong day: passing in his " salon" most of his evenings : eating and drinking as is usual with healthy people (though ever temperate in each of these indulgences), and finally, spending his nights in watching near Arnold's couch, his feelings painfully on the stretch, his rest broken and abridged!

From all these causes—to which some other sources of mental irritation contributed their quota—Scheffer now contracted an affection of the heart, which, in subsequent years, materially interfered with his comfort and physical well-being. To the hurtful effects of his attendance upon his brother, was presently superadded grief for his loss: Arnold's disorder conducting him, after eight months' suffering, to the tomb, about the close of the year 1853.

Scheffer's estimate of his brother's talents and understanding was a high one; but he repeatedly avowed his regret that Arnold's intellectual powers had not been seconded by more steadfast application, and by habits of regular industry. Arnold left one child—a boy—born in the year 1849, his wife dying in childbirth of this infant. Ary Scheffer retained the boy in his own family, treating him as if he had been his son, and, in truth, loving him as such. The child was beautiful as an angel, and always appeared to me to be endowed with fine parts, together

with a tender, generous disposition. He was the
"plaything" of the "ménage," the darling of Scheffer
and his wife, and an object of interest to all who came
within their circle. Yet his upbringing was not
altogether calculated to lead to his becoming a good
and estimable man : for Scheffer's indulgence knew
no bounds, and the clever little Ariel (or " Ary," as
he was always called) failed not to turn both his
uncle's love and weakness to profit.*

---

* It was a touching domestic scene which I witnessed, when, on
one occasion (I think it was in 1855), young Ary, then six years
old, had a slight feverish attack. The child being laid on the sofa
in the salon, Scheffer would, at intervals, feel his little hands, to
judge of the heat of his skin. Then, bending over him, inquire
with the gentlest tones, "as-tu froid, mon enfant," "as-tu soif ?"
&c.; folding a shawl around his limbs; cheering him with assurances
that " he would soon get well," and so on, whilst his own great
heart seemed over full with affectionate solicitude for his infantine
patient.

CHAPTER XII.

1854—1855.

Scheffer completes several works of importance—Remarks upon
some of these—Increased disposition of Scheffer to melancholy
—This revealed in his compositions.

THE year 1854 was one of importance, viewed in reference to Scheffer's pencil; some compositions of high
interest—the Ruth and Naomi, the " Madeleine en
Extase," " Les Gémissemens," and the " Tentation "
—falling among the number of those in progress
about this period.

The last-mentioned picture was, however, "in
hand," during several consecutive years: so much
difficulty did the painter experience in conveying the
ideas which he desired to embody in that ambitious
allegorical piece. He actually effaced the entire figure
of Satan once, and painted it in afresh. Observing
the change, I said to Madame Scheffer, " Why!
the figure of Satan is altogether different from what it
was when I saw it last!" " Yes," replied she, "it *is*
quite changed—the truth of the matter is, Ary
cannot satisfy himself about that figure." " Give me
leave to add," said I, " that he never *will* satisfy
himself, for it is a conception hardly capable of being
rendered to the visual sense."

To his friend Madame Salis Schwabe, Scheffer writes:—

"Mon tableau du Christ et du Satan, je l'ai refait, littéralement, d'un bout à l'autre, excepté la tête du Messie. Le tableau a gagné, mais n'est pas terminé encore." * But whilst Scheffer appreciated, almost in a painful measure, the difficulty of treating this mysterious passage of the Gospel, he was only the more indefatigable in his endeavours to work it out. I conversed about it with him more than once, but he usually appeared disinclined to discuss the matter. The picture, at all events, possessed considerable attraction for many persons, and liberal offers were made for its purchase; but I believe that they were not accepted by the artist: at least it remains in the "studio" at this day.† With the sole exception of "Les Gémissemens," I should be disposed to affirm that "La Tentation" occupied the painter a greater number of hours than any one work beside. He obviously felt his "amour propre" engaged in surmounting the admitted difficulty of the subject. The head of the Christ is, indisputably, fine, as a model of serene dignity; the figure of the Tempter vigorously designed, the attitudes of both natural,

---

* "My picture of Christ and Satan has been, literally, repainted entirely, with the exception of the Saviour's head. The picture is improved, I think, but is still far from finished."

† Since writing the above, information has reached me of the "Tentation" having been sent over to London for the purpose of being engraved. It is probable that it will possess considerable interest for the art world; the objection which I have ventured to take to the colouring of this picture not being valid in the case of an engraving.

and even eloquent. For all this, the picture is one which never possessed much interest for me. Its faults need not be here particularized, but one of them is to be found, in my poor judgment, in the indiscreet selection of rose pink colour for the raiment of the Saviour; it being painted against a full blue ground. After this, the ugliness of the " Satan," the " ex-angel," which seems to me exaggerated. Of " Les Gémissemens" it may be safely affirmed, that the contemplation of numerous examples of human beauty, finely treated, and joined with a kind of holy, elevated expression, can have but one result, viz., the production of an harmonious and captivating effect.

The " sentiment" which is shadowed forth in this allegory, is supposed to teach us that mortal passions and sorrows become purified and refined, in proportion as the beings subjected to them recede from this earth. At foot, are seen various heads, mostly of rather ordinary stamp: as the group ascends heavenward, the countenances assume a more radiant aspect; until, towards the higher portion of the picture, the personages floating in space appear, as it were, spiritualized, in virtue of their approach to the " mansions of the blest!"

Looking attentively into the group, you discern figures already made familiar to memory, from having been introduced in former compositions. Among them, the artist's own sainted mother, under the figure of the St. Monica: Beatrice, Dante, and others. The whole design reveals the promptings of a creative genius, seconded by conscientious labour on the part of the executive hand. It is, in my estimation, one of those pictures which will bear to be viewed again and again, not only without feeling tired of the study, but even with a sense of added pleasure.*

I find a passage in allusion to this subject in one of Scheffer's own letters.   It is as follows:—

. " Je travaille aux ' Gémissemens,' et beaucoup de figures difficiles sont très avancés. J'aime le sujet par dessus tous les autres que j'ai traité, mais la méfiance dans mon talent augmente tous les jours."†

This composition has been objected to, as "metaphysical," as "obscure," as "overleaping the legitimate aim of art," as "mystical," and I know not what else; these terms being intended for disparaging ones. Scheffer certainly aspired to delineate certain forms of humanity in connexion with immortal and religious conceptions; the poetical rendering of Christian traditions and faith, in short.   If, in his hands, these endeavours partook too much of what is commonly termed "the German spirit," we should call to mind Scheffer's paternal origin, and the ineffaceable qualities of " race " whenever, and in whatsoever form, the " æsthetic" vein finds vent.

Furthermore, I would ask whether the department of realistic, material art, be not abundantly furnished with able interpreters? Many renowned painters of our own day have given us splendid examples of felicitous colouring, of imitative texture, of ingenious treatment of light and shade, of truth of " character," of severe

---

* A "replica" of this work, in which some of her family are introduced, is in the possession of Madame Salis Schwabe, at Glyngarth, Anglesea, North Wales.

† " I am occupied upon the ' Gémissemens,' and a good many of the most difficult figures are in a forward stage. I like the subject, perhaps more than any one which I have yet handled ; still, I feel every day more and more conscious of my own incompetency. . ."

and learned "drawing"—of all excellences, indeed, pertaining to the "craft;" excellences, some of which, speaking candidly, cannot be ascribed to Ary Scheffer. I may instance William Etty, Paul de la Roche, Maclise, Herbert, Watts, F. Leighton, Rosa Bonheur, Edwin Landseer, Mulready, Frith, Millais, Hunt, and many more, to illustrate my meaning. Yet although the admiration of mankind be justly due to the exhibition of these qualities, it is nowise regrettable, but is even fortunate for the world, that ministers of art should now and then arise, who, being differently gifted, essay a new flight, and seek to employ their pencil upon other than purely familiar subjects, or great historical passages.

Towards the afternoon of life, (as one may call it,) whilst Scheffer's ability as an inventor and designer maintained its power, his management of the brush may be said to have become more experienced and dexterous; insomuch that it is quite conceivable that had he lived he might have produced works, surpassing, in point of *execution*, those which remain to us. But notwithstanding this undiminished skill, his longings—his dreams, as they may be termed—after an ideal perfection, which he found himself incapable of attaining, tormented and discouraged him: indeed he grew more fastidious, more exigent, in reference to his own work, in proportion as his mental and critical faculties rose higher in tone.

The tendency to depression of spirits, which latterly, (as I have related,) bespread itself over his life, would seem to have had its share in disposing Scheffer to seek, in the speculative and spiritual, a refuge from the poignant disappointments of the "every-day" world. To this source, I conceive that we are in

great measure indebted for the peculiar charm which
distinguishes his later works, to which this same
"sombre" tone of mind doubtless gave the "key-
note" of religious, thoughtful melancholy.

An example of it is furnished in the "Christ
au roseau" (No. 85 in Catalogue of 1859), on
which, be it observed in passing, a vast deal of
comment and criticism has been expended. Without sharing the excessive admiration of this picture
avowed by some recent writers, I recognise, in it,
certain merits which go far to impart value to
compositions of this character. The profound resignation and humility apparent in the head of
the Saviour, the presence of anguish, without *too*
strongly betraying its evidences, the careful drawing
and expressive "pose" of the hands, and, in some
degree, the skilful management of the flesh tones,
(though the anatomical details must be pronounced
to be incompletely made out)—the employment of rich
colour in the garments—these may be regarded as
forming an "ensemble," possessing at once interest
for the eye, and earnest devotional feeling.

Again, the incomplete work, "Jesus Appearing to
Mary Magdalen after his Resurrection," affords an
illustration of Scheffer's "pale cast of thought"—solemn, impressive, colourless—evincing much care in
the distribution of forms; (*learning* displaying itself,
too, here, in the due balancing of lines and angles) this
"sketch" seemed, to my thinking, one of undoubted
excellence. No man could have painted it without
having cultivated that power of thought denoted by
the French word "Récueillement." The effect of
the sketch is, altogether, highly "suggestive," if it
be not all that a painter is required to achieve.

CHAPTER XIII.

1856.

Laborious habits of Scheffer—His eulogy of industry—Illness and death of Augustin Thierry—Sorrow of Scheffer for his loss—Decline of Madame Sophie Scheffer's health—Her death—Its effect upon her husband's mind and life.

SCHEFFER worked, I have said, with a diligence often amounting to toil—all his earnings (and they were large) flowed out as fast as they came in; since he could never refuse his purse to whomsoever asked his assistance, he would have been inconvenienced in his private expenditure had he not plied his pencil incessantly.*

He writes to a friend, in 1855, as under—

" Je travaille toujours, du matin au soir, et je suis forcé de le faire. J'aurois désiré pouvoir prendre des

---

* I quote a passage from a letter of his which will serve to show how settled was Scheffer's habit of labour, and how emphatically he prescribed it to others, as a duty, and even as a valuable means of "distraction."

" Resume your work without delay ; work is the best, the truest support to the mind. It is a positive duty to learn to be able to suffice to oneself (*suffire à soimême*), and in order to do this, one must devote oneself, body and soul, to the obligations which life imposes. Besides, one derives, from the feeling of *duty fulfilled*, a kind of companionship, which helps to smooth our path, and to render less bitter the deceptions we have to bear with . . . ."

bains de mer, mais il me parait peu probable que je trouve le temps. . . ." *

The same pressure is indicated in a letter of 1856, (March): " J'ai beaucoup travaillé ce dernier temps —beaucoup trop, même. Je voudrais pouvoir me reposer, mais la chose m'est impossible; et pourtant je suis tellement fatigué que je n'y vois plus! . . ."†

Yet, notwithstanding the demands made upon his time and energies, Scheffer managed frequently to pass an hour or two with his afflicted friend, Augustin Thierry, who had become both blind and paralytic. I have myself been told, more than once, on asking for Scheffer, at his own house, that he was absent on this pious errand.

But in the spring of 1856, this truly worthy and accomplished friend was released from his manifold sufferings. During the illness which preceded his death, Scheffer visited him daily, and, indeed, for the last two days and nights, never quitted his bed-side.

Thierry's attachment for Scheffer was most faithful and earnest. Their intimacy had been unbroken, from youth to mature age, so that although life had long ceased to possess any value for his poor friend, Scheffer felt real sorrow for his loss.

Scarcely had this cloud passed away, when a fresh

---

* " I work without intermission, from morning till night, and am compelled to do so, indeed. I had wished to be able to get a little sea-bathing this season, but there seems very little chance of my finding leisure for it. . . ."

† "I have worked very hard of late. In truth, *too* hard. It would be a relief to me to obtain some rest, but the thing is impossible; and yet I am literally fagged to death, insomuch that I can scarcely see to paint! . . ."

occasion arose for exertion. Scheffer's nervous system, already cruelly strained by attendance upon
Thierry, now became agitated by the alarming condition of his wife's health. Madame Sophie Scheffer
had, I have already stated, a delicate and susceptible
organization, and was always more or less of an invalid during several years preceding this period.
The wearisome attendance which she had given to
her mother, Madame la Baronne de Charluz, for a
long time,—the incessant striving to mitigate the
sufferings, and dissipate the *ennui* of a person who was,
I feel compelled to add, to the last degree dependent
and helpless, (not to say inconsiderate of the interests
of others)—these protracted demands upon Madame
Scheffer's slender vitality, seem to have exhausted
what little strength remained to her. For, after the
last duties were discharged to Madame la Baronne,
her daughter's health grew more and more feeble, and
in June, 1856, it became obvious that her days were
numbered.

Scheffer consecrated every hour of his time to his
declining partner: watching over, and ministering to
her, with unremitting care and tenderness. Now it
happened that, just at this time, my husband and myself were passing through Paris, on our return from a
tour in Italy; and although we hardly sought out
any one, or meant to stay more than a day or two
in Paris, yet the news reaching us of my poor
friend being seriously ill, we hastened to the Rue
Chaptal to make inquiries after her. All was silence
in that little " enceinte," as we made our way softly
into the court. Madame Marjolin came out of the
"atelier," and spoke with us respecting the patient

above stairs, who, we learned, was sinking day by
day, without hope of recovery. "And how is your
father?" asked I. "He is almost worn out with
attending upon his poor wife;" replied Madame Marjolin; "there is no prevailing upon him to quit her
bedside, and God knows what ill effects may result
from so long a privation of fresh air, and of rest, on
his own health." Whilst we three were standing together, within the inner gates, the door of the house
gently opened, and Ary himself, in his dressing-
gown, came slowly down the steps into the court;
advancing towards us, he took a hand of each of us
two visitors in his, and said "I saw it was you, from
the window of her chamber, and felt that I *must* come
down to you." We asked how she was going on?
Scheffer hardly replied to the question, but by his
manner gave us to understand that it was a hopeless
case. He said to me, "Only an hour since, she
was talking of you! She is perfectly collected, only
weak in the extreme." Here his feelings seemed to
master him, and he quitted us abruptly, saying, "I
will write and tell you when all is over," and so, with
a sign of the hand, he hastened back into the house.

Madame Scheffer lingered only about ten days
longer, dying calmly, in her husband's arms, without
a struggle.

The five months which followed upon this event,
were, with Scheffer, months of blank depression,
almost of prostration. His whole being was unstrung,
as it were. A mental tension, more or less trying,
of several years' duration, terminated by painful and
agitating scenes, such as inevitably attend an eternal

separation, had the effect of weighing down all the energies of his mind. He could not bear even to take up his palette and brush: all vivacity forsook him, and for, probably, the first time in his history, he passed his days unprofitably, listlessly; chiefly alone, musing and pondering upon the chequered circumstances of his life. These five months past, Scheffer seemed to arouse himself by a strong effort, and he began, gradually, to resume his customary avocations.

I regret that the obligations of confidential friendship prevent my quoting more than a portion of a letter which Scheffer addressed to a lady in England, (in January, 1857,) depicting the desolate state of inaction in which he had passed the previous five months. I have rarely met with so touching, so interesting a revelation. One healing balm was there, it is true. Scheffer bore within his breast a conscience void of reproach. This is clearly perceptible in the tone of his letter, otherwise so sad. It concludes thus :—

" J'ai retrouvé du calme, mais de l'énergie pour rien, si non pour le travail. Je suis fort entouré par ma fille, par son mari, qui est de nouveau pour moi le meilleur ami. Je serais ingrat si je me plaignai de mon sort; du fond du cœur je remercie la Providence des biens qu'elle m'accorde; de l'amour du travail, et de l'affection des miens. . . ."*

---

* " I have regained my composure, but have little energy, unless it be in my appetite for work. I am well cared for by my daughter and her husband ; the latter, more than ever a valuable friend to me. I should indeed be ungrateful if I complained of my lot; from my heart I thank Providence for all the blessings granted me; among which the foremost are my own love of occupation, and the affection of those around me."

CHAPTER XIV.

1857.

Ary Scheffer once more in England—Manchester " Exhibition of
Art Treasures"—Scheffer's great enjoyment therein—Goes to
Claremont—Paints portrait of ex-Queen of the French—His
visit to Glyngarth—Beneficial results of this *séjour*—Regret
felt by Scheffer at its termination.

It was fortunate for Scheffer that, towards the spring
of this year (1857), a strong temptation to make a
journey was furnished by the Manchester " Exhibition of Art Treasures." Scheffer was, naturally,
excited by the idea of seeing in one comprehensive
focus, so vast an assemblage of works by both modern
artists and old masters; and, his son-in-law consenting to allow Cornélie to accompany him, he set forth
in the month of May, (taking little Ary, also,) and
accepted the cordial offer of Madame Salis Schwabe
to make her house his home during his stay at Manchester.

Never was change, or recreative occupation, more
needed; nor, it may be added, was it ever more
effectual, in renovating the nervous system and
general physical powers of a careworn being. Scheffer
and his family remained for three weeks at the house
of his esteemed friend, situate a few miles distant
from Manchester: going in to the Exhibition daily,
and poring intently for hours, upon the choice and

precious examples of the various schools of painting
which were there spread out before his eyes. The
delight and instruction which they afforded him,
operated the happiest effect; and when we saw him
in London, shortly afterwards, the decided indications of improved health were most gratifying to
us to observe.

The *existence* of a British school of painters
was known to Scheffer, as it was to most other
foreign connoisseurs. But it had never been un-
derstood or esteemed at its real value, until the
Manchester Exhibition drew forth its manifold
treasures. Scheffer, for his part, was scarcely
less astonished than enchanted with the spectacle
which that collection afforded him. "I had no
conception," said he, "how rich the English school
was! There have lived great painters among you;
that is unquestionable! I have been in a sort of
'*Paradise of art*' for these three weeks past. The
power of dealing with colour, especially, possessed
by the English artists, fills me with admiration. I
only wish it could be imparted to myself!" &c. &c.

From London, Scheffer repaired to the neighbour-
hood of Claremont, (his daughter and young Ary in
company with him,) in order to fulfil a promise he
had made to paint a portrait of Queen Marie Amelie.
Some few weeks were consecrated to this purpose,
during which period Scheffer's health and spirits continued to derive benefit; as well from the tranquil
tenor of his existence, as from the pleasing com-
munion which, in the pursuit of his daily labours, he
enjoyed in the friendly circle at Claremont.

Of the portrait itself, whereon the painter bestowed all the skill and talent at his command, I regret to be nowise qualified to speak, otherwise than on the authority of others. A distinguished Frenchman, (M. Vitet,) has said, in writing of this picture, that " it is, in its way, a masterpiece; expressive of the energy and the resignation of a noble soul, joined with the mingled sorrows and hopes of a tender and Christian character." I have heard, too, more than one competent witness pronounce the " treatment" of the picture to be, in every way, worthy of the painter's reputation.

The Queen's portrait finished—or, as nearly so as it was judged desirable it should be, for the moment —Scheffer now made his dispositions for paying a visit which, in every point of view, promised to afford him the truest satisfaction, and the most suitable restorative that it was possible to furnish to a weary spirit. Accompanied on this journey by M. and Madame Marjolin and his young nephew Ary, Scheffer set forth, some time in July, for the residence of his friend, Madame Salis Schwabe, (now become a widow,) situate on the shores of the Menai Straits, in the Isle of Anglesea, North Wales. At Glyngarth were present, in ample store, all those elements in which an imaginative, sentimental, and affectionate soul, like that of Scheffer, might find delectation and refreshment. The picturesque mountain scenery of Carnarvonshire, the sight of the shipping gliding about in the " Menai;" the novel spectacle of the Welsh people, busy, yet not toilworn; the devoted, kind attentions of the hostess, her daughter, (an attractive girl of seventeen,) and

youthful sons, (all of them esteemed and beloved by
Scheffer and his family,) the salubrity of the air,
the peace, the presence of infantine " entourage,"*
the *pause*, as one may term it, in the arduous journey
of existence—all these circumstances combined to
infuse into the temper and feelings of Scheffer so
efficacious a balm, that it almost revived the whole
man.   The effect might be likened to one of those
serene afternoon skies, which we have, all of us,
frequently gazed upon after a tempestuous day;
seemingly arranging itself, as it were, for a calm
radiant sunset.

And thus it befel, in truth; for I must observe in
passing that this delightful passage was destined to
prove the last of the kind (perhaps I may go farther
and say it was the *only* one of the kind) which it was
permitted to this virtuous and gifted being to enjoy
on earth.

The letters written by Ary to his late hostess,
after returning to Paris, breathe genuine thankful-
ness for the friendly attention and kindness which
he had been treated with, joined with assurances of
regret at having been obliged to leave Glyngarth :—

"Août, 1857.

". . Mais de vous avoir quitté " (he writes) " m'a
fait une peine éxtrême, et il y a de longues années
qu'il ne m'était arrivé d'éprouver un semblable regret;
ne vivant, réellement, de ma vie, que dans mon 'ate-

---

* Ary was continually to be seen walking about near Glyngarth,
with young children for his companions (visitors of the family);
one child holding him by the hand (or finger) on either side—
prattling as they went—Scheffer complacently listening to them.

lier.' Je me suis remis à travailler, après avoir passé trois ou quatre jours à arranger mes ateliers, qui sont maintenant en bon ordre; seulement, j'ai trop à faire, et ne sais pas où commencer !"*

It may well be conceived how welcome had been the recreation resulting from the "séjour" in North Wales, to a man who, for the greater part of his life "in populous cities pent," saw years revolve round him without bringing either pleasant variety, or joy to his hearth. The action of many fresh and unwonted influences—such as arise out of the contact with beautiful nature, and from the *society* of cheerful, congenial companions—told healthfully upon the whole frame of Scheffer's being. Madame Schwabe had observed, with heartfelt pleasure, the healing process going on in her valued friend's person, and cherished the fond hope of a lasting recovery from his previous depressed condition. In this hope, however, she was not long permitted to indulge, as will be seen by what appears in the next chapter.

---

* "It cost me extreme pain to take leave of you all; such regret indeed as I have not experienced for many and many a year; having so rarely set foot outside of my own painting room, all my life long. I fell to, immediately, for three or four days, upon the arrangement of my 'ateliers,' which are now all in good order: but I have so much work on my hands, that I am puzzled how to make a beginning !"

CHAPTER XV.

1857.

Return from England to Paris—Illness and death of Manin—
Scheffer's sorrow for his loss—Effects of it—He falls ill—His
slow recovery—Scheffer's report of his own condition.

IT would seem to have been the destiny of this humane
and generous hearted man, to endure a succession of
painful separations from individuals with whom he had
formed ties of affection.   On Scheffer's return, when
his Paris friends, like his English ones, were cheered
by the improvement perceptible both in his looks and
energies, a new trial awaited him in the serious illness of his friend Manin, the heroic defender of
Venice in 1849.

With this illustrious exile, Scheffer had contracted
a close intimacy, which, during five years, was nurtured by frequent intercourse, and mutual confidences.
All the newly-acquired contentment was therefore
quickly darkened over by the fear of separation from
one whose society had become an almost daily enjoyment, both for father and daughter ; since Madame
Marjolin bore Manin an equally cordial regard and
esteem with Scheffer himself.

A slight indisposition having prevented the latter
from going, for some few days, to his sick friend,
he was shocked and startled by the intelligence
which was one morning brought to him, (it was about

the 22nd of September,) that Manin had expired, rather suddenly. Though it was an act of imprudence on Scheffer's part, to leave his house, he instantly repaired to Manin's lodgings, taking thither his painting materials: and there, from the lifeless features before him, he made a sort of posthumous portrait of the departed patriot: painting during the whole day, until evening put a stop to his work.

On the morrow of this painful exertion, Scheffer, though still far from well, would not be persuaded to renounce the duty of following the corpse of Manin to its last resting place. This place was no other than a private vault belonging to Scheffer, wherein lay the revered remains of his mother, and wherein, alas! he was fated to be, at no distant day, himself deposited by her side.*

The funeral of the respected Italian martyr was attended by most of the distinguished friends of political liberty, members of the press, and liberal men of letters. The ceremony was altogether calculated to awaken strong emotion in those present, and I entertain but little doubt that this whole passage of Manin's illness, death, and burial, caused a serious aggravation of disease of the heart, under which Scheffer had suffered more or less, during the last four years.

Shortly after this ·event, that is to say, in the month of October following, Scheffer fell ill; *so* ill,

---

* The daughter of Manin, who was the solace and support of her poor father whilst alive, had been interred in this same sanctuary, by Scheffer's permission, about a year before. The vault itself is in the cemetery of Montmartre, near Paris.

as to afford much ground for apprehension to his friends. I do not know, precisely, what the character of the disorder was, under which he now laboured: I have been told that its seat was the organ so often alluded to in these pages, but that gout had also fixed itself in that region. I do not, however, quite believe in the accuracy of this statement; leaning rather to the supposition that the action of the arterial system was seriously deranged; thus endangering the very conditions of vitality. Be this as it may, the attack of illness I speak of confined Scheffer to bed for some time, and when, at length, the alarming symptoms disappeared, his convalescence was but a slow process.

It was not until some weeks had been passed in his chamber, that he was enabled to go down stairs to the " atelier," and once more apply himself to his favourite occupation. Here is his own report of himself, in the month of November, 1857 :—

" On me dit que j'ai été fort malade; quoique j'étouffai horriblement, je ne m'en souviens guère. Cornélie m'a soignée nuit et jour; aussi dans ce moment est elle tellement fatiguée qu'elle ne peut rien faire, et auroit grand besoin d'être gardée et soignée elle-même. Elle est encore chez moi, se levant cinq ou six fois chaque nuit pour venir voir comment je me porte, et malgré mes prières, s'obstinant à me traiter encore en malade sérieux. Je suis pourtant entièrement, rétabli, et il ne me reste, qu'une extrême faiblesse, et des douleurs dans tout le corps. Tout cela passera, avec un peu de patience et de soins.

" On m'a permis, depuis quatre jours, de descendre dans mon atelier et de travailler pendant un couple

d'heures, ce qui m'a fait un plaisir extrême. J'espère
que, d'ici à votre arrivée à Paris, j'aurai des choses
nouvelles à vous montrer. Nous parlons constam-
ment des bons jours passés à Glyngarth ; c'est pour
nous, tous, parmi nos meilleurs souvenirs. . . ."*

---

* "They tell me I have been exceedingly ill; I certainly was in
a state of horrible suffocation, but that is all I can remember about
it. Cornélie attended upon me day and night, insomuch that she
is knocked up with her fatigues, and ought to be, herself, nursed
and looked after, in her turn. She is still here, and *will* get up in
the night five or six times, to see how I am going on ; moreover, in
spite of my entreaties, she will have it that I am still a sick patient.
But I am, really, coming round fast, only that I am very weak, and
suffer from pains all over my body. Still, all these symptoms will,
presently, yield to proper treatment, with a little patience.

"I have been allowed, for four days past, to go down stairs, and
to work at my brush for a couple of hours, which has afforded me
excessive pleasure. I hope that by the time you come over to
Paris, I shall be able to show you some new things. We are per-
petually talking of the charming days spent at Glyngarth ; they
rank, indeed, amongst our most agreeable recollections."

CHAPTER XVI.

1858.

In the month of January, Scheffer had so far
recovered from his illness of October in the preceding
year, that he applied himself to his painting with
renovated ardour, and, during the three following
months, appeared to be once more " in good train." In
the atelier were some three or four pictures, on which
Scheffer worked by turns, as the humour dictated.
The "Gémissemens"—now newly named "Les Douleurs de la Terre"—received its final touches, together
with the farewell gaze of its author; a moment fraught
with mingled feelings, partly of self-gratulation, and
partly of regret at quitting a subject which had absorbed so much of his time and thoughts.

The "Faust à la Coupe"—likewise received some
finishing strokes in the winter of 1858: a work
stamped with power and meaning. I have remarked
(at page 22) the ascendancy exercised over the
imagination of Ary by Goethe's wondrous creation:
and his return to the subject, in his mature age,
bears witness to the strength and permanency of that
early impression. To my thinking, the " Faust

holding the Cup" is one of Scheffer's most successful performances; both in point of art, and as forcibly embodying the conception of the poet.   The attitude and face of "Faust" denote agitation and mental ferment, without "grimace" or trick; the tone of the picture is more mellow, more in harmony with the subject, than some others by Scheffer's hand; the accessories, too, (the hands in particular,) are well and artistically painted.   Altogether, the "Faust à la Coupe" may be said to represent effectively the "situation" described in the drama of Goethe.   The "Marguerite à la Fontaine," although it figured among the contributions made to the Manchester Exhibition, was completed after its return to Paris; so that the date of "1858" stands against it, in the catalogue of the Scheffer Exhibition in 1859.*

Of the "Angel Announcing the Resurrection," I could wish to speak as I feel.   But it is a composition which, though only in an early stage of execution, excites one's interest in a peculiar manner; partly from the associations connected with it, partly by its intrinsic charm.   Thus, it is no easy matter to convey, by the medium of language, the deep, mysterious sentiment inspired by this sketch.   The first idea which arises in your mind on looking upon it, is the affinity it displays with the "Antique."   The more attentively you gaze and meditate, the clearer will be the perception—that the Greek Ideal forms, through all "schools," the basis of true nobility "in Art."   But, in the angelic

---

* I postpone the remarks which this picture suggests, to a later page, not to interrupt, too often, the course of the narrative.

personage before your eyes, it is the *form* of Greek beauty, *supremely* instinct with celestial meaning: commanding reverential awe and pious emotion in the persons addressed.

Occupied on the picture here indicated, Scheffer . was at work in his best vein, when, early in the month of May, the unlooked-for tidings of the death of her Royal Highness the Duchess of Orleans were conveyed to him. All considerations, save those linked with the past, faded into nothing before his eyes. To London he at once resolved to go, although, by both friends and physicians, he had been urgently advised to avoid all occasion for either bodily exertion, or painful movement of the feelings. One of his friends —himself a well-known and admired landscape-painter —related to me what follows:—

"I was sitting at my easel one morning, when Ary Scheffer entered the 'atelier,' carrying in his hand a carpet-bag.

"'Je m'en vais en Angleterre, mais je ne voulois point quitter Paris sans venir te dire Adieu!'

"'Comment! en Angleterre! et pourquoi?'

"'C'est que je veux rendre les dernier hommages à Madame la Duchesse d'Orleans, en assistant à ses obséques.'

"'Mais, Scheffer, tu es fou!'

"'Bah, bah, je sais tout ce que tu vais me dire, mais c'est inutile—mon parti est pris; c'est un devoir sacré, et personne au monde ne m'arrêtera.'"*

---

* "I am off to England, but I could not think of quitting Paris without first saying good-bye to you."

"What! going to *England?* and pray what for?"

"It is in order to pay the last duties to the person of her Royal Highness the Duchess of Orleans, by attending her funeral."

So saying, Scheffer, pressing the friendly hand of
Mr. Wyld, (for it was that gentleman to whom this
incident occurred,) straightway hurried to the station
of the Northern Railway : leaving Mr. Wyld in a state
of mind wherein uneasy forebodings predominated,
notwithstanding a certain sympathy with Scheffer's
chivalrous "dévouement" to the memory of the departed Princess.

A hurried and fatiguing journey to England,
followed by participation in all the mournful accom-
paniments of a funeral rite, were perhaps about the
most unfavourable circumstances which a man subject
to heart disease could well undergo. The chill of
the sepulchral building,* coupled with the painful
excitement of the feelings naturally induced by
the solemn scene and service, unavoidably tended to
depress Scheffer's already impaired vital energies.
Nevertheless, he managed to surmount these trials
without any ill effects being apparent at the time;
and, shortly afterwards, made arrangements for
returning home. But the fatal, the latent germs
of evil, were not the less present, alas!

Madame Marjolin (who had borne her father company on this sad occasion) judged it best to divide the
fatigue of the return journey into two parts; going
for one night to London, and proceeding to Paris early
on the morrow. They set forth accordingly; the
weather was fine, and Scheffer, meeting in London
his familiar and congenial friends, M. and Madame

" But, Scheffer! you must be mad!"

" Bah! bah! I know everything you are wanting to say to me,
but it is all of no use—my decision is taken; I have a sacred duty
to perform, and no man alive shall stop me."

        * The Orleans chapel near Weybridge.

Viardot, it was agreed that they should spend the
afternoon together; the whole party dining at a
French "Restaurant's" afterwards.   Ary and his
daughter returned in the evening to M. de Mussy's
house, where they were to sleep:* the former, apparently free from ailment, and tolerably cheerful.

In the course of the night, a bell was heard to ring
in Scheffer's chamber.   Madame Marjolin—always on
the alert where her father was in question—hastened
to his side, and found him seized with a difficulty of
breathing, the unerring sign of an attack of his heart
complaint.   Dr. de Mussy quickly lent his valuable
aid in ministering to the sufferer, and succeeded in
mitigating the most alarming symptoms; so that,
after the first twenty-four hours, the dangerous
character of the attack was, in a measure, subdued.
Dr. Réné Marjolin, being summoned from Paris
by telegraph, now hastened to London, and contributed, both by his affectionate presence and
medical skill, to sustain the reviving powers of his
father-in-law.

It is possible—I will go farther, and say probable—
that the able and attentive management of the
patient pursued by M. de Mussy, (in conjunction with
Dr. Marjolin,) would have enabled Scheffer to rally
from this unfortunate seizure, so far as to survive, for
a period of more or less extent—at all events for a
year or two longer—had Scheffer allowed them to
follow their own judgment.

But the resistless craving—the insatiable longing—

---

* M. de Mussy was (and is) the confidential physician of the
Ex-Queen, and of all the Royal family of Orleans.

to get out of England,* took entire possession of him: insomuch that, fearing to contravene his desires, his friends agreed that he should be conveyed to Dover, and so by railway to Paris, as soon as it was possible for the patient to bear removal, in spite of the risk involved.

It happened that when this moment arrived, the Ascot Races were going forward, and to procure a suitable carriage wherein to remove Scheffer easily to the station, was found excessively difficult. Here however, stepped in the faithful friend, Madame Hollond, who supplied the needed conveyance, and Scheffer was thereby enabled to begin his arduous journey under the least fatiguing circumstances.

The sea passage proved favourable: even seeming to produce a refreshing effect upon him. But on touching French soil, there awaited the trembling, stricken frame of poor Scheffer, the cruel "épreuve" —the "purgatory" it may be termed—of the accursed "Douane." Pent up for half an hour—which seemed three half hours, so distressing were its conditions— in the close, hot, unwholesome waiting-hole of the custom-house—among a crowd of ordinary passengers pushing, as only passengers eager to "save their train" can and *do* push their way—Scheffer was sorely tried. His daughter strove to obtain some indulgence for her fainting companion, by, first of all, naming him, and then explaining that he was an invalid, and a man entitled to consideration, &c. But no "adder" could be more "deaf to the charmer"

---

* "L'air lourd de Londres me tue!" ("I shall die of this heavy London air!") he was continually crying out.

than were the officials during this hateful passage,
and when, at length, the party found egress from
their "durance vile," Scheffer felt himself sensibly
worse.

Nevertheless, by the extreme care and precau-
tionary address of his companions, he was enabled to
reach the country-house from whence he had departed, a month before, to make the sacrifice of
prudence to lofty sentiment.*

To find himself once more in France, and in his
own home, and that "home" offering so much of
" agrément," was for Scheffer an unspeakable comfort.
The balmy air of full summertide, and the quietude
of his retreat, coupled with the presence of those
most dear to him—all combined to shed a momentary
gleam of enjoyment over the brief space of existence
which Scheffer had yet to traverse. And whilst he
did not disguise from himself the improbability of his
recovering this blow, he felt the inward satisfaction
arising from having performed, at all risks, what he
considered his bounden duty. This reflection was
beyond all else valuable in Ary's eyes, and formed
one of the consolations of his now rapidly declining
days.

During the first week which succeeded his return
to the "Pavillon Roquelaure," (such was the desig-
nation borne by the house at Argenteuil), Scheffer
seemed to suffer somewhat less from difficulty of res-

* It was pleasantly situated at Argenteuil, a village some six
miles west of Paris. Attached to the house was a shady and
spacious garden, wherein Scheffer was wont to saunter, at idle
moments, and to watch the little Ary and his companions frisking
about, in holiday hours.

piration, and to regain at least a tranquil, if not a cheerful frame of mind.   He even applied himself to the easel, for several days, at intervals—painting upon the work which I have spoken of above—the " Angel Announcing the Resurrection of Jesus."   But the enfeebled organs connected with the heart grew, daily, more and more incapable of their functions, and it was soon perceived, by his afflicted family, that Scheffer's precious life was ebbing to its close.   A few days later, all hope had ceased, and on the 15th of June, this great and virtuous man yielded up his last breath.   It was a beautiful summer's evening, the calm splendour of which irradiated the scene of his departure from earth.   Not more calm, however—not more serene, was the aspect of the heavens, than were the conscience and pure spirit of him who thus passed to his eternal rest, to suffer, to strive, no more!

CHAPTER XVII.

"Concluding Remarks" — Extracts of Letters — Character of Scheffer—Anecdotes.

ARY SCHEFFER had completed his sixty-third year in the month of February preceding, having been born on the 10th of that month in 1795. Still in possession of his best artistic faculties, he might possibly, I repeat it, have lived to produce more great works, (assuming the requisite prudence to have been observed,) but for the last fatal journey to England. Yet I am not prepared to regret, on Scheffer's own account, that his days were thus, in some sort, abridged: however deeply his loss was, and still is deplored by his surviving friends and relatives. Life had—in sober truth be it said—lost its savour for him. Little enjoyment awaited the remaining span of an existence, the main objects and pleasures of which had successively eluded his grasp. His strenuous and consistent endeavours to forward the liberties, and the sound political progress, of his adopted country, had been, in various forms, completely and painfully frustrated: whilst his most cherished friendships were repeatedly sundered by the hand of death: these two great outlets of his external sympathies were closed, never to be reopened.

In the high consideration borne him by the "élite"

of both sexes in the French capital, and in his now widely-spread fame as a painter, Scheffer found, no doubt, a certain support and solace to his "bruised spirit;" and the tender affection which subsisted among father and daughter, son-in-law, and little Ariel, infused all that remained possible of domestic happiness into his lot. But nothing, I imagine, could have rekindled the embers of Scheffer's interest in the current of human affairs. *That* once active sentiment lay buried under reiterated disappointments and inward chagrin.

Thus, he departed from amongst us not unwillingly —certainly without any *desire* to prolong his course upon earth; although, so long as it was allotted to him to remain, he bore the burthen of his bedimmed existence with fortitude and dignity, and would have done so to the end, had it pleased Providence to extend it to a later period. Madame Marjolin would seem to have been aware of the state of her father's feelings, and indeed she frankly avowed to me (in talking over the melancholy closing scene, together, at Argenteuil, in August, 1858) that " Il éprouvait une profonde satiété de la vie ! "*

My readers have been made acquainted with the principal features of Scheffer's character, whilst I have conducted them along the path of his chequered existence, from childhood down to its close. It will, I venture to think, add to the interest of the foregoing Memoir, to subjoin a few more extracts from his

---

* " He felt himself thoroughly weary of life."

private letters; serving as they do, to furnish additional evidences of the moral rectitude, charity, and generous impulses of the writer. Ary was not much given to corresponding with absent friends, so that memorials of this kind are few in number; his intimates residing for the most part in Paris, whilst from the members of his family he rarely separated himself. It is the more fortunate therefore that I am enabled to introduce the fragments which follow.

"Dieu te garde, toujours, des fautes, chère Cornélie! mais que Dieu te garde surtout, de juger plus sévèrement que lui. Sois sévère pour toi, mais indulgente pour les autres. Toutes les femmes vertueuses qui j'ai connues l'étaient. . . . .

"Sois bien persuadée que tu es la seule occupation de mon cœur et de mon esprit, et ton bonheur mon seul et unique désir et espérance . . . ."*

(1846.)

"Crois moi, le bonheur n'est que dans l'accomplishment généreux du devoir. Il faut repandre le bonheur et le contentement autour de soi. Cela a été l'unique but de ma vie, et peutêtre ma seule vertu. Je l'ai fait aux depens de moi-même, et je te jure que j'en trouve une ample récompense dans ma conscience. . . .

"Avec une âme forte, et une noble intention, on peut tout ce qu'on veut, moralement. . .

---

* "Heaven preserve you, ever, from serious defects, dear Cornélie! but above all, from that of dealing severely with those of others. Be rigorous towards yourself—indulgent to them. Every virtuous woman that I have been acquainted with, has been so. . . . .

"Be assured that you occupy my whole heart and mind, and that all my hopes are centered in seeing you happy. . . . ."

" Vraiment, si on songeait plus souvent à la mort, on vivrait mieux—et pour soi et pour les autres. . ."*

(de Bruxelles, 1849.)

" J'avoue que je suis ravi d'être hors de Paris : si tu étais avec moi je le serais même davantage—mais je sens que j'ai réellement besoin de reposer un peu mon cerveau. . . .

" Ce soir je n'écrirai pas à tes oncles, ainsi charge toi de mes tendresses pour eux. Tache de donner un peu de courage à mon pauvre frère Arnold; si ce n'etait à cause de son fils, je l'aurais forcé de venir avec moi; je suis certain que cela lui auroit fait bien.†

" Etre indulgent pour les autres et sévère pour soi —voilà le premier devoir. Aimer les autres plus que soi-même, la première, la plus grande des vertus. De toute mon existence-passée, il ne me reste de bons souvenirs que des moments ou j'ai pratiqué la leçon que je te donne."

---

* " Believe me, the accomplishing of duties, alone, leads to contentment. We ought to seek to diffuse pleasure and enjoyment around us. To effect this has been the unvarying object of my life; perhaps my only claim to merit, and though it was always pursued at the expense of my own comfort, I vow to you that I have been amply repaid by the consciousness of having done right.

" With a firm soul, and rectitude of purpose, we may achieve what we will—morally speaking.

" If, truly, we would oftener think upon our end, we should live better lives—both for ourselves, and for others' sakes. . . . ."

† " I must own to feeling glad at having got out of Paris ; if you were only with me, more so still. But that my poor brain needs a season of rest, is quite clear. I do not write this evening to your uncles, so you must convey to them all that I feel towards them. Do try and cheer up my poor brother Arnold ; but for his child, I would have forced him to bear me company hither ; I am sure it would have done him good.

(de la Hollande, 1849)

" Donne moi un conseil ; à Weimar, j'avais envie de
faire une étude de la Duchesse d'Orleans et de ses deux
enfans, pour en faire à Paris un tableau, réprésentant
la Duchesse et ses deux fils appuyés contre le
piédestal de la Justice, et y cherchant un abri contre
l'orage.   . ."*

Here is one, containing a little spice of drollery :—

(Hanover, 1840.)

" Si tu etais avec moi, nous nous serions bien
amusés à voir ce bon pays d'outre Rhin ; ces bonnes
faces des femmes endimanchées, et ces graves ' Herren
und Bauern ;" autant de pipes que d'individus !
Pour leur Dimanche, se donnant la satisfaction
d'accourir, pas centaines, voir passer les ' trains,' du
chemin-de-fer.   . . .

" Maintenant je vais—non m'étendre, mais me
plier, dans une boîte de bois peint, entre deux
édredons, et deux petites serviettes.   Cela n'est pas
engageant, mais que veux tu !   C'est comme cela, et
pas autrement, que le Teuton—' der viel Schläfer'—
passe la moitié de sa vie. . . . ."†

" To be tolerant towards others and severe for one's own conduct,
is the first of all duties : to love one's fellow-men more than oneself, the highest virtue.   None of my memories are so pleasing as
those which recal the practice of these maxims."

* " I want a piece of advice.   When at Weimar an idea occurred
to me to make a study of the Duchess of Orleans and her two
children, with a view to make a picture afterwards.   It should represent the Duchess, with her two sons, leaning against the base of
a figure of ' Justice,' seemingly claiming its protection. . . ."

† " If you were with me, we should have enjoyed the diverting
sights of this country beyond the Rhine : the amiable looks of the
good women all in their ' Sunday best,' and the grave men, both
gentlefolk and rustics ; so many *men*, so many *pipes* going !   All,

(Weimar, 1849.)

" J'ai fait aujourd'hui une grande promenade pour voir le Château du Wartburg, et les sites magnifiques qui l'environnent. . . . .

" Tant de grands souvenirs poetiques et historiques se rattachent à ce château, qu'on ne peut le visiter qu'avec une profonde émotion. . . .

" Je sens que j'ai trop peu voyagé: je ne puis rattraper le temps, ni l'occasion utile, perdus; mais je ferai mon possible pour que *tu* voyes, jeune encore, les choses qui peuvent nourrir l'esprit de grands souvenirs; et que ma présence, quand tu en auras reçu l'impression, te rende, plus tard, ces souvenirs plus précieux encore. . . .

" Enfin espérons, et si, comme toujours, mes vœux de bonheur les plus modestes ne peuvent se réaliser, consolons nous en songeant que d'autres souffrent encore plus. . . . . "*

---

by way of pleasant Sunday amusement, running, by hundreds at once, to see the ' trains ' pass. . . . .

"And now, I am about to—not to stretch my person, but—double myself up, into a box of painted deal, between two bags of feathers and two towels. This, to be sure, does not sound over comfortable, but dear me! it is in this fashion that your ' Teuton,' the ' good sleeper,' passes half his existence."

* " I have been to-day to see the château of the Wartburg—(a long *promenade*)—with its magnificent views and scenery around it. . . . .

"So many legends and histories belong to this region, that one cannot visit the castle without experiencing deep emotion. . . .

" I am aware that I ought to have travelled more. It is too late, now, to overtake lost time, and lost opportunities; but I am resolved that *you* shall, whilst yet young, see things calculated to implant valuable impressions; and which, moreover, being seen *with me*, shall associate themselves hereafter in your memory with this added value. . . . .

But I stop here, considering that the above passages will have sufficed to confirm the justice of what has been remarked in these pages, in reference to the pure and elevated moral sentiments of the writer.

It can hardly have escaped the observation of the intelligent reader, that the substance of Ary Scheffer's character was of that kind, which, carried to exaggeration, becomes entitled to the honours of positive martyrdom. He invariably practised the self-sacrifices enjoined in his letters—setting aside his own wishes and inclinations whenever they were crossed by those of other people. I have heard one of his intimate friends say, that " Scheffer could not bear to see a frown, or even a cloud, on the brow of those around him." Here lay his weak point, and no one knew it better than himself. This quality, however, I take to be an element of original temperament and organization, scarcely capable of being effectually modified by its possessor, except at a cost more painful perhaps than profitable to himself. It was, in poor Scheffer's case, remorselessly turned to profit by a number of persons, (of whom it were vain to attempt to give an account,) through whose exigence and importunity the whole of his faculties came to be, as one may say, devoted to the service of others. Toiling without complaining, as we have seen he toiled, to gain the means of supplying the swarm of claimants who besieged his gates, he was nevertheless fully aware of his own slavery. I am tempted to

---

" Well, we must live in hopes, and if, after all, as is so frequently my lot, my schemes of happiness come to nought, we will console ourselves by the reflection that others are worse off than we. . ."

quote one or two short passages more on this subject, as curiously candid effusions of feeling.

"C'est vraiment quelque chose de bizarre, que la manière dont ma vie a toujours été hâtée! Je n'ai jamais pu faire un tableau avec calme et repos. Je n'ai jamais même pu faire un pas dans la vie, sans quelque chose ou quelqu'un qui me presse! . . ."*

Again, in speaking of some one who was *too little* restrained by the obligations of moral duty, he says, "Ne regrette pas la liberté de Madame de ——. Crois moi, le Christ l'a dit, 'mieux être ésclave soumis, qu'ésclave échappé!'"†

None but a thoroughly virtuous mind and heart could have so heartily recognised the force and point of this "dictum."

It was more than once proposed to put Scheffer's name forward as a candidate for the honour of a seat in the "Institut." This coming to his knowledge, he begged that the project might be suffered to drop.

"Jamais (he writes to his daughter) je ne voudrai d'une chose quelconque pour laquelle il faut faire des démarches. . . ."‡

The reluctance habitually entertained by Scheffer, to avail himself of opportunities, leading to the grati-

---

* "It is, positively, something absurd and provoking, to think how my life has always been, as it were, worried and hunted! Never have I been suffered to paint a single picture in peace! Nor have I ever taken a step forwards, without somebody at my back, or some circumstance, which hurried and embarrassed my course!"

† "Do not look with pleasure on the liberty exercised by Madame de ——. Trust me (and Jesus Christ has said it) 'better to be a submissive slave, than an outlaw.'"

‡ "Never will I desire a thing for which one must go about asking help to obtain it. . . . ."

fication of his personal vanity, may be traced to two
causes. First, the extreme value that he set upon
his own self-respect and independence : guarding
these with a vigilance almost bordering, at times, on
rudeness. Dependent, as all artists necessarily are,
more or less, on public favour and esteem, Scheffer
felt, nevertheless, a repugnance to be " patronized,"
which he pushed to the verge of excess. Furthermore, the opinions held by Scheffer on political subjects, strongly tinctured as they were with democratic
sympathies, rendered him an object of jealousy and
dislike in quarters from whence, generally speaking,
marks of distinction emanate. Thus, the two dominant principles of his character, viz., his own self-
respect, and the unalterable convictions of his youth
in regard to republican doctrines, were unquestionably
of the nature of obstacles to social success and honour.
With the higher and wealthier classes of society, again,
Scheffer had but little sympathy, and designedly, indeed, kept aloof from them : even evincing, now and
then, by sallies of " sauvagerie," his unfeigned indifference to worldly distinctions.

One evening, at Scheffer's own house, being myself
on the point of leaving Paris, I said to him, " Mais,
venez donc nous faire une visite en Angleterre, cet
été !" " Je n'aime pas l'Angleterre—c'est à dire,
que je n'aime pas les Anglais—insolens, hautains,
dédaigneux, se croyant au-dessus de tout le monde."

" J'avoue que mes compatriotes portent assez mau-
vaise réputation sur le continent, mais je vous assure
qu'ils se trouvent, chez nous, de bien braves gens, que
vous seriez forcés d'aimer, malgré vos préjugés."

" Je n'en doute pas, au fond ; voilà M—— par

exemple, c'est un homme qui a fait de belles choses, et que j'éstime cordialement—d'ailleurs, il a le cœur républicain; (smiling as he spoke) mais *vous*   . ."

"Eh bien? qu'avez vous à dire de mal, sur mon compte?"

"C'est que vous—*vous* êtes *rien moins* que républicaine: plutôt *aristocrate* qu'autre chose!"* So saying, he darted off to talk to some one else, laughing at the "slap" he had ventured upon giving to "la fière Anglaise."

Among the frequent visitors to the atelier, during the period of the Republic, was Monseigneur Sibour, Archbishop of Paris. His professed leanings towards extreme liberalism recommended him to Scheffer, who used willingly to "chat" with the prelate in the intervals of painting,—taking, indeed, pleasure in his company. In due course of time it came to pass that the "radical" Archbishop found it convenient to give in his adhesion to the Government of Louis Napoleon, and to become, in his turn, an "habitué" of the Elysée Bourbon. As might have been foretold,

---

* "Now, do come over and pay us a visit in England, this summer?"

"I do not like England—that is, I do not like the English. They are such proud, insolent, scornful, conceited people! looking upon themselves as superior to all the rest of the world!"

"I confess that my countrymen are *not* well reputed, on the continent. Still, I assure you that there *are* excellent people in England, and many whom you would find yourself obliged to esteem, in spite of your *prejudices!*"

"Ah, I dare say, in one sense. There is M —— for instance; he has done great things, and I certainly do esteem *him* heartily. Besides, he is a republican *at heart*—whilst *you*   . . ."

"Well, and what have you got to say against *me?*"

"Why, that *you* are *anything* but republican; more *aristocrat*, by a great deal!"

Scheffer saw no more of his reverend visitor for a long time, after this "volte face;" but one day, in 1853, he received a note from the Archbishop, requesting that Scheffer would do him the favour to paint his portrait, &c."

To this note the indignant Ary replied "that he certainly would *not* paint the Archbishop;" adding to his refusal a peremptory desire "that the writer of the note would be so good as never more to set foot in the atelier!"

It was difficult for any one, not personally acquainted with Scheffer, to obtain a sight of his pictures. He disliked being interrupted, and besides this reason, he objected to have his painting-room converted into a lounging-place for idlers. So that admittance could only be obtained through the good offices of a friend of the house. On one occasion a visitor, unknown to Scheffer, called, and asked the servant to go and say "that a lady wished to be permitted to visit the atelier." Antoine brought in the message accordingly. "Ne la connois pas," was Ary's laconic reply. The visitor persisted: "Say it is an English lady;" another negative. The fair applicant, little used, God wot! to repulses, from any quarter, now played what she naturally expected would prove a "winning card," and handed her visiting card to the servant, for presentation to his master. This tentative proved equally infructuous, *for*—it bore, the name of an English Peeress of the highest grade! It is just possible, that had it been "Patty Hopkins," or "Susan Carter," Scheffer *might* have relented; but to admit a Peeress on learning her name and rank, after refusing her as a stranger, was what our stern republican could not bring himself to do. So he returned the same curt answer, "Je ne la connois pas," and the lady went her way.*

The truth is that Scheffer went a step too far, perhaps, in the dislike he felt to being "protegé:" particularly by the rich, by the would-be "patrons" of artists, or by noble *amateurs*. Nothing so rare, however, as the "juste milieu," in states of mind; (or, for that matter, in states of body either.) In his dread of being exposed to the humiliation of "patronage," Ary Scheffer fell not unnaturally into the extravagant phase of independence—becoming testy, or, like Samuel Johnson, bluntly curt and "cassant" towards those who he fancied intended to encourage and flatter him.

Whilst in England, in 1857, he was induced to take an interest in a German youth, named Ludwig Martin, whose dispositions towards the art of sculpture had manifested themselves with some promise of excellence.† With his wonted generosity, Scheffer not only consented to help "Ludwig" forward, but actually took him into his house, and provided the necessary instruction for him; the lad studying diligently under his auspices, up to the period of

---

* The anecdote is illustrative of Scheffer's habits of dealing with strangers, and I have therefore related it here. It may be as well to add that the fair applicant happened to be one of the most amiable, affable, and justly-admired of Englishwomen, so that it was unfortunate for Scheffer that he lost the opportunity of making her acquaintance.

† The boy had been fortunate enough to receive the kind encouragement of His Royal Highness Prince Albert, Prince Consort of England, accompanied with an annual contribution towards defraying the cost of his lessons in drawing, &c.

the disastrous seizure which ultimately closed the labours of Scheffer's own life. I find a word or two referring to this passage, in a letter written (to the friend so often mentioned in these pages) in 1857.

" Je suis très content de Ludwig : et heureux de l'avoir avec moi. C'est une satisfaction que je vous dois, et dont je vous remercie."*

Thus it was, with Scheffer, from childhood to mature age, a native-born, an irresistible impulse, to minister to the necessities, or promote the advantage, of every one connected with art, who came within the circle of his sympathies. It can hardly surprise the reader, after all that has been stated, to learn that Scheffer died poor. I have reason to believe that, in the form of money savings, he did not possess, in 1858, a sum equivalent to half a year's income usually arising from his painting. Whatever it was, however, all that Scheffer had *to* leave became the inheritance of his cherished daughter, along with some few of the later products of his pencil ; these being perhaps among the works best entitled to hand down with honour to posterity the name of Ary Scheffer—" the Painter."

Having now brought this " memoir " to an end, I shall add but little more to that which, I am deeply conscious, falls short of the just claims of my distinguished subject. But having performed the task to the best of my ability, I will hope that, in spite of

---

* " I am quite satisfied with Ludwig, and feel pleased at having him with me. I owe this to you, and must offer you my thanks accordingly."

shortcomings on the part of the writer, the sketch here given, of a life and character so worthy of being known and esteemed, may be regarded as an interesting record of Genius allied with Virtue.

OBSERVATIONS ON THE GENERAL CHARACTERISTICS OF ARY SCHEFFER'S STYLE.

THE "little" which I shall permit myself to append to the narrative here-terminated, will consist in a few comprehensive remarks relating to this painter's style of execution. Indeed, so much of eulogy has been expended on various individual pictures, that it is no more than my duty, as a conscientious critic, to afford utterance to some opinions wherein the deficiencies of the painter will be considered in their turn. I will begin by a quotation from a discerning and capable judge of artistic merit, of my acquaintance.

" The absence of early scientific instruction, is apparent, in the want of knowledge, on Scheffer's part, of certain principles essential to the practice of this divine art. Among these I will note

1st. A neglect of certain leading maxims having reference to the apposition of light and shade. The indiscriminate flood of light which he pours upon his principal figure in many of his best pictures is felt to be at variance, not only with nature, but with the primitive laws according to which imitative art produces its legitimate effects. It is quite painful to me for instance, to look at the unmitigated glare which pervades the " Margaret at the Fountain.". . .

Both of her arms might be on the same plane, owing to their being in equally strong light. . . . .

2ndly. In regard to Scheffer's management of colour, it appears to me that he was wanting in the true instincts of a colourist. He rarely combines different hues so as to produce a pleasing contrast; neither does he reach to anything like real power in this branch of art. What can be less happily chosen than the strong red colour of the ample petticoat, in the " Margaret at the Fountain ? " the violence of which, moreover, has an injurious influence on the flesh tones. The blue petticoat of Margaret " Coming out of Church," again, cuts against a stocking of the very same hue! instead of being agreeably relieved by a lighter shade, or by some other quality of colour. But the faults of his colouring are too obvious to need to be enlarged upon.

3rdly. In respect to the handling of draperies, very considerable progress was made by Scheffer towards the latter stage of his career, attesting earnest industry and meditation on his part.

4thly. To my thinking—Scheffer is never so great, at least in creative art, as where he employs scarcely *any colour,* properly speaking. The " Francesca," the " Calvin," and the "Giaour Monk," will most forcibly illustrate my meaning.

Perhaps the most successful effort in point of colour, is the " Ruth and Naomi "*—painted with

---

* I would call attention to the singularly expressive *pose* of the hands in this noble composition, which indeed, as a whole, I regard with cordial admiration.

H. G.

vigour and care: one of his most recent pictures; proving how steadily he cultivated the technical faculty to the last. . . .

5thly. Among the defects of this master is his ineffective treatment of the nude, more especially of the male figure. He did not indeed attempt it often, knowing that his real "forte" lay in his heads. In the " Christ au Roseau," the absence of all anatomical indications, even to the marking of the "sternum" and ribs, cannot fail to strike the observer.

6thly. A certain sameness prevails in the heads of his principal figures; the Giaour, and the Faust, for example, are very similar in type, and give one an impression that both were drawn from the same model. The heads in " Les Douleurs de la Terre "—lovely as some of these are—also lack *variety*, with the exception of the " St. Monica."

After all, perhaps, the best group of female heads which Scheffer has left to us, is to be found in the " Annunciation to the Shepherds;" in which composition may be also discerned a most skilful employment of contrast in the flesh tones, exhibiting the application of the legitimate principles of art. (See page 61.)

As a painter of heads, I doubt whether there be any living painter who has so successfully cultivated the faculty of expressing profound emotion: and this, too, observe, coupled with a motionless position of the body. Ex. gr. the " Giaour in the Convent," " Faust with the Cup," " Margaret in Church," and " Les Saintes Femmes." . . . .

" Here is the real triumph of Scheffer's genius— the ability to inspire strong sympathy in the

spectator by the power of delineating the emotions of
the soul.   A gift which he shared with Murillo,
and which commands admiration, not only for its
own sake, but also on account of its extreme
rarity.

" H. M."

In the foregoing comments I find myself disposed
to concur—indeed they correspond, in the main, with
the opinions expressed throughout the course of this
work, in reference to various performances therein
mentioned.   There is no denying the want of ability
in this master to deal skilfully with *chiaro oscuro;*
insomuch that, to a cultivated eye, familiar with the
exquisite treatment of flesh in shadow—as displayed
by Paul Veronese, Tintoretto, Albano, and other renowned Italian colourists—Scheffer's unrelieved lights
and pallid tints sensibly detract from the effect of his
pictures.

Could Scheffer have joined to his special faculty of
imparting interest, that of faultless and masterly
handling, we should have possessed one more of those
wondrous Painters who come amongst mortals as
though expressly to furnish examples of perfection,
but whose number is, even now, restricted to some
three or four commanding names.   In the absence of
this rare combination we may be grateful for the enjoyment derivable from works which display a reverential culture of the Ideal, and wherein the modern
world of connoisseurs recognises a peculiar charm and
value, not to be found in those of other painters of
the time.

In another walk of art, I would observe, there are

few amongst us who have not felt the influence of native gifts when exercised by an intelligent *amateur*. The human voice—the violoncello—the violin—let but a child of genius direct their powers, and the listener confesses that an indefinable pleasure steals over his senses: such as the most finished professional *execution*—unaccompanied by the "souffle," or inspiration of genuine sentiment—fails to produce. If, indeed, Magic can be conceived to exist anywhere in the world, surely, it must be in the spiritual domain of art!

My readers need not be invited to apply these reflections to the case of Scheffer.

A couple more extracts, and I have done.

" The two visits which I paid to the atelier of the deceased painter made the deepest, as well as the most elevating impressions which I brought away with me on leaving Paris. . . . . His grandest composition (Les Douleurs de la Terre) shows how sacred history and religious allegory may be associated with humanity, without becoming commonplace."—*Letter from his Excellency M. le Baron de Bunsen*, Feb., 1860.

The passage which follows is contained in a letter to the author, from an English gentleman, whose favourable opinion is of no common value.

" January, 1860.

" I knew Scheffer, and am a great admirer of his genius and his works. I spent two days, last spring, in the Exhibition of his pictures at Paris. In general character—leaving out of the question their respective 'spécialités '—he always reminded me of François

Arago. They were both enthusiasts, fanatics if you will, but always on subjects and principles which entitle them to the admiration and gratitude of the generation for whom they laboured, and to very conspicuous niches in the Temple of Fame.

"E. E."

APPENDIX.

A.

I append to the interesting sketch by Scheffer, a few memoranda supplied from a different source :—

"La Princess Marie d'Orleans avait inspiré à Scheffer des sentiments d'admiration devoués autant que réspectueux. Il trouvait en elle, presque sans modification, ses propres sentiments politiques, avec la même enthousiasme pour les travaux qui atteignent les plus hautes régions de l'art.

"Toute jeune encore, elle ne connaissait d'autres distinctions que celles de l'art, d'autres plaisirs que ceux de l'étude. L'élévation soudaine et violente de sa maison l'effrayait ; elle voyait tous les périls de cette grandeur ; elle en préssentait la chûte avec des angoisses qui, mélées au pressentiment de sa propre mort (dont l'avertissait une santé délabrée) donnaient, à ses traits et à ses manières, la teinte d' une mélancolie resignée. * * * Elle aimait à se renfermer dans son modeste atelier durant ces fêtes, splendidement vulgaires, par lesquelles Louis Philippe croyait acheter une prolongation de popularité.

"Elle dit un jour à Scheffer, qui travaillait avec elle tandis que cinq mille personnes remplissaient les salles du bal et du festin, 'Quand je pensé à ce qui s'agite içi-dessous, d'ambition, de cupidité, de flatterie, combien on y trompe mon père—je me sens heureuse de n'y être pas.'" * * *

---

* "The Princess Mary of Orleans had inspired Scheffer with sentiments of blended admiration and respect :—He found in her a similarity of opinion in regard to political matters, together with an equal enthusiasm for the higher products of art.

B.

It was chiefly owing to the exertions of Scheffer, that King Louis Philippe's consent was obtained to the removal to Versailles, and to the public exhibition, of the " Maid of Orleans." After the early and lamented death of the Princess, Scheffer set apart a recess in his " studio," in honour of her memory. But few visitors were admitted into this sanctuary, where, by the side of the marble effigy of his dying mother (a favourite " souvenir" with her son), Scheffer had placed a bust of the Princess Marie, together with copies from some of her sculptures, and a few of her own original designs.— A. DE C.

" Whilst still young, she took pleasure in no occupations excepting such as related to either the arts, or to instructive books. The sudden and abrupt exaltation of her family alarmed her; she felt all the risks involved in this greatness: she even had a presentiment of its termination, and this, being coupled with certain warnings, derived from very imperfect health, of her own premature decline, produced, both upon the mind and the countenance of the Princess, a settled character of melancholy resignation. She loved to retire within her modest 'studio' (which she had caused to be fitted up in the Palace for herself) when there were given those splendid ' Fêtes,' by which Louis Philippe hoped to sustain his waning popularity.

" On one evening, during which she was working in her atelier in company with Scheffer, there were 5000 people thronging the ' salons' below, wherein dancing and feasting were going on. ' When I reflect,' said the Princess to Scheffer, ' upon what is passing down there; what ambition, what avidity for gain, what flatteries, and upon the way in which my father is cheated and deceived by them—I feel happy to be out of it all!' "

C 1.

Extract of a letter addressed to his daughter, Madame Marjolin, by Ary Scheffer. 1846.

' . . . . Ce mot, ' *il le faut,*' mets le toi bien en tête, ma chère enfant, ta grandmère se le repetait sans cesse.

"C'est que, dans la vie, rien ne porte fruit, que ce qui coute une peine de cœur ou le labeur des mains. Notre vie, pour être bonne et calme, doit être une sacrifice de tous les instants. Maintenant que je suis vieux, je ne me rappelle avec satisfaction, que des biens que j'ai su refuser, des jouissances que j'ai sacrifiées. ' Das Entsagen '* est le devoir et la règle de sagesse ; le sacrifice, le sublime vertu dont Christ nous a donné l'exemple. Dans les grandes occasions, le sacrifice se fait pour ainsi dire plus facilement que dans les choses journalières de la vie. D'abord elles sont rares, et l'âme s'éxalte ; dans les choses de chaque jour, on n'est point en scène : c'est alors entre sa conscience et un monde qui l'ignore que se passe le sacrifice. Mais aussi, comme ceux qui ont cette douce abnegation d'eux-mêmes sont récompensés par le bonheur qu'ils répandent autour d'eux et par la conviction constante de faire le bien. Ce sentiment devient si fort quelquefois, qu'il change presque de nature, et qu'on finit par trouver le bonheur et le joie dans le sacrifice de l'un et de l'autre. . . . . ."†

---

* "The Forbidden."

† "That word—' *must,*' fix it well in your memory, dear child ; your grandmother seldom had it out of hers.

"The truth is that, through our lives, nothing brings any good fruit except what is earned by either the work of the hands, or by the exertion of one's self-denial ; sacrifices must be, in short, ever going on, if we would obtain any comfort or happiness. Now that I am no longer young, I declare that few passages afford me so much satisfaction to look back upon, as those in which I made sacrifices, or denied myself enjoyments. ' The forbidden' is the ' motto' of the

C 2.

On another occasion, having observed in his daughter's letter a tendency towards depression of spirits, he concludes one of his own—itself replete with affectionate yearnings after her society—as follows :—

" Adieu ! ma chère fille, tache toi d'être vaillante et bonne, ce sont les grandes qualités des femmes.   Des peines, tout le monde en a ; contre sa destinée on ne peut qu'une chose ; porter dignement bonheur et malheur.   Il ne faut se laisser amollir ni pour soi ni pour ceux qu'on aime.   Lutter et toujours lutter—c'est la vie, et de ce côté la mienne a été de tout temps complette : mais j'ose dire avec un juste orgueil, que rien n'a jamais abattu mon courage.   Avec un peu plus d'égoisme, j'aurais facilement trouvé plus de repos moral, plus d'aisance matérielle.   J'aurais dû peut-être lutter davantage contre cette faiblesse qui me fait trop craindre les peines des autres. C'est pourtant la seule pardonnable."*

---

wise man.   Self-denial is the quality of which Jesus Christ set us the example.

"It seems to me that sacrifices are, generally speaking, more readily made on great occasions than on ordinary ones.   The first occur rarely, and besides, the mind becomes strung up to them : on slight matters, attention is not awakened to them, and it requires an effort of conscience to perform a sacrifice from which no credit will accrue.   But then, how rich is the reward reaped by those in whom self-postponement is habitual, both in seeing the happiness it diffuses around them, and in their own unfading consciousness of well-doing.   This feeling indeed sometimes gathers such force as to alter our very nature, until we come at last to find pleasure and satisfaction in devoting ourselves to the interests of other people."

* "Farewell ! dear daughter, strive to be of good courage—to be gentle-hearted—these are the true qualities for woman. ' *Troubles*,' everybody must expect.   There is but one way of looking at fate, whatever that be ; whether blessings or afflictions, behave with dignity under both.   We must not lose heart, or it will be worse both for ourselves and for those whom we love.   To struggle, and again and again to renew the conflict—*this* is life's inheritance, and,

D.

In the summer of 1852 I saw, in the atelier of Ary Scheffer, the original painting of " Francesca di Rimini," which had been sent to him from Florence, by Prince Demidoff, in hopes of getting it judiciously repaired and cleaned. It was indeed in a sadly damaged state ; was cracked over the greater portion of its surface, and much of the " impasto " was even " scaling off "—the colours, too, had become disfigured by dirt and spots. I used to see it constantly there, during a space of several months. One day when I happened to be at the Rue Chaptal, I espied a " replica " of this picture, on a slightly reduced scale. It had been executed for the most part (but under Scheffer's eye), by a gentleman possessed of ability as an artist, who was accustomed to work for and with him : Scheffer putting the later and finishing touches himself. This copy, being, in the course of a year or two, sold to a London dealer, it passed from his possession into that of the late Earl of Ellesmere, at, I think, the price of 1100 guineas. No one among the distinguished noble collectors of pictures in London, appear to have been aware that such a picture existed : although abroad, it enjoyed a widely extended fame. Lord Ellesmere hearing, not without some dissatisfaction, that I had pronounced his costly purchase to be a " copy," addressed himself to Scheffer to know whether it was so. Scheffer replied that it certainly *was* a " replica," and had been bought of him as such : that the original was well known on the Continent, and that consequently all amateurs were apprized

---

for that matter, mine has had its full share; but I may add, with somewhat of honest pride, that never have I suffered my mental energy to falter. With a little more selfishness, perhaps, I might easily have passed my life in superior comfort, and have enjoyed greater composure of mind. I ought to have been capable of controlling that weakness in my character, which makes me shrink from the sight of other people's vexation or displeasure. This is, however, the least censurable of weaknesses."

of the fact of its being larger in size than the picture sold in 1856 to Lord Ellesmere.

In the spring of the year 1854, and again in 1855, I was, also, a visitor at the residence of Scheffer, and there beheld the second " replica," which may be regarded, in truth, as surpassing in point of execution the first " Francesca." It would seem that, during the period when the original composition remained with him (as narrated above), Scheffer made a careful study from it (of the same dimensions), which study he subsequently completed, with all the added experience of from eighteen to twenty years' practice in the art. He bestowed even more than usual pains upon this piece. Fine living models were invariably present, from which to paint all portions of the nude—the "contours," as French artists call them—whilst the delicate minute details of drapery, texture, &c., were also executed by the master himself. The product of this assiduous and lengthened application was, as most amateurs are aware, the splendid picture which formed one of the glories of the Exhibition of 1859. Fortunately for us, it remains with M. and Madame Marjolin in Paris, so that *this* work has not disappeared from the scene of his labours, as too many have done. It appeared to me to be a favourite object of contemplation with Scheffer himself. He once said to a friend (who mentioned it afterwards to me), " If I *have* unconsciously borrowed from ANY ONE, in the design of the " Francesca," it must have been from something I had seen among Flaxman's drawings." These were of the number of the works of modern artists which Scheffer highly prized, and it may perhaps be affirmed that there existed a certain affinity between the imaginative gifts which distinguished each of these two eminent men.

Before quitting the subject of the " Francesca," I will add that, since Scheffer's decease, talking with a friend of his concerning the picture bought by Lord Ellesmere, the gentleman observed to me, " that in case Lord Ellesmere's family wished to part with the picture, there would be no difficulty in finding a purchaser, at, possibly, an advance upon the price given by his lordship." When one hears of the large sums paid even for copies of this painter's works, it is somewhat surprising that people are to be found who refuse to recognise his claim to the title of a great artist.

E.

Scheffer's loyalty towards the Queen Marie Amelie (which, I have already said, constituted one of his most durable sentiments) induced him to make, during the year 1853, a second, but hasty, journey to England. It was undertaken in deference to her Majesty's earnest wish that he would come and take leave of her, prior to her intended departure for Spain.

Madame Scheffer accompanied her husband on this occasion. The midsummer season was warm; they travelled "through" from Paris to London, without a halt, so that on her arrival she was fairly exhausted with fatigue. I was surprised by receiving a brief note, about seven o'clock one evening, inviting me to come over and see them, in Albemarle-street. As I was just then stepping into the carriage, to go and dine at Kensington, I was forced to postpone my visit till about half-past ten p.m. I found them at that hour, alone; Scheffer, visibly out of spirits—much "dérangé" by the obligation of coming over—said he could hardly bring himself to quit his brother Arnold—that he should return with as little delay as might be, &c. &c. Madame Scheffer, having spoken a few words with me, retired to repose, but I stayed on for half-an-hour, talking with her husband; chiefly about the impending rupture with Russia, on account of Turkey. He now grew more animated: expressed himself (as was natural) averse to the idea of a common action on the part of France and England, but augured no other result than a war. Speaking of the Emperor Nicholas, I remember (or rather it is recorded in my note-book in connexion with this passage) Scheffer's saying with emphasis, "Il—ne—dé—mor—dra—pas!"

They both left town early on the morrow ; Scheffer paid his visit to the Queen Marie Amelie, took farewell of her and the family, and sped his way back to Paris; resuming the fraternal office of ministering to the dying guest, for dying his brother Arnold may be said to have been, even at that stage of his disorder.

F.

Tableaux d'Ary Scheffer, non exposés en 1859.

1810 Annibal jurant de venger la mort de son frère.
1811 Malvina.
—   La Mort de Pline l'ancien.
1812 Les Anges chez Abraham.
—   Pyrrhus cherchant à intimider Fabricius.
—   Abel et Tirza.
1813 Pétrarque et Laure.
1814 Orphée et Euridice.
1815 Entre Chien et Loup.
—   L'Orage.
1816 Le Grandpère.
—   La Grandmère.
1817 Le Vieux Sergent.
—   La Visite chez le Grandpère.
—   Le Vengeur.
1815 St. Louis recevant le Viatique.
—   Le Vieux Berger.
1816 La Déclaration.
1817 La Mort de St. Louis.
1819 Dévouement des Bourgeois de Calais.
—   Socrate défendant Alcibiade à Potidié.
1818 Les Enfants Glaneurs.
—   Le Champ grelé.
1820 Sujet pastoral pendant et après l'orage.
—   Le Premier Chagrin.
1821 Scène de Naufrage.
1822 St. Louis attaqué de la peste visitant les malades.
1824 Jeune Fille à genoux au pied d'un tombeau.

1824 Gaston de Foy trouvé mort à Ravenne.
— St. Thomas d'Aquin pendant une Tempête.
— La fin d'une incendie de ferme.
— L'Enterrement du Jeune Pécheur de *l'Antiquaire*.
— La Pauvre Femme en Couche.
— Les Enfants Egarés.
— L'Enfant Malade.
— Le Retour du Jeune Invalide.
— La Bonne Vieille.
— L'Enfant qui pleure pour être porté.
— La Mère Convalescente.
— Le Jeune Malade.
— Morton, scène des Puritains d'Ecosse.
— Le Départ du Conscrit.
1823 Les Orphelins
— La Ferme Abandonnée.
— Jeune Fille au bord de la Mer.
— Scène d'Invasion.
1825 Le Chant du Départ.
1827 Macbeth (de Shakspear.)
— Scène d'Inondation.
— Jeunes Filles Grècques implorant la Vierge.
— Le Sommeil du Grandpère.
— La Mort de Jeanne d'Arc.
— Hénri IV. à cheval.
1826 Ulysse réconnu par sa Nourrice.
— Ode de Pétrarque.
1825 Jeune Grec defendant son Père.
— Gulnare.
— La Vierge et l'enfant Jesus.
1828 Episode de la Retraite de Russie.
— La Dame de Charité.
— Jeannie Deans dans la prison d'Edinbourg.
1829 Marguerite implorant la Vierge.
— Charlemagne dictant les Capitulaires.
1831 Portrait du Duc d'Orleans.
— Scène des Journées de Juillet, 1830.

M

1831 La ronde, "Scène de l'orage," de Beranger.
— Le Roi Louis Phillippe à cheval.
— Anne d'Autriche et le Coadjuteur.
1833 Portrait en pied de la Reine des Belges.
— ——————— ، du Maréchal Lobau.
1832 Enfant Endormi.
1834 Les Anges endormant l'enfant Jesus.
1836 Portrait du Roi Louis Philippe.
— ——————— du Prince de Joinville.
1830 La Mort de Géricault.
1836 Charlemagne recevant la soumission de Witikind.
— Les Anges pleurant sur la Mort de Jesus Christ.
1837 Le Christ Consolateur.
— Bataille de Tolbiac.
— La Plainte de la Jeune Fille, ballade de Schiller.
— Rachel en Prière (Ahasverus de Quinet.)
1840 Ste. Cecile.
1841 Adoration des Mages.
1842 Mater Dolorosa.
— Heureux ceux qui ont le cœur pur.
— Un Ange endormant un Enfant.
1843 Achille et Priam.
1844 Tête de Christ.
1845 Madeleine au pied de la Croix.
1846 Le Simples de Cœur.
1833 Marguerite contemplant les Bijoux.
— Portrait de la Duchesse de Broglie
1846 Le Christ Rémunerateur.
— Dante et Beatrice.
— Faust et Marguerite au Jardin.
— Faust au Sabbat.
— Le Christ portant la Croix.
1847 Les Quatre Ages.
— Retour de Philippe Auguste après Bouvines.
— Entrée de Jeanne d'Arc à Orléans.
1848 Le Christ pleurant sur Jerusalem.
— La Madeleine au Tombeau.

1849 La Prière.
— Les Plaintes de la Jeune Fille.
1851 Eberhard le Larmoyeur.
— Eberhard le Coupeur de Nappe.
— St. Jean.
1852 Ange enlevant un Enfant au Ciel.
— L'Age de fer.
— La Vierge à la Moisson.
1853 St. Jean.
1855 Le Christ avec l'Enfant.
1857 L'Enfant Prodigue.
1858 La Lutte de Jacob et de l'Ange.
1857 Portrait de Léon Faucher.
— Portrait en pied de Lord Dufferin, en costume de Pair
      d'Angleterre.
1857 Portrait de la Reine Marie Amélie.
                Album lithographique.
1832 Vignettes pour l'Histoire de la Révolution Française,
      par Thiers.

G.

Ary Scheffer was " Chevalier et Officier de la Légion d'Honneur." After the memorable conflict of June, 1848, in which, as " Chef de Bataillon," he had shown a capacity for military conduct not less remarked than his cool courage— General Changarnier, then commanding the National Guard of Paris, tendered to Scheffer's acceptance the cross of " Commandeur." He replied, " Had this honourable distinction been offered to me in my quality of ' Artist,' and as a recognition of the merit of my works, I should receive it with deference and satisfaction. But, to carry about me a decoration, reminding me only of the horrors of civil war, is what I cannot consent to do :" and he firmly declined the offer.

He also was " Officier de l'Ordre de Léopold (Belgique), de l'Ordre du Chêne (Hollande), et de l'Ordre du Faucon Blanc" (de Weimar). Of no one of these foreign orders did he ever display the insignia, however.

H.

The portrait given in this work, of Ary Scheffer, is photographed from that painted by Henri Scheffer, of his brother, about the year 1850. Ary considered it a very good likeness of himself, and, in a letter to the possessor of the picture, speaks with just commendation of it as a painting. I can vouch for its being a good resemblance also.

I.

An engraving from Scheffer's large picture of " Le Christ Consolateur" has been, I am informed, published in the United States ; but the " Slave" does not appear in the print ! The feelings entertained in America towards the negro race are strikingly exemplified by this fact. I suppose it would have been regarded as offensive to introduce a slave to the presence of the Redeemer !

K.

I ought to have made mention, when speaking of Scheffer's attack of illness in London, in 1858, of the kind and respectful feeling which was shown by the Orleans Princes, in coming to see the old and constant friend of their house whilst he lay ill. The Comte de Paris and the Duc de Chartres appeared to take a deep concern in Scheffer's condition, and their interview, I was told, proved most interesting to all three. The words of counsel which Scheffer then addressed to the youthful Princes would doubtless sink into their hearts, as being the last they would probably hear from their wise and experienced preceptor and friend.

L.

The mother of Ary Scheffer was sufficiently skilled to practise miniature portrait painting during the first years of her residence in Paris, in order to augment the slender fund on which she supported herself and her young family. Thus the boys would seem to have breathed an art atmosphere from earliest childhood—both the parents possessing a certain amount of talent for painting.

M.

The friends who remained to Ary Scheffer to the end were few. Perhaps M. Krasinski, and Mr. Wyld, and M. and Madame Viardot, may be named as those to whose society he latterly attached most value. The first-named was a noble Pole (an exile), possessed of a highly endowed mind, and who had produced some poems (in his own native tongue) said to be extremely admired by his countrymen. Some of Scheffer's earliest friendships, I have said, were terminated by death, years before. Among his intimates, the most prized (not to recur to the names of Thierry and Manin) had been, perhaps, M. Geo. Lafayette, General Cavaignac, Lamartine, Alexis de Tocqueville, M. Oscar de Lafayette, M. de Broglie, and one or two more. With M. de la Mennais he was once closely familiar, but his feelings underwent a change towards the last years of his life.

POSTSCRIPT.

I stated what was not correct, in speaking (at p. 105) of the picture of " Christ Tempted by Satan," or the " Tentation," of Scheffer. It is now the property of the French Government. Messrs. Goupil et Comp^{le}. are the parties in whose hands this work is placed by the French authorities, with the view of getting it engraved by subscription.

THE END.

LONDON:
SAVILL AND EDWARDS, PRINTERS, CHANDOS STREET,
COVENT GARDEN.

ALBEMARLE STREET, LONDON.
January, 1860.

MR. MURRAY'S

GENERAL LIST OF WORKS.

ABBOTT'S (Rev. J.) Philip Musgrave; or, Memoirs of a Church of England Missionary in the North American Colonies. Post 8vo. 2s. 6d.

ABERCROMBIE'S (John, M.D.) Enquiries concerning the Intellectual Powers and the Investigation of Truth. *Fifteenth Edition.* Fcap. 8vo. 6s. 6d.

———————— Philosophy of the Moral Feelings. *Twelfth Edition.* Fcap. 8vo. 4s.

———————— Pathological and Practical Researches on the Diseases of the Stomach, &c. *Third Edition.* Fcap. 8vo. 6s.

ACLAND'S (Rev. Charles) Popular Account of the Manners and Customs of India. Post 8vo. 2s. 6d.

ADDISON'S WORKS. A New Edition, with a New Life and Notes. By Rev. Whitwell Elwin. 4 Vols. 8vo. *In preparation.*

ADOLPHUS'S (J. L.) Letters from Spain, in 1856 and 1857. Post 8vo. 10s. 6d.

ÆSCHYLUS. (The Agamemnon and Choephoroe.) Edited, with Notes. By Rev. W. Peile, D.D. *Second Edition.* 2 Vols. 8vo. 9s. each.

ÆSOP'S FABLES. A New Translation. With Historical Preface. By Rev. Thomas James, M.A. With 100 Woodcuts, by John Tenniel and J. Wolf. *26th Thousand.* Post 8vo. 2s. 6d.

AGRICULTURAL (The) Journal. Of the Royal Agricultural Society of England. 8vo. 10s. *Published half-yearly.*

AMBER-WITCH (The). The most interesting Trial for Witchcraft ever known. Translated from the German by Lady Duff Gordon. Post 8vo. 2s. 6d.

ARABIAN NIGHTS ENTERTAINMENT. Translated from the Arabic, with Explanatory Notes. By E. W. Lane. *A New Edition.* Edited by E. Stanley Poole. With 600 Woodcuts. 3 Vols. 8vo. 42s.

ARTHUR'S (Little) History of England. By Lady Callcott. *Nineteenth Edition.* With 20 Woodcuts. Fcap. 8vo. 2s. 6d.

AUNT IDA'S Walks and Talks; a Story Book for Children. By a Lady. Woodcuts. 16mo. 5s.

AUSTIN'S (Sarah) Fragments from German Prose Writers. With Biographical Notes. Post 8vo. 10s.

———————— Translation of Ranke's History of the Popes of Rome. *Third Edition.* 2 Vols. 8vo. 24s.

B

ADMIRALTY PUBLICATIONS; Issued by direction of the Lords
Commissioners of the Admiralty:—

. A MANUAL OF SCIENTIFIC ENQUIRY, for the Use of Travellers in General. By Various Hands. Edited by Sir John F. Herschel, Bart. *Third Edition*, revised by Rev. Robert Main. Woodcuts. Post 8vo. 9s.

2. AIRY'S ASTRONOMICAL OBSERVATIONS made at Greenwich. 1836 to 1847. Royal 4to. 50s. each.

———— ASTRONOMICAL RESULTS. 1848 to 1857. 4to. 8s. each.

3. ———— APPENDICES TO THE ASTRONOMICAL OBSERVA-TIONS.

    1836.—I. Bessel's Refraction Tables.
          II. Tables for converting Errors of R.A. and N.P.D. into Errors of Longitude and Ecliptic P.D. } 8s.
    1837.—I. Logarithms of Sines and Cosines to every Ten Seconds of Time.
          II. Table for converting Sidereal into Mean Solar Time. } 8s.
    1842.—Catalogue of 1439 Stars. 8s.
    1845.—Longitude of Valentia. 8s.
    1847.—Twelve Years' Catalogue of Stars. 14s.
    1851.—Maskelyne's Ledger of Stars. 6s.
    1852.—I. Description of the Transit Circle. 5s.
          II. Regulations of the Royal Observatory. 2s.
    1853.—Bessel's Refraction Tables. 3s.
    1854.—I. Description of the Zenith Tube. 3s.
          II. Six Years' Catalogue of Stars. 10s.
    1856.—Description of the Galvanic Apparatus at Greenwich Observatory. 8s.

4. ———— MAGNETICAL AND METEOROLOGICAL OBSERVA-TIONS. 1840 to 1847. Royal 4to. 50s. each.

———— MAGNETICAL AND METEOROLOGICAL RESULTS. 1848 to 1857. 4to. 8s. each.

5. ———— ASTRONOMICAL, MAGNETICAL, AND METEOROLO-GICAL OBSERVATIONS, 1848 to 1857. Royal 4to. 50s. each.

6. ———— REDUCTION OF THE OBSERVATIONS OF PLANETS, 1750 to 1830. Royal 4to. 50s.

7. ———————————— LUNAR OBSERVATIONS. 1750 to 1830. 2 Vols. Royal 4to. 50s. each.

8. BERNOULLI'S SEXCENTENARY TABLE. *London*, 1779. 4to.

9. BESSEL'S AUXILIARY TABLES FOR HIS METHOD OF CLEAR-ING LUNAR DISTANCES. 8vo.

10. ————FUNDAMENTA ASTRONOMIÆ: *Regiomontii*, 1818. Folio. 60s.

11. BIRD'S METHOD OF CONSTRUCTING MURAL QUADRANTS. *London*, 1768. 4to. 2s. 6d.

12. ———— METHOD OF DIVIDING ASTRONOMICAL INSTRU-MENTS. *London*, 1767. 4to. 2s. 6d.

13. COOK, KING, and BAYLY'S ASTRONOMICAL OBSERVATIONS. *London*, 1782. 4to. 21s.

14. EIFFE'S ACCOUNT OF IMPROVEMENTS IN CHRONOMETERS. 4to. 2s.

15. ENCKE'S BERLINER JAHRBUCH, for 1830. *Berlin*, 1828. 8vo. 9s.

16. GROOMBRIDGE'S CATALOGUE OF CIRCUMPOLAR STARS. 4to. 10s.

17. HANSEN'S TABLES DE LA LUNE. 4to. 20s.

17. HARRISON'S PRINCIPLES OF HIS TIME-KEEPER. Plates. 1767. 4to. 5s.

18. HUTTON'S TABLES OF THE PRODUCTS AND POWERS OF NUMBERS. 1781. Folio. 7s. 6d.

19. LAX'S TABLES FOR FINDING THE LATITUDE AND LONGI-TUDE. 1821. 8vo. 10s.

ADMIRALTY PUBLICATIONS—*continued.*

20. LUNAR OBSERVATIONS at GREENWICH. 1783 to 1819. Compared with the Tables, 1821. 4to. 7*s.* 6*d.*

22. MASKELYNE'S ACCOUNT OF THE GOING OF HARRISON'S WATCH. 1767. 4to. 2*s.* 6*d.*

21. MAYER'S DISTANCES of the MOON'S CENTRE from the PLANETS. 1822, 3*s.*; 1823, 4*s.* 6*d.* 1824 to 1835, 8vo. 4*s.* each.

23. —————— THEORIA LUNÆ JUXTA SYSTEMA NEWTONIANUM 4to. 2*s.* 6*d.*

24. —————— TABULÆ MOTUUM SOLIS ET LUNÆ. 1770. 4to. 5*s.*

25. —————— ASTRONOMICAL OBSERVATIONS MADE AT GOTTINGEN, from 1756 to 1761. 1826. Folio. 7*s.* 6*d.*

26. NAUTICAL ALMANACS, from 1767 to 1861. 8vo. 2*s.* 6*d.* each.

27. —————— SELECTIONS FROM THE ADDITIONS up to 1812. 8vo. 5*s.* 1834-54. 8vo. 5*s.*

28. —————— SUPPLEMENTS, 1828 to 1833, 1837 and 1838. 8vo. 2*s.* each.

29. —————— TABLE requisite to be used with the N.A. 1781. 8vo. 5*s.*

30. POND'S ASTRONOMICAL OBSERVATIONS. 1811 to 1835. 4to. 21*s.* each.

31. RAMSDEN'S ENGINE for DIVIDING MATHEMATICAL INSTRUMENTS. 4to. 5*s.*

32. —————— ENGINE for DIVIDING STRAIGHT LINES. 4to. 5*s.*

33. SABINE'S PENDULUM EXPERIMENTS to DETERMINE THE FIGURE OF THE EARTH. 1825. 4to. 40*s.*

34. SHEPHERD'S TABLES for CORRECTING LUNAR DISTANCES. 1772. Royal 4to. 21*s.*

35. —————— TABLES, GENERAL, of the MOON'S DISTANCE from the SUN, and 10 STARS. 1787. Folio. 5*s.* 6*d.*

36. TAYLOR'S SEXAGESIMAL TABLE. 1780. 4to. 15*s.*

37. —————— TABLES OF LOGARITHMS. 4to. 3*l.*

38. TIARK'S ASTRONOMICAL OBSERVATIONS for the LONGITUDE of MADEIRA. 1822. 4to. 5*s.*

39. —————— CHRONOMETRICAL OBSERVATIONS for DIFFERENCES of LONGITUDE between DOVER, PORTSMOUTH, and FALMOUTH. 1823. 4to. 5*s.*

40. VENUS and JUPITER: OBSERVATIONS of, compared with the TABLES. *London*, 1822. 4to. 2*s.*

41. WALES' AND BAYLY'S ASTRONOMICAL OBSERVATIONS. 1777. 4to. 21*s.*

42. WALES' REDUCTION OF ASTRONOMICAL OBSERVATIONS MADE IN THE SOUTHERN HEMISPHERE. 1764—1771. 1788. 4to. 10*s.* 6*d.*

BABBAGE'S (CHARLES) Economy of Machinery and Manufactures. *Fourth Edition.* Fcap. 8vo. 6*s.*

—————— Ninth Bridgewater Treatise. 8vo. 9*s.* 6*d.*

—————— Reflections on the Decline of Science in England, and on some of its Causes. 4to. 7*s.* 6*d.*

——— Views of the Industry, the Science, and the Government of England, 1851. *Second Edition.* 8vo. 7*s.* 6*d.*

BAIKIE'S (W. B.) Narrative of an Exploring Voyage up the Rivers Quorra and Tshadda in 1854. Map. 8vo. 16s.

BANKES' (GEORGE) STORY OF CORFE CASTLE, with documents relating to the Time of the Civil Wars, &c. Woodcuts. Post 8vo. 10s. 6d.

BASSOMPIERRE'S Memoirs of his Embassy to the Court of England in 1626. Translated with Notes. 8vo. 9s. 6d.

BARROW'S (SIR JOHN) Autobiographical Memoir, including Reflections, Observations, and Reminiscences at Home and Abroad. From Early Life to Advanced Age. Portrait. 8vo. 16s.

———— Voyages of Discovery and Research within the Arctic Regions, from 1818 to the present time. Abridged and arranged from the Official Narratives. 8vo. 15s.

———— (SIR GEORGE) Ceylon; Past and Present. Map. Post 8vo. 6s. 6d.

———— (JOHN) Naval Worthies of Queen Elizabeth's Reign, their Gallant Deeds, Daring Adventures, and Services in the infant state of the British Navy. 8vo. 14s.

———— Life and Voyages of Sir Francis Drake. With numerous Original Letters. Post 8vo. 2s. 6d.

BEES AND FLOWERS. Two Essays. By Rev. Thomas James. Reprinted from the "Quarterly Review." Fcap. 8vo. 1s. each.

BELL'S (SIR CHARLES) Mechanism and Vital Endowments of the Hand as evincing Design. Sixth Edition. Woodcuts. Post 8vo. 7s. 6d.

BENEDICT'S (JULES) Sketch of the Life and Works of Felix Mendelssohn Bartholdy. Second Edition. 8vo. 2s. 6d.

BERTHA'S Journal during a Visit to her Uncle in England. Containing a Variety of Interesting and Instructive Information. Seventh Edition. Woodcuts. 12mo. 7s. 6d.

BIRCH'S (SAMUEL) History of Ancient Pottery and Porcelain: Egyptian, Assyrian, Greek, Roman, and Etruscan. With 200 Illustrations. 2 Vols. Medium 8vo. 42s.

BLUNT'S (REV. J. J.) Principles for the proper understanding of the Mosaic Writings, stated and applied, together with an Incidental Argument for the truth of the Resurrection of our Lord. Being the Hulsean Lectures for 1832. Post 8vo. 6s. 6d.

———— Undesigned Coincidences in the Writings of the Old and New Testament, an Argument of their Veracity: with an Appendix containing Undesigned Coincidences between the Gospels, Acts, and Josephus. Sixth Edition. Post 8vo. 7s. 6d.

———— History of the Church in the First Three Centuries. Second Edition. 8vo. 9s. 6d.

———— Parish Priest; His Duties, Acquirements and Obligations. Third Edition. Post 8vo. 7s. 6d.

———— Lectures on the Right Use of the Early Fathers. Second Edition. 8vo. 15s.

———— Plain Sermons Preached to a Country Congregation. Second Edition. 2 Vols. Post 8vo. 7s. 6d. each.

BLACKSTONE'S COMMENTARIES on the Laws of England. A New Edition, adapted to the present state of the law. By R. MALCOLM KERR, LL.D. 4 Vols. 8vo. 42s.

——————————— - FOR STUDENTS. Being those Portions of the above work which relate to the BRITISH CONSTITUTION and the RIGHTS OF PERSONS. By R. MALCOLM KERR, LLD. *Second Thousand.* Post 8vo. 9s.

BLAINE (ROBERTON) on the Laws of Artistic Copyright and their Defects, for Artists, Engravers, Printsellers, &c. 8vo. 3s. 6d.

BOOK OF COMMON PRAYER. With 1000 Illustrations of Borders, Initials, and Woodcut Vignettes. *A New Edition.* Medium 8vo. 21s. *cloth,* 31s. 6d. *calf,* or 42s. *morocco.*

BOSWELL'S (JAMES) Life of Dr. Johnson. Including the Tour to the Hebrides. Edited by Mr. CROKER. *Third Edition.* Portraits. Royal 8vo. 10s. sewed, 12s. cloth.

BORROW'S (GEORGE) Lavengro ; The Scholar—The Gipsy—and the Priest. Portrait. 3 Vols. Post 8vo. 30s.

——————————— Romany Rye ; a Sequel to Lavengro. *Second Edition.* 2 Vols. Post 8vo. 21s.

——————————— Bible in Spain; or the Journeys, Adventures, and Imprisonments of an Englishman in an Attempt to circulate the Scriptures in the Peninsula. 3 Vols. Post 8vo. 27s., or *Popular Edition.* 16mo, 6s.

——————————— Zincali, or the Gipsies of Spain ; their Manners, Customs, Religion, and Language. 2 Vols. Post 8vo. 18s., or *Popular Edition.* 16mo, 6s.

BRAY'S (MRS.) Life of Thomas Stothard, R.A. With Personal Reminiscences. Illustrated with Portrait and 60 Woodcuts of his chief works. 4to.

BREWSTER'S (SIR DAVID) Martyrs of Science, or the Lives of Galileo, Tycho Brahe, and Kepler. *Fourth Edition.* Fcap. 8vo. 4s. 6d.

——————————— More Worlds than One. The Creed of the Philosopher and the Hope of the Christian. *Eighth Edition.* Post 8vo. 6s.

——————————— Stereoscope : its History, Theory, Construction, and Application to the Arts and to Education. Woodcuts. 12mo. 5s. 6d.

——————————— Kaleidoscope: its History, Theory, and Construction, with its application to the Fine and Useful Arts. *Second Edition.* Woodcuts. Post 8vo. 5s. 6d.

BRITISH ASSOCIATION REPORTS. 8vo. York and Oxford, 1831-32, 13s. 6d. Cambridge, 1833, 12s. Edinburgh, 1834, 15s. Dublin, 1835, 13s. 6d. Bristol, 1836, 12s. Liverpool, 1837, 16s. 6d. Newcastle, 1838, 15s. Birmingham, 1839, 13s. 6d. Glasgow, 1840, 15s. Plymouth, 1841, 13s. 6d. Manchester, 1842, 10s. 6d. Cork, 1843, 12s. York, 1844. 20s. Cambridge, 1845, 12s. Southampton, 1846, 15s. Oxford, 1847, 18s. Swansea, 1848, 9s. Birmingham, 1849, 10s. Edinburgh, 1850, 15s. Ipswich, 1851, 16s. 6d. Belfast, 1852, 15s. Hull, 1853, 10s. 6d. Liverpool, 1854, 18s. Glasgow, 1855, 15s.; Cheltenham, 1856, 18s; Dublin, 1857, 15s ; Leeds 1858, 20s.

BRITISH CLASSICS. A New Series of Standard English
Authors, printed from the most correct text, and edited with elucidatory notes. Published occasionally in demy 8vo. Volumes.

Already Published.

GOLDSMITH'S WORKS. Edited by Peter Cunningham, F.S.A. Vignettes. 4 Vols. 30s.

GIBBON'S DECLINE AND FALL OF THE ROMAN EMPIRE. Edited by William Smith, LL.D. Portrait and Maps. 8 Vols. 60s.

JOHNSON'S LIVES OF THE ENGLISH POETS. Edited by Peter Cunningham, F.S.A. 3 Vols. 22s. 6d.

BYRON'S POETICAL WORKS. Edited, with Notes. 6 vols. 45s.

In Preparation.

WORKS OF POPE. Edited, with Notes.

WORKS OF DRYDEN. Edited, with Notes.

HUME'S HISTORY OF ENGLAND. Edited, with Notes.

LIFE, LETTERS, AND JOURNALS OF SWIFT. By John Forster.

WORKS OF SWIFT. Edited by John Forster.

BROUGHTON'S (Lord) Journey through Albania and other Provinces of Turkey in Europe and Asia, to Constantinople, 1809—10. *Third Edition.* Maps and Woodcuts. 2 Vols. 8vo. 30s.

———————— Visits to Italy, from the Year 1816 to 1824. *Second Edition.* 2 vols. Post 8vo. 18s.

BUBBLES FROM THE BRUNNEN OF NASSAU. By an Old Man. *Sixth Edition.* 16mo. 5s.

BUNBURY'S (C. J. F.) Journal of a Residence at the Cape of Good Hope; with Excursions into the Interior, and Notes on the Natural History and Native Tribes of the Country. Woodcuts. Post 8vo. 9s.

BUNYAN (John) and Oliver Cromwell. Select Biographies. By Robert Southey. Post 8vo. 2s. 6d.

BUONAPARTE'S (Napoleon) Confidential Correspondence with his Brother Joseph, sometime King of Spain. *Second Edition.* 2 vols. 8vo. 26s.

BURGHERSH'S (Lord) Memoir of the Operations of the Allied Armies under Prince Schwarzenberg and Marshal Blucher during the latter end of 1813—14. 8vo. 21s.

———————— Early Campaigns of the Duke of Wellington in Portugal and Spain. 8vo. 8s. 6d.

BURGON'S (Rev. J. W.) Portrait of a Christian Gentleman: a Memoir of the late Patrick Fraser Tytler, author of "The History of Scotland." *Second Edition.* Post 8vo. 9s.

BURN'S (Lieut-Col.) French and English Dictionary of Naval and Military Technical Terms. *Third Edition.* Crown 8vo. 15s.

BURNS' (Robert) Life. By John Gibson Lockhart. Fifth Edition. Fcap. 8vo. 3s.

BURR'S (G. D.) Instructions in Practical Surveying, Topographical Plan Drawing, and on sketching ground without Instruments. *Third Edition.* Woodcuts. Post 8vo. 7s. 6d.

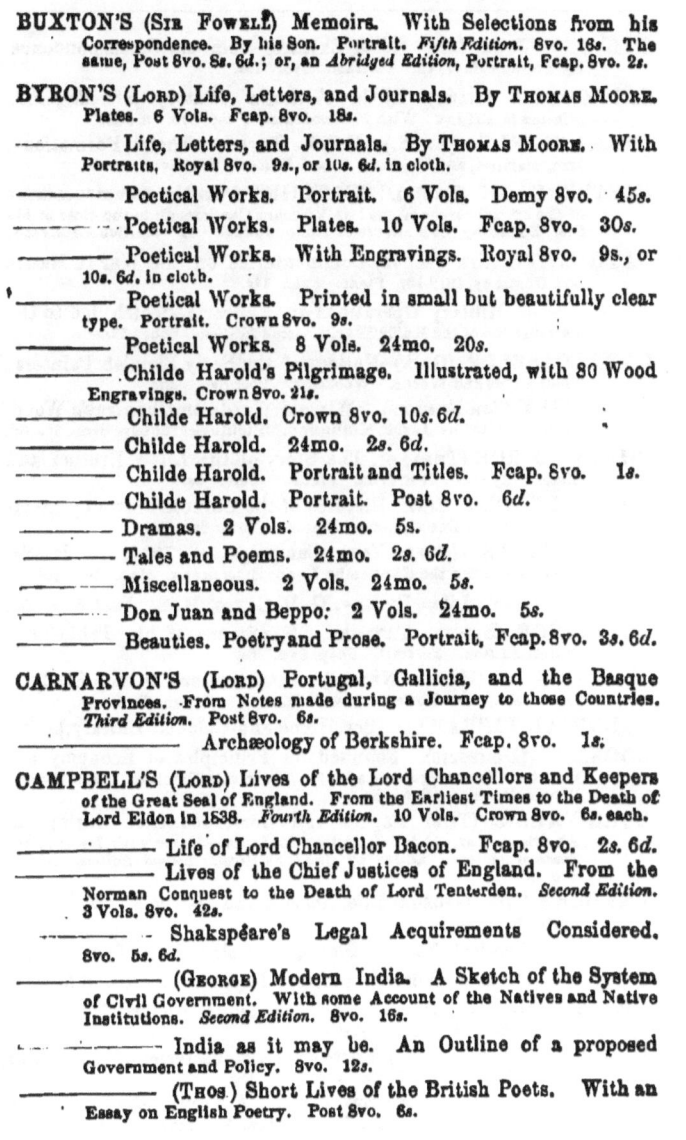

BUXTON'S (Sir Fowell) Memoirs. With Selections from his Correspondence. By his Son. Portrait. *Fifth Edition.* 8vo. 16s. The same, Post 8vo. 8s. 6d.; or, an *Abridged Edition*, Portrait, Fcap. 8vo. 2s.

BYRON'S (Lord) Life, Letters, and Journals. By Thomas Moore. Plates. 6 Vols. Fcap. 8vo. 18s.

———— Life, Letters, and Journals. By Thomas Moore. With Portraits, Royal 8vo. 9s., or 10s. 6d. in cloth.

———— Poetical Works. Portrait. 6 Vols. Demy 8vo. 45s.

———— Poetical Works. Plates. 10 Vols. Fcap. 8vo. 30s.

———— Poetical Works. With Engravings. Royal 8vo. 9s., or 10s. 6d. in cloth.

———— Poetical Works. Printed in small but beautifully clear type. Portrait. Crown 8vo. 9s.

———— Poetical Works. 8 Vols. 24mo. 20s.

———— Childe Harold's Pilgrimage. Illustrated, with 80 Wood Engravings. Crown 8vo. 21s.

———— Childe Harold. Crown 8vo. 10s. 6d.

———— Childe Harold. 24mo. 2s. 6d.

———— Childe Harold. Portrait and Titles. Fcap. 8vo. 1s.

———— Childe Harold. Portrait. Post 8vo. 6d.

———— Dramas. 2 Vols. 24mo. 5s.

———— Tales and Poems. 24mo. 2s. 6d.

———— Miscellaneous. 2 Vols. 24mo. 5s.

———— Don Juan and Beppo. 2 Vols. 24mo. 5s.

———— Beauties. Poetry and Prose. Portrait, Fcap. 8vo. 3s. 6d.

CARNARVON'S (Lord) Portugal, Gallicia, and the Basque Provinces. From Notes made during a Journey to those Countries. *Third Edition.* Post 8vo. 6s.

———— Archæology of Berkshire. Fcap. 8vo. 1s.

CAMPBELL'S (Lord) Lives of the Lord Chancellors and Keepers of the Great Seal of England. From the Earliest Times to the Death of Lord Eldon in 1838. *Fourth Edition.* 10 Vols. Crown 8vo. 6s. each.

———— Life of Lord Chancellor Bacon. Fcap. 8vo. 2s. 6d.

———— Lives of the Chief Justices of England. From the Norman Conquest to the Death of Lord Tenterden. *Second Edition.* 3 Vols. 8vo. 42s.

———— Shakspéare's Legal Acquirements Considered. 8vo. 5s. 6d.

———— (George) Modern India. A Sketch of the System of Civil Government. With some Account of the Natives and Native Institutions. *Second Edition.* 8vo. 16s.

———— India as it may be. An Outline of a proposed Government and Policy. 8vo. 12s.

———— (Thos.) Short Lives of the British Poets. With an Essay on English Poetry. Post 8vo. 6s.

CALVIN'S (JOHN) Life. With Extracts from his Correspondence By THOMAS H. DYER. Portrait. 8vo. 15s.

CALLCOTT'S (LADY) Little Arthur's History of England. *Nineteenth Edition.* With 20 Woodcuts. Fcap. 8vo. 2s. 6d.

CARMICHAEL'S (A. N.) Greek Verbs. Their Formations, Irregularities, and Defects. *Second Edition.* Post 8vo. 8s. 6d.

CASTLEREAGH (THE) DESPATCHES, from the commencement of the official career of the late Viscount Castlereagh to the close of his life. Edited by the MARQUIS OF LONDONDERRY. 12 Vols. 8vo. 14s. each.

CATHCART'S (SIR GEORGE) Commentaries on the War in Russia and Germany, 1812-13. Plans. 8vo. 14s.

————— Military Operations in Kaffraria, which led to the Termination of the Kaffir War. *Second Edition.* 8vo. 12s.

CAVALCASELLE (G. B.) Notices of the Early Flemish Painters; Their Lives and Works. Woodcuts. Post 8vo. 12s.

CHANTREY (SIR FRANCIS). Winged Words on Chantrey's Woodcocks. Edited by JAS. P. MUIRHEAD. Etchings. Square 8vo. 10s. 6d.

CHARMED ROE (THE); or, The Story of the Little Brother and Sister. By OTTO SPECKTER. Plates. 16mo. 5s.

COBBOLD'S (REV. R. H.) Pictures of the Chinese drawn by themselves. With Descriptions. Plates. Crown 8vo. 9s.

CLAUSEWITZ'S (CARL VON) Campaign of 1812, in Russia. Translated from the German by LORD ELLESMERE. Map. 8vo. 10s. 6d.

CLIVE'S (LORD) Life. By REV. G. R. GLEIG, M.A. Post 8vo. 6s.

COLERIDGE (SAMUEL TAYLOR). Specimens of his Table-Talk. *Fourth Edition.* Portrait. Fcap. 8vo. 6s.

————— (HENRY NELSON) Introductions to the Study of the Greek Classic Poets. *Third Edition.* Fcap. 8vo. 5s. 6d.

COLONIAL LIBRARY. [See Home and Colonial Library.]

COOKERY (DOMESTIC). Founded on Principles of Economy and Practical Knowledge, and adapted for Private Families. *New Edition.* Woodcuts. Fcap. 8vo. 5s.

CORNWALLIS (THE) Papers and Correspondence during the American War,—Administrations in India,—Union with Ireland, and Peace of Amiens. Edited by CHARLES ROSS. *Second Edition.* 3 Vols. 8vo. 63s.

CRABBE'S (REV. GEORGE) Life, Letters, and Journals. By his SON. Portrait. Fcap. 8vo. 3s.

————— Poetical Works. Plates. 8 Vols. Fcap. 8vo. 24s.

————— Poetical Works. Plates. Royal 8vo. 10s. 6d.

CRAIK'S (G. L.) Pursuit of Knowledge under Difficulties. *New Edition.* 2 Vols. Post 8vo. 12s.

CURZON'S (HON. ROBERT) Visits to the Monasteries of the Levant. *Fourth Edition.* Woodcuts. Post 8vo. 15s.

————— ARMENIA AND ERZEROUM. A Year on the Frontiers of Russia, Turkey, and Persia. *Third Edition.* Woodcuts. Post 8vo. 7s. 6d.

CUNNINGHAM'S (ALLAN) Life of Sir David Wilkie. With his Journals and Critical Remarks on Works of Art. Portrait. 3 Vols. 8vo. 42s.

——————————— Poems and Songs. Now first collected and arranged, with Biographical Notice. 24mo 2s. 6d.

———— ——— — (CAPT. J. D.) History of the Sikhs. From the Origin of the Nation to the Battle of the Sutlej. *Second Edition.* Maps. 8vo. 15s.

——————————— (PETER) London—Past and Present. A Handbook to the Antiquities, Curiosities, Churches, Works of Art, Public Buildings, and Places connected with interesting and historical associations. *Second Edition.* Post 8vo. 16s.

——————————— Modern London. A complete Guide for Visitors to the Metropolis. Map. 16mo. 5s.

——————————— Westminster Abbey. Its Art, Architecture, and Associations. Woodcuts. Fcap. 8vo. 1s.

——————————— Works of Oliver Goldsmith. Edited with Notes. Vignettes. 4 vols. 8vo. 30s. (Murray's British Classics.)

——————————— Lives of Eminent English Poets. By SAMUEL JOHNSON, LL.D. Edited with Notes. 3 vols. 8vo. 22s. 6d. (Murray's British Classics.)

CROKER'S (J. W.) Progressive Geography for Children. *Fifth Edition.* 18mo. 1s. 6d.

——————————— Stories for Children, Selected from the History of England. *Fifteenth Edition.* Woodcuts. 16mo. 2s. 6d.

——— ——— Boswell's Life of Johnson. Including the Tour to the Hebrides. *Third Edition.* Portraits. Royal 8vo. 10s. sewed, or 12s. cloth.

———————— LORD HERVEY'S Memoirs of the Reign of George the Second, from his Accession to the death of Queen Caroline. Edited with Notes. *Second Edition.* Portrait. 2 Vols. 8vo. 21s.

———— Essays on the Early Period of the French Revolution. Reprinted from the Quarterly Review. 8vo. 15s.

——— Historical Essay on the Guillotine. Fcap. 8vo. 1s.

CROMWELL (OLIVER) and John Bunyan. By ROBERT SOUTHEY. Post 8vo. 2s. 6d.

CROWE'S (J. A.) Notices of the Early Flemish Painters; their Lives and Works. Woodcuts. Post 8vo. 12s.

CURETON (REV. W.) Remains of a very Ancient Recension of the Four Gospels in Syriac, hitherto unknown in Europe. Discovered, Edited, and Translated. 4to. 24s.

DARWIN'S (CHARLES) Journal of Researches into the Natural History and Geology of the Countries visited during a Voyage round the World. Post 8vo. 8s. 6d.

——————————— Origin of Species by Means of Natural Selection; or, the Preservation of Favoured Races in the Struggle for Life. Post 8vo. 14s.

DAVIS'S (SIR J. F.) China: A General Description of that Empire and its Inhabitants, down to 1857. *New Edition.* Woodcuts. 2 Vols. Post 8vo. 14s.

DAVY'S (SIR HUMPHRY) Consolations in Travel; or, Last Days of a Philosopher. *Fifth Edition.* Woodcuts. Fcap. 8vo. 6s.

——————————— Salmonia; or, Days of Fly Fishing. With some Account of the Habits of Fishes belonging to the genus Salmo. *Fourth Edition.* Woodcuts. Fcap. 8vo. 6s.

DENNIS' (George) Cities and Cemeteries of Etruria. Plates.
2 Vols. 8vo. 42s.

DOG-BREAKING; the Most Expeditious, Certain, and Easy
Method, whether great excellence or only mediocrity be required. By
Lieut.-Col. Hutchinson. *Third Edition.* Revised and enlarged.
Woodcuts. Post 8vo. 9s.

DOMESTIC MODERN COOKERY. Founded on Principles of
Economy and Practical Knowledge, and adapted for Private Families.
New Edition. Woodcuts. Fcap. 8vo. 5s.

DOUGLAS'S (General Sir Howard) Treatise on the Theory
and Practice of Gunnery. *Fourth Edition.* Plates. 8vo. 21s.

———————— Treatise on Military Bridges, and the Passages of
Rivers in Military Operations. *Third Edition.* Plates. 8vo. 21s.

———————— Naval Warfare with Steam. 8vo. 8s. 6d.

———————— Modern Systems of Fortification, with special reference to the Naval, Littoral, and Internal Defence of England. Plans.
8vo. 12s.

DRAKE'S (Sir Francis) Life, Voyages, and Exploits, by Sea and
Land. By John Barrow. *Third Edition.* Post 8vo. 2s. 6d.

DRINKWATER'S (John) History of the Siege of Gibraltar,
1779-1783. With a Description and Account of that Garrison from the
Earliest Periods. Post 8vo. 2s. 6d.

DUDLEY'S (Earl of) Letters to the late Bishop of Llandaff.
Second Edition. Portrait. 8vo. 10s. 6d.

DUFFERIN'S (Lord) Letters from High Latitudes, being some
Account of a Yacht Voyage to Iceland, &c., in 1856. *Fourth Edition.*
Woodcuts. Post 8vo. 9s.

DURHAM'S (Admiral Sir Philip) Naval Life and Services. By
Capt. Alexander Murray. 8vo. 5s. 6d.

DYER'S (Thomas H.) Life and Letters of John Calvin. Compiled
from authentic Sources. Portrait. 8vo. 15s.

EASTLAKE (Sir Charles) The Schools of Painting in Italy.
From the Earliest times. From the German of Kugler. Edited, with
Notes. *Third Edition.* Illustrated from the Old Masters. 2 Vols.
Post 8vo. 30s.

EASTWICK'S (E. B.) Handbook for Bombay and Madras, with
Directions for Travellers, Officers, &c. Map. 2 Vols. Post 8vo. 24s.

EDWARDS' (W. H.) Voyage up the River Amazon, including a
Visit to Para. Post 8vo. 2s. 6d.

EGERTON'S (Hon. Capt. Francis) Journal of a Winter's Tour in
India; with a Visit to Nepaul. Woodcuts. 2 Vols. Post 8vo. 18s.

ELDON'S (Lord Chancellor) Public and Private Life, with Selections from his Correspondence and Diaries. By Horace Twiss. *Third
Edition.* Portrait. 2 Vols. Post 8vo. 21s.

ELIOT'S (Hon. W. G. C.) Khans of the Crimea. Being a Narrative of an Embassy from Frederick the Great to the Court of Krim
Geral. Translated from the German. Post 8vo. 6s.

ELLIS (Mrs.) On the Education of Character, with Hints on Moral
Training. Post 8vo. 7s. 6d.

———— **(Rev. W.)** Three Visits to Madagascar. During 1853, '54,
and '56, including a Journey to the Capital, with notices of Natural
History, and Present Civilisation of the People. *Fifth Thousand.* Map
and Woodcuts. 8vo. 16s.

ELLESMERE'S (LORD) Two Sieges of Vienna by the Turks. Translated from the German. Post 8vo. 2s. 6d.

———————— Second Campaign of Radetzky in Piedmont. The Defence of Temeswar and the Camp of the Ban. From the German. Post 8vo. 6s. 6d.

——————— Campaign of 1812 in Russia, from the German of General Carl Von Clausewitz. Map. 8vo. 10s. 6d.

——————— Pilgrimage, and other Poems. Crown 4to. 24s.

——————— Essays on History, Biography, Geography, and Engineering. 8vo. 12s.

ELPHINSTONE'S (HON. MOUNTSTUART) History of India—the Hindoo and Mahomedan Periods. *Fourth Edition*. With an Index. Map. 8vo. 18s.

ELWIN'S (REV. W.) Lives of Eminent British Poets. From Chaucer to Wordsworth. 4 Vols. 8vo. *In Preparation.*

ENGLAND (HISTORY OF) from the Peace of Utrecht to the Peace of Versailles, 1713—83. By LORD MAHON. *Library Edition*, 7 Vols. 8vo, 93s.; or, *Popular Edition*, 7 Vols. Post 8vo. 35s.

——————— From the First Invasion by the Romans, down to the 14th year of Queen Victoria's Reign. By MRS. MARKHAM. 98th Edition. Woodcuts. 12mo. 6s.

——————— AS IT IS: Social, Political, and Industrial, in the 19th Century. By W. JOHNSTON. 2 Vols. Post 8vo. 18s.

——————— and France under the House of Lancaster. With an Introductory View of the Early Reformation. *Second Edition*. 8vo. 15s.

ENGLISHWOMAN IN AMERICA. Post 8vo. 10s. 6d.

——————— RUSSIA: or, Impressions of Manners and Society during a Ten Years' Residence in that Country. *Fifth Thousand*. Woodcuts. Post 8vo. 10s. 6d.

EOTHEN; or, Traces of Travel brought Home from the East. *A New Edition*. Post 8vo. 7s. 6d.

ERSKINE'S (CAPT., R.N.) Journal of a Cruise among the Islands of the Western Pacific, including the Fejees, and others inhabited by the Polynesian Negro Races. Plates. 8vo. 16s.

ESKIMAUX (THE) and English Vocabulary, for the use of Travellers in the Arctic Regions. 16mo. 3s. 6d.

ESSAYS FROM "THE TIMES." Being a Selection from the LITERARY PAPERS which have appeared in that Journal. *Seventh Thousand*. 2 vols. Fcap. 8vo. 8s.

EXETER'S (BISHOP OF) Letters to the late Charles Butler, on the Theological parts of his Book of the Roman Catholic Church; with Remarks on certain Works of Dr. Milner and Dr. Lingard, and on some parts of the Evidence of Dr. Doyle. *Second Edition*. 8vo. 16s.

FAIRY RING (THE), A Collection of TALES and STORIES for Young Persons. From the German. By J. E. TAYLOR. Illustrated by RICHARD DOYLE. *Second Edition*. Fcap. 8vo.

FALKNER'S (FRED.) Muck Manual for the Use of Farmers. A Treatise on the Nature and Value of Manures. *Second Edition*, with a Glossary of Terms and an Index. Fcap. 8vo. 5s.

FAMILY RECEIPT-BOOK. A Collection of a Thousand Valuable and Useful Receipts. Fcap. 8vo. 5s. 6d.

FANCOURT'S (Col.) History of Yucatan, from its Discovery to the Close of the 17th Century. With Map. 8vo. 10s. 6d.

FARRAR'S (Rev. A. S.) Science in Theology. Sermons Preached before the University of Oxford. 8vo. 9s.

FEATHERSTONHAUGH'S (G. W.) Tour through the Slave States of North America, from the River Potomac, to Texas and the Frontiers of Mexico. Plates. 2 Vols. 8vo. 26s.

FELLOWS' (Sir Charles) Travels and Researches in Asia Minor, more particularly in the Province of Lydia. New Edition. Plates. Post 8vo. 9s.

FERGUSSON'S (James) Palaces of Nineveh and Persepolis Restored: an Essay on Ancient Assyrian and Persian Architecture. With 45 Woodcuts. 8vo. 16s.

————— Handbook of Architecture. Being a Concise and Popular Account of the Different Styles prevailing in all Ages and Countries in the World. With a Description of the most remarkable Buildings. Fourth Thousand. With 550 Illustrations. 8vo. 26s.

FERRIER'S (T. P.) Caravan Journeys in Persia, Affghanistan, Herat, Turkistan, and Beloochistan, with Descriptions of Meshed, Balk, and Candahar, and Sketches of the Nomade Tribes of Central Asia. Second Edition. Map. 8vo. 21s.

————— History of the Afghans. Map. 8vo. 21s.

FEUERBACH'S Remarkable German Crimes and Trials. Translated from the German by Lady Duff Gordon. 8vo. 12s.

FISHER'S (Rev. George) Elements of Geometry, for the Use of Schools. Fifth Edition. 18mo. 1s. 6d.

————— First Principles of Algebra, for the Use of Schools. Fifth Edition. 18mo. 1s. 6d.

FLOWER GARDEN (The). An Essay. By Rev. Thos. James. Reprinted from the "Quarterly Review." Fcap. 8vo. 1s.

FORD'S (Richard) Handbook for Spain, Andalusia, Ronda, Valencia, Catalouia, Granada, Gallicia, Arragon, Navarre, &c. Third Edition. 2 Vols. Post 8vo. 30s.

————— Gatherings from Spain. Post 8vo. 6s.

FORSTER'S (John) Historical & Biographical Essays. 2 Vols. Post 8vo. 21s.

I. The Grand Remonstrance, 1641.	IV. Daniel De Foe.
II. The Plantagenets and the Tudors.	V. Sir Richard Steele.
III. Civil Wars & Oliver Cromwell.	VI. Charles Churchill.
	VII. Samuel Foote.

FORSYTH'S (William) Hortensius, or the Advocate: an Historical Essay on the Office and Duties of an Advocate. Post 8vo. 12s.

————— History of Napoleon at St. Helena. From the Letters and Journals of Sir Hudson Lowe. Portrait and Maps. 3 Vols. 8vo. 45s.

FORTUNE'S (Robert) Narrative of Two Visits to China, between the years 1843-52, with full Descriptions of the Culture of the Tea Plant. Third Edition. 2 Vols. Post 8vo. 18s.

————— Residence among the Chinese: Inland, on the Coast, and at Sea, during 1853-56. Woodcuts. 8vo. 16s.

FRANCE (History of). From the Conquest by the Gauls to the Death of Louis Phillippe. By Mrs. Markham. 56th Thousand. Woodcuts. 12mo. 6s.

FRENCH (THE) in Algiers; The Soldier of the Foreign Legion— and the Prisoners of Abd-el-Kadir. Translated by Lady DUFF GORDON. Post 8vo. 2s. 6d.

GALTON'S (FRANCIS) Art of Travel ; or, Hints on the Shifts and Contrivances available in Wild Countries. *Third Edition, enlarged.* Woodcuts. Post 8vo. 7s. 6d.

GEOGRAPHICAL (THE) Journal. Published by the Royal Geo- graphical Society of London. 8vo.

GERMANY (HISTORY OF). From the Invasion by Marius, to the present time. On the plan of Mrs. MARKHAM. *Fifteenth Thousand.* Woodcuts. 12mo. 6s.

GIBBON'S (EDWARD) Decline and Fall of the Roman Empire. A *New Edition.* Preceded by his Autobiography. Edited with Notes by Dr. WM. SMITH. Maps. 8 Vols. 8vo. 60s.

———— **The Student's Gibbon ; Being the History of the** Decline and Fall, Abridged, incorporating the Researches of Recent Commentators. By Dr. WM. SMITH. *Sixth Thousand.* Woodcuts. Post 8vo. 7s. 6d.

GIFFARD'S (EDWARD) Deeds of Naval Daring; or, Anecdotes of the British Navy. 2 Vols. Fcap. 8vo. 5s.

GISBORNE'S (THOMAS) Essays on Agriculture. *Third Edition.* Post 8vo.

GLADSTONE'S (W. E.) Prayers arranged from the Liturgy for Family Use. *Second Edition.* 12mo. 2s. 6d.

GOLDSMITH'S (OLIVER) Works. A New Edition. Printed from the last editions revised by the Author. Edited by PETER CUNNING-HAM. Vignettes. 4 Vols. 8vo. 30s. (Murray's British Classics.)

GLEIG'S (REV. G. R.) Campaigns of the British Army at Washing- ton and New Orleans. Post 8vo. 2s. 6d.

———— **Story of the Battle of Waterloo. Compiled from Public** and Authentic Sources. Post 8vo. 5s.

———— **Narrative of Sir Robert Sale's Brigade in Afghanistan,** with an Account of the Seizure and Defence of Jellalabad. Post 8vo. 2s. 6d.

———— **Life of Robert Lord Clive. Post 8vo. 5s.**

———— **Life and Letters of General Sir Thomas Munro. Post** 8vo. 5s.

GORDON'S (SIR ALEX. DUFF) Sketches of German Life, and Scenes from the War of Liberation. From the German. Post 8vo. 6s.

———— **(LADY DUFF) Amber-Witch : the most interesting** Trial for Witchcraft ever known. From the German. Post 8vo. 2s. 6d.

———— **French in Algiers. 1. The Soldier of the Foreign** Legion. 2. The Prisoners of Abd-el-Kadir. From the French. Post 8vo. 2s. 6d.

————**Remarkable German Crimes and Trials. From the** German of Fuerbach. 8vo. 12s.

GRANT'S (ASAHEL) Nestorians, or the Lost Tribes ; containing Evidence of their Identity, their Manners, Customs, and Ceremonies ; with Sketches of Travel in Ancient Assyria, Armenia, and Mesopotamia ; and Illustrations of Scripture Prophecy. *Third Edition.* Fcap 8vo. 6s.

GRENVILLE (THE) PAPERS. Being the Public and Private Correspondence of George Grenville, his Friends and Contemporaries, during a period of 30 years.— Including his DIARY OF POLITICAL EVENTS while First Lord of the Treasury. Edited, with Notes, by W. J. SMITH. 4 Vols. 8vo. 16s. each.

GREEK GRAMMAR FOR SCHOOLS. Abridged from Matthiæ. By the BISHOP OF LONDON. *Ninth Edition*, revised by Rev. J. EDWARDS. 12mo. 3s.

GREY'S (SIR GEORGE) Polynesian Mythology, and Ancient Traditional History of the New Zealand Race. Woodcuts. Post 8vo. 10s. 6d.

GROTE'S (GEORGE) History of Greece. From the Earliest Times to the close of the generation contemporary with the death of Alexander the Great. *Third Edition*. Maps and Index. 12 vols. 8vo. 16s. each.

———— (MRS.) Memoir of the Life of the late Ary Scheffer. Portrait. 8vo. (Nearly Ready.)

GROSVENOR'S (LORD ROBERT) Leaves from my Journal during the Summer of 1851. *Second Edition*. Plates. Post 8vo. 3s. 6d.

GUSTAVUS VASA (History of), King of Sweden. With Extracts from his Correspondence. Portrait. 8vo. 10s. 6d.

HALLAM'S (HENRY) Constitutional History of England, from the Accession of Henry the Seventh to the Death of George the Second. *Seventh Edition*. 3 Vols. 8vo. 30s.

———————— History of Europe during the Middle Ages. *Tenth Edition*. 3 Vols. 8vo. 30s.

———— — Introduction to the Literary History of Europe, during the 16th, 17th, and 18th Centuries. *Fourth Edition*. 3 Vols. 8vo. 36s.

———————— Literary Essays and Characters. Selected from the last work. Fcap. 8vo. 2s.

—— ———— Historical Works. Containing the History of England,—The Middle Ages of Europe,—and the Literary History of Europe. *Complete Edition*. 10 Vols. Post 8vo. 6s. each.

HAMILTON'S (JAMES) Wanderings in Northern Africa, Benghazi, Cyrene, the Oasis of Siwah, &c. *Second Edition*. Woodcuts. Post 8vo. 12s.

———————— (WALTER) Hindostan, Geographically, Statistically, and Historically. Map. 2 Vols. 4to. 94s. 6d.

HAMPDEN'S (BISHOP) Essay on the Philosophical Evidence of Christianity, or the Credibility obtained to a Scripture Revelation from its Coincidence with the Facts of Nature. 8vo. 9s. 6d.

HARCOURT'S (EDWARD VERNON) Sketch of Madeira; with Map and Plates. Post 8vo. 8s. 6d.

HART'S ARMY LIST. (*Quarterly and Annually*.) 8vo.

HAY'S (J. H. DRUMMOND) Western Barbary, its wild Tribes and savage Animals. Post 8vo. 2s. 6d.

HEBER (BISHOP) Parish Sermons; on the Lessons, the Gospel, or the Epistle, for every Sunday in the Year, and for Week-day Festivals. *Sixth Edition*. 2 Vols. Post 8vo. 16s.

———————— Sermons Preached in England. *Second Edition*. 8vo. 9s. 6d.

———————— Hymns written and adapted for the Weekly Church Service of the Year. *Twelfth Edition*. 16mo. 2s.

———————— Poetical Works. *Fifth Edition*. Portrait. Fcap. 8vo. 7s. 6d.

———————— Journey through the Upper Provinces of India, From Calcutta to Bombay, with a Journey to Madras and the Southern Provinces. 2 Vols. Post 8vo. 12s.

HAND-BOOK OF TRAVEL-TALK; or, Conversations in English, German, French, and Italian. 18mo. 3s. 6d.

———— NORTH GERMANY—Holland, Belgium, and the Rhine to Switzerland. Map. Post 8vo. 10s.

———— SOUTH GERMANY—Bavaria, Austria, Salzberg, the Austrian and Bavarian Alps, the Tyrol, and the Danube, from Ulm to the Black Sea. Map. Post 8vo. 10s.

———— PAINTING—the German, Flemish, and Dutch Schools. From the German of Kugler. A New Edition. Edited by Dr. Waagen. Woodcuts. Post 8vo. (In the Press.)

———— SWITZERLAND—the Alps of Savoy, and Piedmont. Maps. Post 8vo. 9s.

———— FRANCE—Normandy, Brittany, the French Alps, the Rivers Loire, Seine, Rhone, and Garonne, Dauphiné, Provence, and the Pyrenees. Maps. Post 8vo. 10s.

———— SPAIN—Andalusia, Ronda, Granada, Valencia, Catalonia, Gallicia, Arragon, and Navarre. Maps. 2 Vols. Post 8vo. 30s.

———— PORTUGAL, LISBON, &c. Map. Post 8vo. 9s.

———— PAINTING—Spanish and French Schools. By Sir Edmund Head, Bart. Woodcuts. Post 8vo. 12s.

———— NORTH ITALY—Florence, Sardinia, Genoa, the Riviera, Venice, Lombardy, and Tuscany. Map. Post 8vo. 2 Vols. 12s.

———— CENTRAL ITALY—South Tuscany and the Papal States. Map. Post 8vo. 7s.

———— ROME—AND ITS ENVIRONS. Map. Post 8vo. 9s.

———— SOUTH ITALY—Naples, Pompeii, Herculaneum, Vesuvius, &c. Map. Post 8vo. 10s.

———— SICILY. Map. Post 8vo. (In the Press.)

———— PAINTING—the Italian Schools. From the German of Kugler. Edited by Sir Charles Eastlake, R. A. Woodcuts. 2 Vols. Post 8vo. 30s.

———— Early Italian Painters and Progress of Painting in Italy. By Mrs. Jameson. Woodcuts. Post 8vo. 12s.

———— Biographical Dictionary of Italian Painters. With a Chart. Post 8vo. 6s. 6d.

———— GREECE—the Ionian Islands, Albania, Thessaly, and Macedonia. Maps. Post 8vo. 15s.

———— TURKEY—Malta, Asia Minor, Constantinople, Armenia, Mesopotamia, &c. Maps. Post 8vo.

———— EGYPT—Thebes, the Nile, Alexandria, Cairo, the Pyramids, Mount Sinai, &c. Map. Post 8vo. 15s.

———— SYRIA AND PALESTINE; the Peninsula of Sinai, Edom, and the Syrian Desert. Maps. 2 Vols. Post 8vo. 24s.

———— BOMBAY AND MADRAS. Map. 2 Vols. Post 8vo. 24s.

———— DENMARK—Norway and Sweden. Maps. Post 8vo. 15s.

———— RUSSIA—The Baltic and Finland. Maps. Post 8vo. 12s.

HANDBOOK OF LONDON, Past and Present. Alphabetically arranged. *Second Edition.* Post 8vo. 16s.

——— MODERN LONDON. A Guide to all objects of interest in the Metropolis. Map. 16mo. 5s.

——— ENVIRONS OF LONDON. Including a Circle of 30 Miles round St. Paul's. Maps. Post 8vo. (*In preparation.*)

——— DEVON AND CORNWALL. Maps. Post 8vo. 7s. 6d.

——— WILTS, DORSET, AND SOMERSET. Map. Post 8vo. 7s. 6d.

——— KENT AND SUSSEX. Map. Post 8vo. 10s.

——— SURREY, HANTS, and the Isle of Wight. Maps. Post 8vo 7s. 6d.

——— WESTMINSTER ABBEY—its Art, Architecture, and Associations. Woodcuts. 16mo. 1s.

——— SOUTHERN CATHEDRALS OF ENGLAND. Woodcuts. Post 8vo. (*Nearly Ready.*)

——— PARIS. Post 8vo. (*In preparation.*)

——— FAMILIAR QUOTATIONS. Chiefly from English Authors. *Third Edition.* Fcap. 8vo. 5s.

——— ARCHITECTURE. Being a Concise and Popular Account of the Different Styles prevailing in all Ages and Countries. By James Fergusson. *Fourth Thousand.* With 850 Illustrations. 8vo. 26s.

——— ARTS OF THE MIDDLE AGES AND RE-naissance. By M. Jules Labarte. With 200 Illustrations. 8vo. 18s.

HEAD'S (Sir Francis) Rough Notes of some Rapid Journeys across the Pampas and over the Andes. Post 8vo. 2s. 6d.

——— Descriptive Essays : contributed to the "Quarterly Review." 2 Vols. Post 8vo. 18s.

——— Bubbles from the Brunnen of Nassau. By an Old Man. *Sixth Edition.* 16mo. 5s.

——— Emigrant. *Sixth Edition.* Fcap. 8vo. 2s. 6d.

——— Stokers and Pokers; or, the London and North-Western Railway. Post 8vo. 2s. 6d.

——— Defenceless State of Great Britain. Post 8vo. 12s.

——— Faggot of French Sticks; or, Sketches of Paris. *New Edition.* 2 Vols. Post 8vo. 12s.

——— Fortnight in Ireland. *Second Edition.* Map. 8vo. 12s.

——— (Sir George) Forest Scenes and Incidents in Canada. *Second Edition.* Post 8vo. 10s.

——— Home Tour through the Manufacturing Districts of England, Scotland, and Ireland, including the Channel Islands, and the Isle of Man. *Third Edition.* 2 Vols. Post 8vo. 12s.

——— (Sir Edmund) Handbook of Painting—the Spanish and French Schools. With Illustrations. Post 8vo.

——— Shall and Will; or, Two Chapters on Future Auxiliary Verbs. *Second Edition, Enlarged.* Fcap. 8vo. 4s.

HEIRESS (The) in Her Minority; or, The Progress of Character. By the Author of "Bertha's Journal." 2 Vols. 12mo. 18s.

HERODOTUS. A New English Version. Edited with Notes, and Essays. By Rev. G. Rawlinson, assisted by Sir Henry Rawlinson, and Sir J. G. Wilkinson. Maps and Woodcuts. 4 Vols. 8vo. 18s. each.

HERVEY'S (Lord) Memoirs of the Reign of George the Second, from his Accession to the Death of Queen Caroline. Edited, with Notes by Mr. Croker. Second Edition. Portrait. 2 Vols. 8vo. 21s.

HICKMAN'S (Wm.) Treatise on the Law and Practice of Naval Courts Martial. 8vo. 10s. 6d.

HILLARD'S (G. S.) Six Months in Italy. 2 Vols. Post 8vo. 16s.

HISTORY OF ENGLAND AND FRANCE under the House of Lancaster. With an Introductory View of the Early Reformation. Second Edition. 8vo. 15s.

HOLLAND'S (Rev. W. B.) Psalms and Hymns, selected and adapted to the various Solemnities of the Church. Third Edition. 24mo. 1s. 3d.

HOLLWAY'S (J. G.) Month in Norway. Fcap. 8vo. 2s.

HONEY BEE (The). An Essay. By Rev. Thomas James. Reprinted from the "Quarterly Review." Fcap. 8vo. 1s.

HOOK'S (Dean) Church Dictionary. Eighth Edition. 8vo. 16s.

———— Discourses on the Religious Controversies of the Day. 8vo. 9s.

———— (Theodore) Life. By J. G. Lockhart. Reprinted from the "Quarterly Review." Fcap. 8vo. 1s.

HOOKER'S (Dr. J. D.) Himalayan Journals; or, Notes of an Oriental Naturalist in Bengal, the Sikkim and Nepal Himalayas, the Khasia Mountains, &c. Second Edition. Woodcuts. 2 vols. Post 8vo. 18s.

HOOPER'S (Lieut.) Ten Months among the Tents of the Tuski; with Incidents of an Arctic Boat Expedition in Search of Sir John Franklin. Plates, 8vo. 14s.

HORACE (Works of). Edited by Dean Milman. With 300 Woodcuts. Crown 8vo. 21s.

———— (Life of). By Dean Milman. Woodcuts, and coloured Borders. 8vo. 9s.

HOSPITALS AND SISTERHOODS. By a Lady. Fcap. 8vo. 3s. 6d.

HOUSTOUN'S (Mrs.) Yacht Voyage to Texas and the Gulf of Mexico. Plates. 2 Vols. Post 8vo. 21s.

c

HOME AND COLONIAL LIBRARY. Complete in 70 Parts.
Post 8vo, 2s. 6d. each, or bound in 31 Volumes, cloth.

CONTENTS OF THE SERIES.

THE BIBLE IN SPAIN. By GEORGE BORROW.
JOURNALS IN INDIA. By BISHOP HEBER.
TRAVELS IN THE HOLY LAND. By CAPTAINS IRBY and MANGLES.
THE SIEGE OF GIBRALTAR. By JOHN DRINKWATER.
MOROCCO AND THE MOORS. By J. DRUMMOND HAY.
LETTERS FROM THE BALTIC. By a LADY.
THE AMBER-WITCH. By LADY DUFF GORDON.
OLIVER CROMWELL & JOHN BUNYAN. By ROBERT SOUTHEY.
NEW SOUTH WALES. By MRS. MEREDITH.
LIFE OF SIR FRANCIS DRAKE. By JOHN BARROW.
FATHER RIPA'S MEMOIRS OF THE COURT OF CHINA.
A RESIDENCE IN THE WEST INDIES. By M. G. LEWIS.
SKETCHES OF PERSIA. By SIR JOHN MALCOLM.
THE FRENCH IN ALGIERS. By LADY DUFF GORDON.
VOYAGE OF A NATURALIST. By CHARLES DARWIN.
HISTORY OF THE FALL OF THE JESUITS.
LIFE OF LOUIS PRINCE OF CONDE. By LORD MAHON.
GIPSIES OF SPAIN. By GEORGE BORROW.
THE MARQUESAS. By HERMANN MELVILLE.
LIVONIAN TALES. By a LADY.
MISSIONARY LIFE IN CANADA. By REV. J. ABBOTT.
SALE'S BRIGADE IN AFFGHANISTAN. By REV. G. R. GLEIG.
LETTERS FROM MADRAS. By a LADY.
HIGHLAND SPORTS. By CHARLES ST. JOHN.
JOURNEYS ACROSS THE PAMPAS. By SIR F. B. HEAD.
GATHERINGS FROM SPAIN. By RICHARD FORD.
SIEGES OF VIENNA BY THE TURKS. By LORD ELLESMERE.
SKETCHES OF GERMAN LIFE. By SIR A. GORDON.
ADVENTURES IN THE SOUTH SEAS. By HERMANN MELVILLE.
STORY OF BATTLE OF WATERLOO. By REV. G. R. GLEIG.
A VOYAGE UP THE RIVER AMAZON. By W. H. EDWARDS.
THE WAYSIDE CROSS. By CAPT. MILMAN.
MANNERS & CUSTOMS OF INDIA. By REV. C. ACLAND.
CAMPAIGNS AT WASHINGTON. By REV. G. R. GLEIG.
ADVENTURES IN MEXICO. By G. F. RUXTON.
PORTUGAL AND GALLICIA. By LORD CARNARVON.
LIFE OF LORD CLIVE. By REV. G. R. GLEIG.
BUSH LIFE IN AUSTRALIA. By H. W. HAYGARTH.
THE AUTOBIOGRAPHY OF HENRY STEFFENS.
SHORT LIVES OF THE POETS. By THOMAS CAMPBELL.
HISTORICAL ESSAYS. By LORD MAHON.
LONDON & NORTH-WESTERN RAILWAY. By SIR F. B. HEAD.
ADVENTURES IN THE LIBYAN DESERT. By BAYLE ST. JOHN.
A RESIDENCE AT SIERRA LEONE. By a LADY.
LIFE OF GENERAL MUNRO. By REV. G. R. GLEIG.
MEMOIRS OF SIR FOWELL BUXTON. By his SON.

HUME (THE STUDENT'S). A History of England, from the Invasion of Julius Cæsar. Based on HUME's History, and continued to 1858. *Tenth Thousand.* Woodcuts. Post 8vo. 7s. 6d.

HUTCHINSON (COLONEL) on Dog-Breaking; the most expeditious, certain, and easy Method, whether great Excellence or only Mediocrity be required. *Third Edition.* Woodcuts. Post 8vo. 9s.

HUTTON'S (H. E.) Principia Græca; an Introduction to the Study of Greek. Comprehending Grammar, Delectus, and Exercise-book, with Vocabularies. 12mo. 2s. 6d.

IRBY AND MANGLES' Travels in Egypt, Nubia, Syria, and the Holy Land, including a Journey round the Dead Sea, and through the Country east of the Jordan. Post 8vo. 2s. 6d.

JAMES' (REV. THOMAS) Fables of Æsop. A New Translation, with Historical Preface. With 100 Woodcuts by TENNIEL and WOLF. *Twenty-sixth Thousand.* Post 8vo. 2s. 6d.

JAMESON'S (MRS.) Memoirs of the Early Italian Painters, and of the Progress of Italian Painting in Italy. *New Edition, revised and enlarged.* With very many Woodcuts. Post 8vo. 12s. (*Uniform with Kugler's Handbooks.*)

JAPAN AND THE JAPANESE. Described from the Accounts of Recent Dutch Travellers. *New Edition.* Post 8vo. 6s.

JARDINE'S (DAVID) Narrative of the Gunpowder Plot. *New Edition.* Post 8vo. 7s. 6d.

JERVIS'S (CAPT.) Manual of Operations in the Field, for the Use of Officers. Post 8vo. 9s. 6d.

JESSE'S (EDWARD) Favorite Haunts and Rural Studies; or Visits to Spots of Interest in the Vicinity of Windsor and Eton. Woodcuts. Post 8vo. 12s.

———— Scenes and Occupations of Country Life. With Recollections of Natural History. *Third Edition.* Woodcuts. Fcap. 8vo. 6s.

———— Gleanings in Natural History. With Anecdotes of the Sagacity and Instinct of Animals. *Eighth Edition.* Fcap. 8vo. 6s.

JOHNSON'S (DR. SAMUEL) Life: By James Boswell. Including the Tour to the Hebrides. Edited by the late MR. CROKER. *Third Edition.* Portraits. Royal 8vo. 10s. sewed; 12s. c'oth.

————, ———— Lives of the most eminent English Poets. Edited by PETER CUNNINGHAM. 3 vols. 8vo. 22s. 6d. (Murray's British Classics.)

JOHNSTON'S (WM.) England: Social, Political, and Industrial, in 19th Century. 2 Vols. Post 8vo. 18s.

JOURNAL OF A NATURALIST. *Fourth Edition.* Woodcuts. Post 8vo. 9s. 6d.

JOWETT'S (Rev. B.) Commentary on St. Paul's Epistles to the Thessalonians, Galatians, and Romans. *Second Edition.* 2 Vols. 8vo. 30s.

JONES' (Rev. R.) Literary Remains. With a Prefatory Notice. By Rev. W. WHEWELL, D.D. Portrait. 8vo. 14s.

KEN'S (BISHOP) Life. By A LAYMAN. *Second Edition.* Portrait. 2 Vols. 8vo. 18s.

———— (BISHOP) Exposition of the Apostles' Creed. Extracted from his "Practice of Divine Love." *New Edition.* Fcap. 1s. 6d.

———— Approach to the Holy Altar. Extracted from his "Manual of Prayer" and "Practice of Divine Love." *New Edition.* Fcap. 8vo 1s. 6d.

KING'S (Rev. S. W.) Italian Valleys of the Alps; a Tour through all the Romantic and less-frequented "Vals" of Northern Piedmont, from the Tarentaise to the Gries. With Illustrations. Crown 8vo. 18s.

KING EDWARD VIth's Latin Grammar; or, an Introduction to the Latin Tongue, for the Use of Schools. 12th Edition. 12mo. 3s. 6d.

————————————— First Latin Book; or, the Accidence, Syntax and Prosody, with an English Translation for the Use of Junior Classes. Third Edition. 12mo. 2s.

KINGLAKE'S (A. W.) History of the War in the Crimea. Based chiefly upon the Private Papers of Field Marshal Lord Raglan, and other authentic materials. Vols. I. and II. 8vo.

KNAPP'S (J. A.) English Roots and Ramifications; or, the Derivation and Meaning of Divers Words. Fcap. 8vo. 4s.

KUGLER'S (Dr. Franz) Handbook to the History of Painting (the Italian Schools). Translated from the German. Edited, with Notes, by Sir Charles Eastlake. Third Edition. Woodcuts. 2 Vols. Post 8vo. 30s.

—————— (the German, Dutch, and Flemish Schools). Translated from the German. A New Edition. Edited, with Notes. By Dr. Waagen. Woodcuts. Post 8vo. Nearly Ready.

LABARTE'S (M. Jules) Handbook of the Arts of the Middle Ages and Renaissance. With 200 Woodcuts. 8vo. 18s.

LABORDE'S (Leon de) Journey through Arabia Petræa, to Mount Sinai, and the Excavated City of Petræa,—the Edom of the Prophecies. Second Edition. With Plates. 8vo. 18s.

LANE'S (E. W.) Arabian Nights. Translated from the Arabic, with Explanatory Notes. A New Edition. Edited by E. Stanley Poole. With 600 Woodcuts. 3 Vols. 8vo. 42s.

—————— Manners and Customs of the Modern Egyptians. A New Edition, with Additions and Improvements by the Author. Edited by E. Stanley Poole. Woodcuts. 8vo. 18s.

LATIN GRAMMAR (King Edward the VIth's.) For the Use of Schools. Twelfth Edition. 12mo. 3s. 6d.

—————— First Book (King Edward VI.); or, the Accidence, Syntax, and Prosody, with English Translation for Junior Classes. Third Edition. 12mo. 2s.

LAYARD'S (A. H.) Nineveh and its Remains. Being a Narrative of Researches and Discoveries amidst the Ruins of Assyria. With an Account of the Chaldean Christians of Kurdistan; the Yezedis, or Devil-worshippers; and an Enquiry into the Manners and Arts of the Ancient Assyrians. Sixth Edition. Plates and Woodcuts. 2 Vols. 8vo. 36s.

—————————————— Nineveh and Babylon; being the Result of a Second Expedition to Assyria. Fourteenth Thousand. Plates. 8vo. 21s. Or Fine Paper, 2 Vols. 8vo. 30s.

—————— Popular Account of Nineveh. 15th Edition. With Woodcuts. Post 8vo. 5s.

LESLIE'S (C. R.) Handbook for Young Painters. With Illustrations. Post 8vo. 10s. 6d.

—————— Life of Sir Joshua Reynolds. With an Account of his Works, and a Sketch of his Cotemporaries. Fcap. 4to. In the Press.

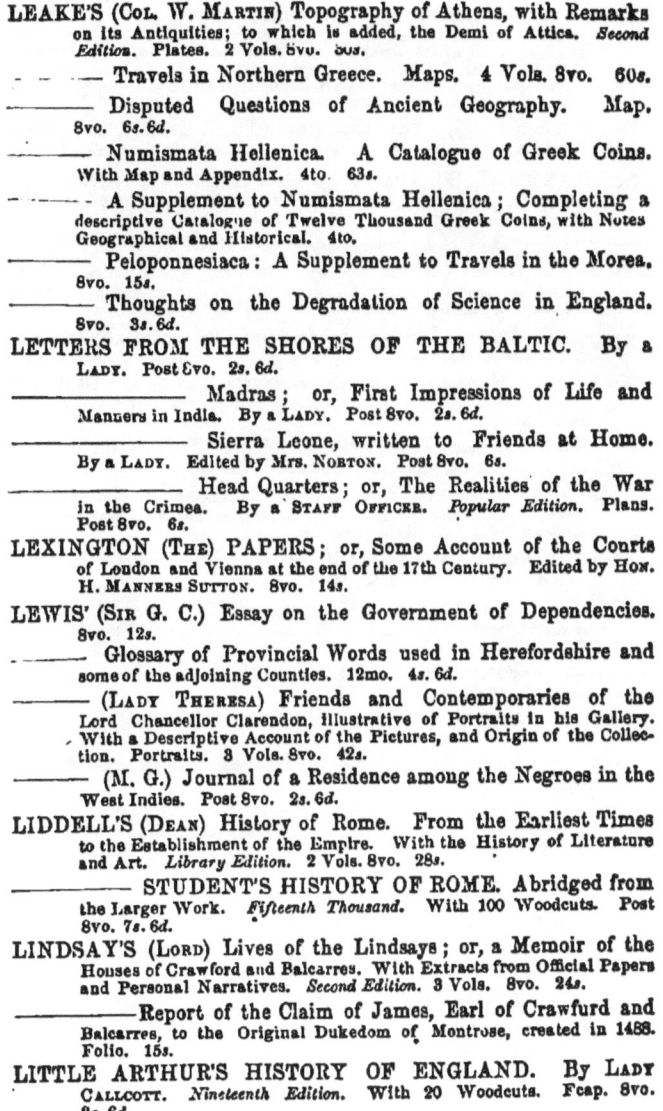

LEAKE'S (COL. W. MARTIN) Topography of Athens, with Remarks on its Antiquities; to which is added, the Demi of Attica. *Second Edition.* Plates. 2 Vols. 8vo. 30s.

———— Travels in Northern Greece. Maps. 4 Vols. 8vo. 60s.

———— Disputed Questions of Ancient Geography. Map. 8vo. 6s. 6d.

———— Numismata Hellenica. A Catalogue of Greek Coins. With Map and Appendix. 4to. 63s.

———— A Supplement to Numismata Hellenica; Completing a descriptive Catalogue of Twelve Thousand Greek Coins, with Notes Geographical and Historical. 4to.

———— Peloponnesiaca: A Supplement to Travels in the Morea. 8vo. 15s.

———— Thoughts on the Degradation of Science in England. 8vo. 3s. 6d.

LETTERS FROM THE SHORES OF THE BALTIC. By a LADY. Post 8vo. 2s. 6d.

———————— Madras; or, First Impressions of Life and Manners in India. By a LADY. Post 8vo. 2s. 6d.

———————— Sierra Leone, written to Friends at Home. By a LADY. Edited by Mrs. NORTON. Post 8vo. 6s.

———————— Head Quarters; or, The Realities of the War in the Crimea. By a STAFF OFFICER. *Popular Edition.* Plans. Post 8vo. 6s.

LEXINGTON (THE) PAPERS; or, Some Account of the Courts of London and Vienna at the end of the 17th Century. Edited by HON. H. MANNERS SUTTON. 8vo. 14s.

LEWIS' (SIR G. C.) Essay on the Government of Dependencies. 8vo. 12s.

———— Glossary of Provincial Words used in Herefordshire and some of the adjoining Counties. 12mo. 4s. 6d.

———— (LADY THERESA) Friends and Contemporaries of the Lord Chancellor Clarendon, illustrative of Portraits in his Gallery. With a Descriptive Account of the Pictures, and Origin of the Collection. Portraits. 3 Vols. 8vo. 42s.

———— (M. G.) Journal of a Residence among the Negroes in the West Indies. Post 8vo. 2s. 6d.

LIDDELL'S (DEAN) History of Rome. From the Earliest Times to the Establishment of the Empire. With the History of Literature and Art. *Library Edition.* 2 Vols. 8vo. 28s.

———— STUDENT'S HISTORY OF ROME. Abridged from the Larger Work. *Fifteenth Thousand.* With 100 Woodcuts. Post 8vo. 7s. 6d.

LINDSAY'S (LORD) Lives of the Lindsays; or, a Memoir of the Houses of Crawford and Balcarres. With Extracts from Official Papers and Personal Narratives. *Second Edition.* 3 Vols. 8vo. 24s.

———— Report of the Claim of James, Earl of Crawfurd and Balcarres, to the Original Dukedom of Montrose, created in 1488. Folio. 15s.

LITTLE ARTHUR'S HISTORY OF ENGLAND. By LADY CALLCOTT. *Nineteenth Edition.* With 20 Woodcuts. Fcap. 8vo. 2s. 6d.

LIVINGSTONE'S (Rev. Dr.) Missionary Travels and Researches in South Africa; including a Sketch of Sixteen Years' Residence in the Interior of Africa, and a Journey from the Cape of Good Hope to Loanda on the West Coast; thence across the Continent, down the River Zambesi, to the Eastern Ocean. *Thirtieth Thousand.* Map, Plates, and Index. 8vo. 21s.

LIVONIAN TALES.—The Disponent.—The Wolves.—The Jewess. By the Author of "Letters from the Baltic." Post 8vo. 2s. 6d.

LOCKHART'S (J. G.) Ancient Spanish Ballads. Historical and Romantic. Translated, with Notes. *Illustrated Edition.* 4to. 21s. Or, *Popular Edition.* Post 8vo. 2s. 6d.

———— Life of Robert Burns. *Fifth Edition.* Fcap. 8vo. 3s.

LOUDON'S (Mrs.) Instructions in Gardening for Ladies. With Directions and Calendar of Operations for Every Month. *Eighth Edition.* Woodcuts. Fcap. 8vo. 5s.

———— Modern Botany; a Popular Introduction to the Natural System of Plants. *Second Edition.* Woodcuts. Fcap. 8vo. 6s.

LOWE'S (Sir Hudson) Letters and Journals, during the Captivity of Napoleon at St. Helena. By William Forsyth. Portrait. 3 Vols. 8vo. 45s.

LUCKNOW: A Lady's Diary of the Siege. Written for Friends at Home. *Fourth Thousand.* Fcap. 8vo. 4s. 6d.

LYELL'S (Sir Charles) Principles of Geology; or, the Modern Changes of the Earth and its Inhabitants considered as illustrative of Geology. *Ninth Edition.* Woodcuts. 8vo. 18s.

———— Visits to the United States, 1841-46. *Second Edition.* Plates. 4 Vols. Post 8vo. 24s.

MAHON'S (Lord) History of England, from the Peace of Utrecht to the Peace of Versailles, 1713—83. *Library Edition.* 7 Vols. 8vo. 93s. *Popular Edition.* 7 Vols. Post 8vo. 35s.

———— "Forty-Five;" a Narrative of the Rebellion in Scotland. Post 8vo. 3s.

———— History of British India from its Origin till the Peace of 1783. Post 8vo. 3s. 6d.

———— History of the War of the Succession in Spain. *Second Edition.* Map. 8vo. 15s.

———— Spain under Charles the Second; or, Extracts from the Correspondence of the Hon. Alexander Stanhope, British Minister at Madrid from 1690 to 1700. *Second Edition.* Post 8vo. 6s. 6d.

———— Life of Louis Prince of Condé, surnamed the Great. Post 8vo. 6s.

———— Life of Belisarius. *Second Edition.* Post 8vo. 10s. 6d.

———— Historical and Critical Essays. Post 8vo. 6s.

———— Story of Joan of Arc. Fcap. 8vo. 1s.

———— Addresses Delivered at Manchester, Leeds, and Birmingham. Fcap. 8vo. 1s.

McCLINTOCK'S (Capt.) Narrative of the Discovery of the Fate of Sir John Franklin and his Companions, in the Arctic Seas. With Preface, by Sir Roderick Murchison. Map and Illustrations. 8vo. 16s.

McCOSH (Rev. Dr.) On the intuitive Convictions of the Mind. 8vo.

M'CULLOCH'S (J. R.) Collectéd Edition of RICARDO'S Political Works. With Notes and Memoir. *Second Edition.* 8vo. 16s.

MALCOLM'S (SIR JOHN) Sketches of Persia. *Third Edition.* Post 8vo. 6s.

MANSEL'S (REV. H. L.) Bampton Lectures. The Limits of Religious Thought Examined. *Fourth and cheaper Edition.* Post 8vo. 7s. 6d.

———— Examination of Professor Maurice's Strictures on the Bampton Lectures of 1858. *Second Edition* 8vo. 2s. 6d.

MANTELL'S (GIDEON A.) Thoughts on Animalcules; or, the Invisible World, as revealed by the Microscope. *Second Edition.* Plates. 16mo. 6s.

MANUAL OF SCIENTIFIC ENQUIRY, Prepared for the Use of Officers and Travellers. By various Writers. *Third Edition revised* by the Rev. R. MAIN. Maps. Post 8vo. 9s. *(Published by order of the Lords of the Admiralty.)*

MARKHAM'S (MRS.) History of England. From the First Invasion by the Romans, down to the fourteenth year of Queen Victoria's Reign. *118th Edition.* Woodcuts. 12mo. 6s.

———— History of France. From the Conquest by the Gauls, to the Death of Louis Philippe. *Sixtieth Edition.* Woodcuts. 12mo. 6s.

———— History of Germany. From the Invasion by Marius, to the present time. *Fifteenth Edition.* Woodcuts. 12mo. 6s..

———— History of Greece. From the Earliest Times to the Roman Conquest. With the History of Literature and Art. By Dr. WM. SMITH. *Twentieth Thousand.* Woodcuts. 12mo. 7s. 6d. *(Questions.* 12mo. 2s.)

———— History of Rome, from the Earliest Times to the Establishment of the Empire. With the History of Literature and Art. By DEAN LIDDELL. *Fifteenth Thousand.* Woodcuts. 12mo. 7s. 6d.

MARKLAND'S (J. H.) Reverence due to Holy Places. *Third Edition.* Fcap. 8vo. 2s.

MARRYAT'S (JOSEPH) History of Modern and Mediæval Pottery and Porcelain. With a Description of the Manufacture, a Glossary, and a List of Monograms. *Second Edition.* Plates and Woodcuts. 8vo. 31s. 6d.

MATTHIÆ'S (AUGUSTUS) Greek Grammar for Schools. Abridged from the Larger Grammar. By Blomfield. *Ninth Edition.* Revised by EDWARDS. 12mo. 3s.

MAUREL'S (JULES) Essay on the Character, Actions, and Writings of the Duke of Wellington. *Second Edition.* Fcap. 8vo. 1s. 6d.

MAWE'S (H. L.) Journal of a Passage from the Pacific to the Atlantic, crossing the Andes in the Northern Provinces of Peru, and descending the great River Maranon. 8vo. 12s.

MAXIMS AND HINTS for an Angler, and the Miseries of Fishing. By RICHARD PENN. *New Edition.* Woodcuts. 12mo. 1s.

MAYO'S (DR.) Pathology of the Human Mind. Fcap. 8vo. 5s. 6d.

MELVILLE'S (HERMANN) Typee and Omoo; or, Adventures amongst the Marquesas and South Sea Islands. 2 Vols. Post 8vo.

MENDELSSOHN'S (FELIX BARTHOLDY) Life. By JULES BENEDICT. 8vo. 2s. 6d.

MEREDITH'S (Mrs. Charles) Notes and Sketches of New South Wales, during a Residence from 1839 to 1844. Post 8vo. 2s. 6d.

———— Tasmania, during a Residence of Nine Years. With Illustrations. 2 Vols. Post 8vo. 18s.

MERRIFIELD (Mrs.) on the Arts of Painting in Oil, Miniature, Mosaic, and Glass; Gilding, Dyeing, and the Preparation of Colours and Artificial Gems, described in several old Manuscripts. 2 Vols. 8vo. 30s.

MILLS (Arthur) India in 1858: A Summary of the Existing Administration—Political, Fiscal, and Judicial; with Laws and Public Documents, from the earliest to the present time. Second Edition. With Coloured Revenue Map. 8vo. 10s. 6d.

MITCHELL'S (Thomas) Plays of Aristophanes. With English Notes. 8vo.—1. CLOUDS, 10s.—2. WASPS, 10s.—3. FROGS, 15s.

MILMAN'S (Dean) History of Christianity, from the Birth of Christ to the Extinction of Paganism in the Roman Empire. 3 Vols. 8vo. 36s.

———— History of Latin Christianity; including that of the Popes to the Pontificate of Nicholas V. Second Edition. 6 Vols. 8vo. 72s.

———— Character and Conduct of the Apostles considered as an Evidence of Christianity. 8vo. 10s. 6d.

———— Life and Works of Horace. With 300 Woodcuts. New Edition. 2 Vols. Crown 8vo. 30s.

———— Poetical Works. Plates. 3 Vols. Fcap. 8vo. 18s.

———— Fall of Jerusalem. Fcap. 8vo. 1s.

———— (Capt. E. A.) Wayside Cross; or, the Raid of Gomez. A Tale of the Carlist War. Post 8vo. 2s. 6d.

MODERN DOMESTIC COOKERY. Founded on Principles of Economy and Practical Knowledge, and adapted for Private Families. New Edition. Woodcuts. Fcap. 8vo. 5s.

MOLTKE'S (Baron) Russian Campaigns on the Danube and the Passage of the Balkan, 1828–9. Plans. 8vo. 14s.

MONASTERY AND THE MOUNTAIN CHURCH. By Author of "Sunlight through the Mist." Woodcuts. 16mo. 4s.

MOORE'S (Thomas) Life and Letters of Lord Byron. 6 Vols. Fcap. 8vo. 18s.

———— Life and Letters of Lord Byron. With Portraits. Royal 8vo. 9s. sewed, or 10s. 6d. in cloth.

MOZLEY'S (Rev. J. B.) Treatise on the Augustinian Doctrine of Predestination. 8vo. 14s.

———— Primitive Doctrine of Baptismal Regeneration. 8vo. 7s. 6d.

MUCK MANUAL (The) for the Use of Farmers. A Practical Treatise on the Chemical Properties, Management, and Application of Manures. By Frederick Falkner. Second Edition. Fcap. 8vo. 5s.

MUNDY'S (Gen.) Pen and Pencil Sketches during a Tour in India. Third Edition. Plates. Post 8vo. 7s. 6d.

MUNRO'S (General Sir Thomas) Life and Letters. By the Rev. G. R. Gleig. Post 8vo. 6s.

MURCHISON'S (Sir Roderick) Russia in Europe and the Ural Mountains; Geologically Illustrated. With Coloured Maps, Plates, Sections, &c. 2 Vols. Royal 4to.

———————— Siluria ; or, a History of the Oldest Rocks containing Organic Remains. *Third Edition.* Map and Plates. 8vo. 42s.

MURRAY'S (Capt. A.) Naval Life and Services of Admiral Sir Philip Durham. 8vo. 5s. 6d.

MURRAY'S RAILWAY READING. For all classes of Readers.

[The following are published:]

Wellington. By Lord Ellesmere. 6d.	Mahon's Joan of Arc. 1s.
Nimrod on the Chase, 1s.	Head's Emigrant. 2s. 6d.
Essays from "The Times." 2 Vols. 8s.	Nimrod on the Road. 1s.
Music and Dress. 1s.	Wilkinson's Ancient Egyptians. 12s.
Layard's Account of Nineveh. 5s.	Croker on the Guillotine. 1s.
Milman's Fall of Jerusalem. 1s.	Hollway's Norway. 2s.
Mahon's "Forty-Five." 3s.	Maurel's Wellington. 1s. 6d.
Life of Theodore Hook. 1s.	Campbell's Life of Bacon. 2s. 6d.
Deeds of Naval Daring. 2 Vols. 6s.	The Flower Garden. 1s.
The Honey Bee. 1s.	Lockhart's Spanish Ballads. 2s. 6d.
James' Æsop's Fables. 2s. 6d.	Lucas on History. 6d.
Nimrod on the Turf. 1s. 6d.	Beauties of Byron. 3s.
Oliphant's Nepaul. 2s. 6d.	Taylor's Notes from Life. 2s.
Art of Dining. 1s. 6d.	Rejected Addresses. 1s.
Hallam's Literary Essays. 2s.	Penn's Hints on Angling. 1s.

MUSIC AND DRESS. Two Essays, by a Lady. Reprinted from the "Quarterly Review." Fcap. 8vo. 1s.

NAPIER'S (Sir Wm.) English Battles and Sieges of the Peninsular War. *Third Edition.* Portrait. Post 8vo. 10s. 6d.

———————— Life and Opinions of General Sir Charles Napier; chiefly derived from his Journals, Letters, and Familiar Correspondence. *Second Edition.* Portraits. 4 Vols. Post 8vo. 48s.

NAUTICAL ALMANACK (The). Royal 8vo. 2s. 6d. (*Published by Authority.*)

NAVY LIST (The Quarterly). (*Published by Authority.*) Post 8vo. 2s. 6d.

NELSON (The Pious Robert), his Life and Times. By Rev. C. T. Secretan, M.A. Portrait. 8vo. 12s.

NEWBOLD'S (Lieut.) Straits of Malacca, Penang, and Singapore. 2 Vols. 8vo. 26s.

NEWDEGATE'S (C. N.) Customs' Tariffs of all Nations; collected and arranged up to the year 1855. 4to. 30s.

NICHOLLS' (Sir George) History of the British Poor : Being an Historical Account of the English, Scotch, and Irish Poor Law : in connection with the Condition of the People. 4 Vols. 8vo.

The work may be had separately :—
English Poor-Laws. 2 Vols. 8vo. 28s.
Irish Poor. 8vo. 14s.—Scotch Poor. 8vo. 12s.

———————— (Rev. H. G.) Historical and Descriptive Account of the Forest of Dean, derived from Personal Observation and other Sources, Public, Private, Legendary, and Local. Woodcuts, &c. Post 8vo. 10s. 6d.

NICOLAS' (Sir Harris) Historic Peerage of England. Exhibiting, under Alphabetical Arrangement, the Origin, Descent, and Present State of every Title of Peerage which has existed in this Country since the Conquest. Being a New Edition of the "Synopsis of the Peerage." Revised, Corrected, and Continued to the Present Time. By William Courthope, Somerset Herald. 8vo. 30s.

NIMROD On the Chace—The Turf—and The Road. Reprinted from the "Quarterly Review." Woodcuts. Fcap. 8vo. 3s. 6d.

O'CONNOR'S (R.) Field Sports of France; or, Hunting, Shooting, and Fishing on the Continent. Woodcuts. 12mo. 7s. 6d.

OLIPHANT'S (LAURENCE) Journey to Katmandu, with Visit to the Camp of the Nepaulese Ambassador. Fcap. 8vo. 2s. 6d.

OWEN'S (PROFESSOR) Manual of Fossil Mammals. Including the substance of the course of Lectures on Osteology and Palæontology of the class Mammalia, delivered at the Metropolitan School of Science, Jermyn Street. Illustrations. 8vo. [In the Press.

OXENHAM'S (REV. W.) English Notes for Latin Elegiacs; designed for early Proficients in the Art of Latin Versification, with Prefatory Rules of Composition in Elegiac Metre. Third Edition. 12mo. 4s.

PAGET'S (JOHN) Hungary and Transylvania. With Remarks on their Condition, Social, Political, and Economical. Third Edition. Woodcuts. 2 Vols. 8vo. 18s.

PARIS' (Dr.) Philosophy in Sport made Science in Earnest; or, the First Principles of Natural Philosophy inculcated by aid of the Toys and Sports of Youth. Eighth Edition. Woodcuts. Post 8vo. 9s.

PARKYNS' (MANSFIELD) Personal Narrative of Three Years' Residence and Adventures in Abyssinia. Woodcuts. 2 Vols. 8vo. 30s.

PEEL'S (SIR ROBERT) Memoirs. Left in MSS. Edited by EARL STANHOPE and the Right Hon. EDWARD CARDWELL. 2 Vols. Post 8vo. 7s. 6d. each.

PEILE'S (REV. DR.) Agamemnon and Choephoræ of Æschylus. A New Edition of the Text, with Notes. Second Edition. 2 Vols. 8vo. 9s. each.

PENN'S (RICHARD) Maxims and Hints for an Angler, and the Miseries of Fishing. To which is added, Maxims and Hints for a Chess-player. New Edition. Woodcuts. Fcap. 8vo. 1s.

PENROSE'S (REV. JOHN) Faith and Practice; an Exposition of the Principles and Duties of Natural and Revealed Religion. Post 8vo. 8s. 6d.

———————— (F. C.) Principles of Athenian Architecture, and the Optical Refinements exhibited in the Construction of the Ancient Buildings at Athens, from a Survey. With 40 Plates. Folio. 5l. 5s. (Published under the direction of the Dilettanti Society.)

PERCY'S (JOHN, M.D.) Metallurgy; or, the Art of Extracting Metals from their Ores and adapting them to various purposes of Manufacture. Illustrations. 8vo. [In the Press.

PERRY'S (SIR ERSKINE) Bird's-Eye View of India. With Extracts from a Journal kept in the Provinces, Nepaul, &c. Fcap. 8vo. 5s.

PHILLIPS' (JOHN) Memoirs of William Smith, LL.D. (the Geologist). Portrait. 8vo. 7s. 6d.

———————— Geology of Yorkshire, The Yorkshire Coast, and the Mountain-Limestone District. Plates 4to. Part I., 20s.—Part II., 30s.

———————— Rivers, Mountains, and Sea Coast of Yorkshire. With Essays on the Climate, Scenery, and Ancient Inhabitants of the Country. Second Edition, with 36 Plates. 8vo. 15s.

PHILPOTT'S (BISHOP) Letters to the late Charles Butler, on the Theological parts of his "Book of the Roman Catholic Church;" with Remarks on certain Works of Dr. Milner and Dr. Lingard, and on some parts of the Evidence of Dr. Doyle. Second Edition. 8vo. 16s.

PHIPPS' (HON. EDMUND) Memoir, Correspondence, Literary and Unpublished Diaries of Robert Plumer Ward. Portrait. 2 Vols. 8vo. 28s.

POPE'S (ALEXANDER) Works. An entirely New Edition. Edited, with Notes. 8vo. [In the Press.

PORTER'S (Rev. J. L.) Five Years in Damascus. With Travels to Palmyra, Lebanon, and other Scripture Sites. Map and Woodcuts. 2 vols. Post 8vo. 21s.

———— Handbook for Syria and Palestine: including an Account of the Geography, History, Antiquities, and Inhabitants of these Countries, the Peninsula of Sinai, Edom, and the Syrian Desert. Maps. 2 Vols. Post 8vo. 24s.

———— (Mrs.) Rational Arithmetic for Schools and for Private Instruction. 12mo. 3s. 6d.

PRAYER-BOOK (The Illustrated), with 1000 Illustrations of Borders, Initials, Vignettes, &c. Medium 8vo. Cloth, 21s.; Calf, 31s. 6d.; Morocco, 42s.

PRECEPTS FOR THE CONDUCT OF LIFE. Exhortations to a Virtuous Course and Dissuasions from a Vicious Career. Extracted from the Scriptures. *Second Edition.* Fcap. 8vo. 1s.

PRINSEP'S (Jas.) Essays on Indian Antiquities, Historic, Numismatic, and Palæographic, with Tables, illustrative of Indian History, Chronology. Modern Coinage, Weights, Measures, &c. Edited by Edward Thomas. Illustrations. 2 Vols. 8vo. 52s. 6d.

PROGRESS OF RUSSIA IN THE EAST. An Historical Summary, continued to the Present Time. With Map by Arrowsmith. *Third Edition.* 8vo. 6s. 6d.

PUSS IN BOOTS. With 12 Illustrations; for Old and Young. By Otto Speckter. *A New Edition.* 16mo. 1s. 6d.

QUARTERLY REVIEW (The). 8vo. 6s.

RANKE'S (Leopold) Political and Ecclesiastical History of the Popes of Rome, during the Sixteenth and Seventeenth Centuries. Translated from the German by Mrs. Austin. *Third Edition.* 2 Vols. 8vo. 24s.

RAWLINSON'S (Rev. George) Herodotus. A New English Version. Edited with Notes and Essays. Assisted by Sir Henry Rawlinson and Sir J. G. Wilkinson. Maps and Woodcuts. 4 Vols. 8vo. 18s. each.

———— Historical Evidences of the truth of the Scripture Records stated anew, with special reference to the Doubts and Discoveries of Modern Times; being the Bampton Lectures for 1859. 8vo. 14s.

REJECTED ADDRESSES (The). By James and Horace Smith. With Biographies of the Authors, and additional Notes. *New Edition, with the Author's latest Corrections.* Fcap. 8vo. 1s., or *Fine Paper,* with Portrait. Fcap. 8vo. 5s.

RENNIE'S (James) Insect Architecture. To which are added Chapters on the Ravages, the Preservation, for Purposes of Study, and the Classification of Insects. *New Edition.* Woodcuts. Post 8vo. 5s.

RICARDO'S (David) Political Works. With a Notice of his Life and Writings. By J. R. M'Culloch. *New Edition.* 8vo. 16s.

RIPA'S (Father) Memoirs during Thirteen Years' Residence at the Court of Peking, in the Service of the Emperor of China. Translated from the Italian. By Fortunato Prandi. Post 8vo. 2s. 6d.

ROBERTSON'S (Rev. J. C.) History of the Christian Church, From the Apostolic Age to the Pontificate of Gregory the Great, A.D. 590. *Second and Revised Edition.* Vol. 1. 8vo. 16s.

———— Second Period, from A.D. 590 to the Concordat of Worms. A.D. 1123. Vol. 2. 8vo. 18s.

———— Becket; Archbishop of Canterbury; a Biography. Illustrations. Post 8vo. 9s.

ROBINSON'S (Rev. Dr.) Biblical Researches in the Holy Land. Being a Journal of Travels in 1838, and of Later Researches in 1852. With New Maps. 3 Vols. 8vo. 36s.
₊ The *"Later Researches"* may be had separately. 8vo. 15s.

ROMILLY'S (SIR SAMUEL) Memoirs and Political Diary. By his
Sons. *Third Edition*. Portrait. 2 Vols. Fcap. 8vo. 12s.

ROSS'S (SIR JAMES) Voyage of Discovery and Research in the
Southern and Antarctic Regions during the years 1839-43. Plates.
2 Vols. 8vo. 36s.

ROWLAND'S (DAVID) Manual of the English Constitution; a
Review of its Rise, Growth, and Present State. Post 8vo. 10s. 6d.

RUNDELL'S (MRS.) Domestic Cookery, founded on Principles
of Economy and Practice, and adapted for Private Families. *New and
Revised Edition*. Woodcuts. Fcap. 8vo. 5s.

RUSSIA; A Memoir of the Remarkable Events which attended
the Accession of the Emperor Nicholas. By BARON M. KORFF, Secretary
of State. 8vo. 10s. 6d. (*Published by Imperial Command.*)

RUXTON'S (GEORGE F.) Travels in Mexico; with Adventures
among the Wild Tribes and Animals of the Prairies and Rocky Mountains. Post 8vo. 6s.

SALE'S (LADY) Journal of the Disasters in Affghanistan. *Eighth
Edition*. Post 8vo. 12s.

———— (SIR ROBERT) Brigade in Affghanistan. With an Account of
the Seizure and Defence of Jellalabad. By REV. G. R. GLEIG. Post 8vo. 2s. 6d.

SANDWITH'S (HUMPHRY) Narrative of the Siege of Kars
and of the Six Months' Resistance by the Turkish Garrison under
General Williams. *Seventh Thousand*. Post 8vo. 3s. 6d.

SCOTT'S (G. GILBERT) Remarks on Secular and Domestic
Architecture, Present and Future. *Second Edition*. 8vo. 9s.

SCROPE'S (WILLIAM) Days of Deer-Stalking in the Forest of Atholl;
with some Account of the Nature and Habits of the Red Deer. *Third
Edition*. Woodcuts. Crown 8vo. 20s.

———— Days and Nights of Salmon Fishing in the Tweed;
with a short Account of the Natural History and Habits of the Salmon.
Second Edition. Woodcuts. Royal 8vo. 31s. 6d.

———— (G. P.) Memoir of Lord Sydenham, and his Administration in Canada. *Second Edition*. Portrait. 8vo. 9s. 6d.

———— Geology and Extinct Volcanos of Central France.
Second Edition, revised and enlarged. Illustrations. Medium 8vo. 30s.

SHAFTESBURY (LORD CHANCELLOR), Memoirs of his Early Life.
With his Letters, Speeches, and other Papers. By W. D. CHRISTIE.
Portrait. 8vo. 10s. 6d.

SHAW'S (THOS. B.) Outlines of English Literature, for the Use of
Young Students. Post 8vo. 12s.

SIERRA LEONE; Described in a Series of Letters to Friends at
Home. By A LADY. Edited by MRS. NORTON. Post 8vo. 6s.

SMILES' (SAMUEL) Life of George Stephenson. *Fifth Edition*.
Portrait. 8vo. 16s.

———— Story of the Life of Stephenson. With Woodcuts.
Fifth Thousand. Post 8vo. 6s.

———— Self Help. With Illustrations of Character and Conduct.
Post 8vo. 6s.

SOMERVILLE'S (MARY) Physical Geography. *Fourth Edition*.
Portrait. Post 8vo. 9s.

———————— Connexion of the Physical Sciences. *Ninth
Edition*. Woodcuts. Post 8vo. 9s.

SOUTH'S (JOHN F.) Household Surgery; or, Hints on Emergen-
cies. *Seventeenth Thousand*. Woodcuts. Fcp. 8vo. 4s. 6d.

SOUTHEY'S (ROBERT) Book of the Church; with Notes containing the Authorities, and an Index. *Seventh Edition*. Post 8vo. 7s. 6d.

———————— Lives of John Bunyan & Oliver Cromwell. Post 8vo. 2s. 6d.

SMITH'S (WM., LL.D.) Dictionary of Greek and Roman Antiquities. *Second Edition.* With 500 Woodcuts. 8vo. 42*s.*
——— Smaller Dictionary of Greek and Roman Antiquities. Abridged from the above work. *Fourth Edition.* With 200 Woodcuts. Crown 8vo. 7*s.* 6*d.*

——— Dictionary of Greek and Roman Biography and Mythology. With 500 Woodcuts. 3 Vols. 8vo. 5*l.* 15*s.* 6*d.*

——— Dictionary of Greek and Roman Geography. With Woodcuts. 2 Vols. 8vo. 80*s.*

——— Atlas of Ancient Geography. 4to. [*In préparation.*

——— Classical Dictionary for the Higher Forms in Schools. Compiled from the above two works. *Fifth Edition.* With 750 Woodcuts. 8vo. 18*s.*

——— Smaller Classical Dictionary. Abridged from the above work. *Fifth Edition.* With 200 Woodcuts. Crown 8vo. 7*s.* 6*d.*

——— Latin-English Dictionary. Based upon the Works of Forcellini and Freund. *Seventh Thousand.* 8vo. 21*s.*

——— Smaller Latin-English Dictionary. Abridged from the above work. *Sixteenth Thousand.* Square 12mo. 7*s.* 6*d.*

——— English-Latin Dictionary. 8vo. & 12mo. [*In preparation.*

——— Mediæval Latin-English Dictionary. Selected from the great work of DUCANGE. 8vo. [*In preparation.*

——— Dictionary of the Bible, including its Antiquities, Biography, Geography, and Natural History. Woodcuts. Vol. 1. 8vo. 42*s.* [*Nearly ready.*

——— Gibbon's History of the Decline and Fall of the Roman Empire. Edited, with Notes. Portrait and Map. 8 Vols. 8vo. 60*s.* (Murray's British Classics.)

——— Student's Gibbon; being the History of the Decline and Fall, Abridged. Incorporating the Researches of Recent Commentators. *Sixth Thousand.* Woodcuts. Post 8vo. 7*s.* 6*d.*

——— Student's History of Greece; from the Earliest Times to the Roman Conquest. With the History of Literature and Art. *Twentieth Thousand.* Woodcuts. Crown 8vo. 7*s.* 6*d.* (Questions. 12mo. 2*s.*)

——— Smaller History of Greece for Junior Classes. Woodcuts. 12mo. 3*s.* 6*d.*

——— Student's Hume. A History of England from the Invasion of Julius Cæsar. Based on Hume's History, and continued to 1858. *Tenth Thousand.* Woodcuts. Post 8vo. 7*s.* 6*d.*

——— Student's History of Rome; from the Earliest Times to the Establishment of the Empire. With the History of Literature and Art. By H. G. LIDDELL, D.D. *Fifteenth Thousand.* Woodcuts. Crown 8vo. 7*s.* 6*d.*

——— Principia Latina; a First Latin Course, comprehending Grammar, Delectus, and Exercise Book, with Vocabularies, for the lower forms in Public and Private Schools. 12mo. 3*s.* 6*d.*

——— Principia Græca; an Introduction to the Study of Greek. Comprehending Grammar, Delectus, and Exercise-book with Vocabularies. For the Lower Forms. By H. E. HUTTON, M.A. 12mo. 2*s.* 6*d.*

——— (WM. JAS.) Grenville Letters and Diaries, including MR. GRENVILLE'S DIARY OF POLITICAL EVENTS, while First Lord of the Treasury. Edited, with Notes. 4 Vols. 8vo. 64*s.*

——— (JAMES & HORACE) Rejected Addresses. *Twenty-third Edition.* Fcap. 8vo. 1*s.*, or *Fine Paper*, with Portrait. Fcap. 8vo. 5*s.*

——— (THOMAS ASSHETON) Reminiscences of his Life and Pursuits. By SIR EARDLEY WILMOT. Illustrations. 8vo.

SPECKTER'S (OTTO) Puss in Boots, suited to the Tastes of Old and Young. *A New Edition.* With 12 Woodcuts. Square 12mo. 1s. 6d.
—————— Charmed Roe; or, the Story of the Little Brother and Sister. Illustrated. 16mo.
STANLEY'S (Rev. A. P.) ADDRESSES AND CHARGES OF THE LATE BISHOP STANLEY. With a Memoir of his Life. *Second Edition.* 8vo. 10s. 6d.
—————— Sermons preached in Canterbury Cathedral, on the Unity of Evangelical and Apostolical Teaching. Post 8vo. 7s. 6d.
—————— Commentary on St. Paul's Epistles to the Corinthians, with Notes and Dissertations. *Second, and revised Edition.* 8vo. 18s.
—————— Historical Memorials of Canterbury. The Landing of Augustine—The Murder of Becket—The Black Prince—The Shrine of Becket. *Third Edition.* Woodcuts. Post 8vo. 7s. 6d.
—————— Sinai and Palestine, in Connexion with their History. *Sixth Edition.* Map. 8vo. 16s.
ST. JOHN'S (CHARLES) Wild Sports and Natural History of the Highlands. Post 8vo. 6s.
—————— (BAYLE) Adventures in the Libyan Desert and the Oasis of Jupiter Ammon. Woodcuts. Post 8vo. 2s. 6d.
STEPHENSON'S (GEORGE) Life. The Railway Engineer. By SAMUEL SMILES. *Fifth Edition.* Portrait. 8vo. 16s.
—————— The Story of his Life. By SAMUEL SMILES. *Fifth Thousand.* Woodcuts. Post 8vo. 6s.
STOTHARD'S (THOS., R. A.) Life. With Personal Reminiscences. By Mrs. BRAY. With Portrait and 60 Woodcuts. 4to.
STREET'S (G. E.) Brick and Marble Architecture of Italy, in the Middle Ages. Plates. 8vo. 21s.
STRIFE FOR THE MASTERY. Two Allegories. With Illustrations. Crown 8vo. 6s.
SWIFT'S (JONATHAN) Life, Letters and Journals. By JOHN FORSTER. 8vo. *In Preparation.*
—————— Works. Edited, with Notes. By JOHN FORSTER. 8vo. *In Preparation.*
SYDENHAM'S (LORD) Memoirs. With his Administration in Canada. By G. POULETT SCROPE, M.P. *Second Edition.* Portrait. 8vo. 9s.6d.
SYME'S (JAS.) Principles of Surgery. *Fourth Edition.* 8vo. 14s.
TAYLOR'S (HENRY) Notes from Life. Fcap 8vo. 2s.
—————— (J. E.) Fairy Ring. A Collection of Stories for Young Persons. From the German. With Illustrations by RICHARD DOYLE. *Second Edition.* Woodcuts. Fcap. 8vo.
TENNENT'S (SIR J. E.) Christianity in Ceylon. Its Introduction and Progress under the Portuguese, Dutch, British, and American Missions. With an Historical Sketch of the Brahmanical and Buddhist Superstitions. Woodcuts. 8vo. 14s.
THOMSON'S (DR. A. S.) Story of New Zealand; Past and Present —Savage and Civilised. Maps and Illustrations. 2 Vols. Post 8vo. 24s.
THREE-LEAVED MANUAL OF FAMILY PRAYER; arranged so as to save the trouble of turning the Pages backwards and forwards. Royal 8vo. 2s.
TICKNOR'S (GEORGE) History of Spanish Literature. With Criticisms on particular Works, and Biographical Notices of Prominent Writers. *Second Edition.* 3 Vols. 8vo. 24s.
TOCQUEVILLE'S (M. DE) State of France before the Revolution, 1789, and on the Causes of that Event. Translated by HENRY REEVE, Esq. 8vo. 14s.

TREMENHEERE'S (H. S.) Political Experience of the Ancients, in its bearing on Modern Times. Fcap. 8vo. 2s. 6d.

———————— Notes on Public Subjects, made during a Tour in the United States and Canada. Post 8vo. 10s. 6d.

———————— Constitution of the United States compared with our own. Post 8vo. 9s. 6d.

TWISS' (HORACE) Public and Private Life of Lord Chancellor Eldon, with Selections from his Correspondence. Portrait. *Third Edition.* 2 Vols. Post 8vo. 21s.

TYNDALL'S (JOHN) Glaciers of the Alps. Being a Narrative of various Excursions among them, and an Account of Three Years' Observations and Experiments on their Motion, Structure, and General Phenomena. Post 8vo. *In the Press.*

TYTLER (PATRICK FRASER), A Memoir of. By his Friend, REV. J. W. BURGON, M.A. *Second Edition.* 8vo. 9s.

UBICINI'S (M. A.) Letters on Turkey and its Inhabitants—the Moslems, Greeks, Armenians, &c. Translated by LADY EASTHOPE. 2 Vols. Post 8vo. 21s.

VAUGHAN'S (REV. DR.) Sermons preached in Harrow School. 8vo. 10s. 6d.

———————— New Sermons. 12mo. 5s.

VENABLES' (REV. R. L.) Domestic Scenes in Russia during a Year's Residence, chiefly in the Interior. *Second Edition.* Post 8vo. 5s.

VOYAGE to the Mauritius and back, touching at the Cape of Good Hope, and St. Helena. By Author of "PADDIANA." Post 8vo. 9s. 6d.

WAAGEN'S (DR.) Treasures of Art in Great Britain. Being an Account of the Chief Collections of Paintings, Sculpture, Manuscripts, Miniatures, &c. &c., in this Country. Obtained from Personal Inspection during Visits to England. 3 Vols. 8vo. 36s.

———————— Galleries and Cabinets of Art in England. Being an Account of more than Forty Collections, visited in 1854-56 and never before described. With Index. 8vo. 18s.

WADDINGTON'S (DEAN) Condition and Prospects of the Greek Church. *New Edition.* Fcap. 8vo. 3s. 6d.

WAKEFIELD'S (E. J.) Adventures in New Zealand. With some Account of the Beginning of the British Colonisation of the Island. Map. 2 Vols. 8vo. 28s.

WALKS AND TALKS. A Story-book for Young Children. By AUNT IDA. With Woodcuts. 16mo. 5s.

WARD'S (ROBERT PLUMER) Memoir, Correspondence, Literary and Unpublished Diaries and Remains. By the HON. EDMUND PHIPPS. Portrait. 2 Vols. 8vo. 28s.

WATT'S (JAMES) Life. Incorporating the most interesting passages from his Private and Public Correspondence. By JAMES P. MUIRHEAD, M.A. *Second Edition.* Portraits and Woodcuts. 8vo. 16s.

———————— Origin and Progress of his Mechanical Inventions. Illustrated by his Correspondence with his Friends. Edited by J. P. MUIRHEAD. Plates. 3 vols. 8vo. 45s., or Large Paper. 3 Vols. 4to.

WILKIE'S (SIR DAVID) Life, Journals, Tours, and Critical Remarks on Works of Art, with a Selection from his Correspondence. By ALLAN CUNNINGHAM. Portrait. 3 Vols. 8vo. 42s.

WOOD'S (LIEUT.) Voyage up the Indus to the Source of the River Oxus, by Kabul and Badakhshan. Map. 8vo. 14s.

WELLINGTON'S (THE DUKE OF) Despatches during his various Campaigns. Compiled from Official and other Authentic Documents. By COL. GURWOOD, C.B. *New Enlarged Edition.* 8 Vols. 8vo. 21s. each.

———————— Supplementary Letters, Despatches, and other Papers relating to India. Edited by his Son. 4 Vols. 8vo. 20s. each.

———————— Civil Correspondence and Memoranda, while Chief Secretary for Ireland, from 1807 to 1809. 8vo. 20s.

———————— Selections from his Despatches and General Orders. By COLONEL GURWOOD. 8vo. 18s.

———————— Speeches in Parliament. 2 Vols. 8vo. 42s.

WILKINSON'S (SIR J. G.) Popular Account of the Private Life, Manners, and Customs of the Ancient Egyptians. *New Edition.* Revised and Condensed. With 500 Woodcuts. 2 Vols. Post 8vo. 12s.

———————— Dalmatia and Montenegro; with a Journey to Mostar in Hertzegovina, and Remarks on the Slavonic Nations. Plates and Woodcuts. 2 Vols. 8vo. 42s.

———————— Handbook for Egypt.—Thebes, the Nile, Alexandria, Cairo, the Pyramids, Mount Sinai, &c. Map. Post 8vo. 15s.

———————— On Colour, and on the Necessity for a General Diffusion of Taste among all Classes; with Remarks on laying out Dressed or Geometrical Gardens. With Coloured Illustrations and Woodcuts. 8vo. 18s.

———————— (G. B.) Working Man's Handbook to South Australia; with Advice to the Farmer, and Detailed Information for the several Classes of Labourers and Artisans. Map. 18mo. 1s. 6d.

WILSON'S (REV. D., late Lord Bishop of Calcutta) Life, with Extracts from his Letters and Journals. By Rev. JOSIAH BATEMAN, M.A. Portrait and Illustrations. 2 Vols. 8vo. 28s.

———————— (GENL. SIR ROBERT) Journal, while employed at the Head Quarters of the Russian Army on a special mission during the Invasion of Russia, and Retreat of the French Army, 1812. 8vo.

WORDSWORTH'S (REV. DR.) Athens and Attica. Journal of a Tour. *Third Edition.* Plates. Post 8vo. 8s. 6d.

———————— Greece: Pictorial, Descriptive, and Historical, with a History of Greek Art, by G. SCHARF, F.S.A. *New Edition.* With 600 Woodcuts. Royal 8vo. 28s.

———————— King Edward VIth's Latin Grammar, for the Use of Schools. *12th Edition,* revised. 12mo. 3s. 6d.

———————— First Latin Book, or the Accidence, Syntax and Prosody, with English Translation for Junior Classes. *Third Edition.* 12mo. 2s.

WORNUM (RALPH). A Biographical Dictionary of Italian Painters: with a Table of the Contemporary Schools of Italy. By a LADY. Post 8vo. 6s. 6d.

———————— Epochs of Painting Characterised; a Sketch of the History of Painting, showing its gradual and various development from the earliest ages to the present time. *New Edition.* Woodcuts. Post 8vo. 6s.

WROTTESLEY'S (LORD) Thoughts on Government and Legislation. Post 8vo. 7s. 6d.

YOUNG'S (DR. THOS.) Life and Miscellaneous Works, edited by DEAN PEACOCK and JOHN LEITCH. Portrait and Plates. 4 Vols. 8vo. 15s. each.

BRADBURY AND EVANS, PRINTERS, WHITEFRIARS.

www.ingramcontent.com/pod-product-compliance
Lightning Source LLC
Chambersburg PA
CBHW020618030726
47497CB00007B/2309